For Geri Crooke
26 November 1989 – 17 June 2019

Everyone who knew you, couldn't help but love you.
Everyone who knew you was touched by your light

The Host

7.45 p.m.

The Host watched with anticipation. He was clear in his instruction. The rules of The Game had been relayed and understood. And although The Player, twenty-six-year-old Dean Winters, seemed to agree to them, it wasn't clear if he would play.

If Dean did, The Host knew that the next phase would begin.

Dean shifted from one foot to the other, his eyes darting from left to right. It was obvious he was nervous; The Host could tell he had never done anything like this. Nerves were good, nerves produced adrenaline, and cortisol, the fight or flight hormones. Nerves told The Host he was taking The Game seriously.

A few people walked by, oblivious that Dean was assessing them; deciding if they would be the one he would confront. But none of them so far matched the specific requirements laid out in the rules of The Game. And so, Dean let them pass and continue with their evening not knowing just how lucky they had been. This went on for nearly an hour. People passed, untouched, because of the instructions The Host had set out.

Then, Dean stopped. His eyes fixed on someone to his right, beyond The Host's eyeline. His reaction told The Host that Dean had found the one. The Host enjoyed watching his Player ready himself. Dean looked around, making sure no one would see what he was about to do. He took his hands out of his pockets, tightened his fists, as the person came into view. The Host felt his skin begin to tingle with anticipation.

The target was just one hundred feet away.

In a matter of minutes, The Host would know if his Game worked.

When The Host first told Dean about The Game he wanted to play, Dean reacted with confusion. After the rules had been explained and questions answered, quiet excitement began to build. The idea was simple. Dean had to wait until he saw someone with a red coat. Then, he was to attack them. If he was able to render them unconscious, he would receive £500 cash in hand. If he lost his nerve, he would receive nothing. It didn't matter if the person wearing the coat was male or female, young or old. The only thing that mattered was whether Dean would do it. When asked why a person in a red coat, The Host responded, why not?

The Game was simple, he just had to play.

The Host knew it wasn't without risk as most people would ring the police on hearing such a proposition. The first two red coat experiments had proved inconclusive. But The Host had chosen his next Player well. Dean was in debt – a payday loan he'd taken out three months ago of just £100 had now spiralled to £500. Dean needed that money, he needed it badly. Financial reward was a strong motivator. The Host just hoped it would be strong enough.

As the red coat drew closer to Dean, The Host could now see the figure was a woman, perhaps in her mid-twenties so a similar age to The Player. Dean began to shift again, unable to stand still. The woman in the red coat became aware of the man on the footpath in front of her. She hesitated for just a beat, before she lowered her head and continued advancing cautiously. The Host suspected she felt something was wrong, but she didn't react, because if she crossed the street, if she turned around and walked the other way, she would appear rude, and as with most people, the shame of appearing rude was more of a motivator than self-preservation.

She was just twenty feet away.

Calm now, Dean turned his back to her, pretending to read something on his phone. The Host understood, he was going to wait for her to pass, and then, attack from behind.

She was ten feet away.

It was about to happen. The Game was hurtling towards its brutal finale.

The woman in red upped her pace. Her shoulders hunched, her head cast down, but her eyes were not looking at the ground, they were scanning to see if anyone else was around to help. She knew something was wrong and still she didn't cross the road. She knew but she didn't turn around and walk the other way. The Host didn't understand that about people. Life was supposed to be cherished, and yet people seldom respected it.

The woman walked past his Player and continued along the path. Three steps, that would be how many she should take before Dean acted – one less would mean she was too close to strike properly, any more would put her out of range. Just three steps. The Host counted them, expecting to watch his Player pounce, but three became five, became ten, became twenty. And still, his Player hadn't moved.

The third red coat experiment had failed.

When the woman had disappeared, Dean looked across the road to find The Host, but he had already vanished into the night. The Host was disappointed. Despite the desperation for it, money wasn't enough of a motivator to play.

But if money wasn't enough, then surely, love would be. Once it had been tested, a new Game would begin, and everyone would be a Player.

DAY 1

3 February 2019

CHAPTER ONE

9.56 a.m.

With my palm wrapped around the cool metal of the door handle, I paused before opening. Several people from work had been here over the years, but this was my first visit. As soon as I opened the door, there would be no going back. When I stepped inside I knew that I'd be forced to confront the nightmare I'd been living in for over a week.

Just open the door, Karen, I told myself.

The second hand on the clock behind the reception desk ticked loudly as it approached 10 a.m. I waited until it ticked a full half minute before moving.

'Is everything all right? You can just knock and go in,' the receptionist said when I still had not moved.

I knew I couldn't delay this moment anymore. I took a deep breath, pushed the door open and tentatively stepped in.

I'd not been inside a therapist's office before, and my first thought as I entered was how dark the room was. The reception had been light and airy and I expected this too to be bright, welcoming, with pictures of beautiful landscapes or quotes about not waiting for storms to pass but learning to dance in the rain. But this room felt entirely different. It was the kind of place that hid things in its shadows, the kind of room that watched, that judged. I shivered, knowing that this room was one that never felt quite warm enough, even on the hottest summer's day.

The woman who had allowed me to look around the room and familiarise myself with my new surroundings stood up from her armchair and offered her hand. As she did, I glimpsed the doctorate certificate over her shoulder, centred on the wall behind her desk.

'Good morning, DI Holt, I'm Shauna,' she said with the hint of an Irish accent. I nodded and took her hand. A firm shake. I considered her accent for a moment – if I had to guess, I'd say she was from Dublin, but it was diluted, suggesting she had been in the UK for several years.

'Take a seat, Karen. May I call you Karen?'

'Sure.'

'How are you feeling today?'

I wasn't ready for a direct question about my feelings. It caught me off guard, and as I took a breath to respond, my chest felt tight. 'All right, I guess. I mean, as well as can be expected.' Then I remembered my manner. 'Thank you for seeing me at the weekend. I hope it's not too inconvenient.'

She waved my apology aside. 'No problem at all. I understand you've had a turbulent time recently.'

She paused, waited for me to comment, but I simply nodded. I wasn't ready to show my cards, not yet. First, I wanted to assess the woman in front of me and work out whose side she was on.

'Do you know the purpose of our time together?'

'I do.' Despite my best efforts, I heard apprehension in my voice.

'Good, that's good.' She waited for me to say something again, but again I didn't bite. I placed my hands in my lap, interlocking my fingers, squeezing so tight that my knuckles whitened. The therapist noticed. She was observant, smart. I felt my guard go up.

'This is a safe space, Karen, where you can talk about whatever you want. It goes without saying that what we discuss is confidential. I understand you're currently suspended due to the investigation, but my role is to listen, offer support, and ultimately make the decision of when I think you're fit to return to work.'

'OK.'

'Why don't you start by talking about what happened the morning you went to arrest Grayson James?'

Hearing his name spoken out loud for the first time in over a week made my chest squeeze harder, like someone was squashing me. I had actively avoided thinking of him. Of that day. It was too much. I flicked my fingernails on my right hand, thumb to little finger and back, it calmed me, to a point.

'Karen?'

'I'm fine,' I replied too quickly, responding to a question she hadn't asked. From the outside I knew exactly the kind of person I appeared to be. I had seen it hundreds of times in interview rooms. I looked guilty. But then, I was guilty, wasn't I?

'I need to stress, this isn't a criminal investigation.'

'No?' I said.

'No. I'm here to help you process what happened the day of the incident.'

'And establish if it was lawful.'

'That's for the IOPC review board. My job, Karen, is to make sure that you're OK, so that when you are allowed to return to active duty, you feel up to it. I'm sure you already know this, but I just want to reiterate that although we work closely with Cambridge Constabulary in looking after the wellbeing of its officers, we do not in fact work *for* them. We are independent, intentionally so. The Office for Police Conduct deals with any investigations. We're just here to support you.'

I nodded but didn't pass any further comment. I knew there was more to it. The IOPC were examining the facts of that day; they would look at the bodycam footage and would read the incident reports. The softly spoken therapist was examining the psychological state of the police officer involved.

'Let's get to know one another,' she continued, attempting to redirect the conversation.

'What do you want to know?'

'Whatever you want to say. Let me start. I'm originally from Ireland, a small town called Bray, on the coast just south of Dublin.'

I nodded, pleased that at least some parts of my judgement hadn't failed.

'I have one brother and grew up with my dad. What about you, Karen? Any brothers or sisters?'

'I've got a brother.'

'What's his name?'

'Jacob.'

'Are you close?'

'I don't mean to be rude, but we're not really here to talk about my brother, are we?'

'No,' she agreed.

'So shall we get this over with and discuss what we are here for?'

'You seemed hesitant, which is why I suggested we talked about other things. But if you are sure you want to get straight into it—'

'I'm not, but we have to, don't we?'

'At some point, yes,' she agreed. 'But we have time, weeks, if necess—'

'I'd rather get this done, so I can get back to work.'

'OK then,' she said decisively, slapping her palms against her thighs. 'Where would you be comfortable starting?'

I had prepared what I was going to say, rehearsed it a thousand times, but as I went to speak, my throat closed as hot bile forced its way up. I tried to disguise it by coughing.

Come on, Karen, speak.

My hands felt hot, and I had to blink hard as white dots had appeared in the corners of my vision.

SPEAK.

'On the morning of the 23rd of January, myself and Detective Howard Carlson entered the property of Gray…'

I stopped, took a breath. I knew today was about opening up and discussing the arrest, but knowing and doing were two very different things.

'Karen?'

'Detective Howard Carlson and I entered the property as part of a planned arrest. As we approached…'

I was aware that my mouth was moving, that words were falling out, and yet I couldn't hear them. The sound of blood rushing around my head was drowning out my voice. Despite it being cool in the office, I felt my skin start to itch as I began to sweat. I had prepared my words carefully, I had selected the right ones to explain what had happened that day, and yet, now I was here, I couldn't finish them. My hands began to tremble and I tried to discreetly massage the blood back into them. When I saw the therapist watching, I ever so slightly tucked them into the sleeves of my favourite blue cardigan.

'Karen, do you need to take a moment?'

'Please,' I managed to say between jagged breaths. I needed to be outside, there wasn't enough oxygen in the room. I needed the wind on my skin, the clouds above my head. I needed to run. 'Is there a bathroom I could use?'

'Outside, second door on the left. Take your time.'

Without thanking her or excusing myself, I stood up, my legs feeling hollow and unsteady and left the room. I walked past the receptionist, who looked at me with concern, and stumbled into the bathroom. The room shifted on its axis and I had to grab onto the sink to stop myself from falling. I didn't know what was happening to me, the tingle in my hands had moved to my face and numbed my lips. My heart began to gallop. Looking into the mirror I saw my skin was completely washed out and my eyes had glazed over.

I tried to call for help, but as I opened my mouth, the sound that came out was inaudible, my throat had seized and wouldn't release any words. It wouldn't allow anything in either, and I began to feel like I was choking. Stumbling against the wall I slid to the floor, cradled my head in my hands, forced myself to try and take a breath. It was like I was sipping oxygen through a blocked straw.

'Please. Someone—'

I couldn't finish my sentence; bile forced its way up my constricted throat and crawling into a cubical I lifted the toilet lid and heaved. I hadn't eaten, so it was mostly liquid. I heaved three times, my burning forehead resting on the porcelain bowl, fighting to get my breathing back under control. The bathroom door opened and closed as I retched again, without bringing anything up this time. I felt a hand on my shoulder; I hated that it made me jump.

'Karen, are you all right?'

'Just, give me a minute, please?'

'Come on, let me help you.'

The therapist scooped me under my armpits and dragged me to my feet. I still didn't trust my legs, so she held onto me as we half walked, half dragged ourselves to the sink. As I leant against the wall, she ran the cold tap and told me to put my wrists under the water.

'It helps, trust me.'

I felt powerless to challenge, so complied, and as the water ran over my wrists and hands, I felt myself begin to calm. My chest started to feel lighter, air started to flow into my lungs once more.

'That's it, just concentrate on your breathing. It will pass. In and out, you're doing a grand job.'

'I'm sorry,' I said.

'Nothing to be sorry for. It happens.'

'Can I have a minute?'

'Are you sure?'

The more I felt centred, the more I understood what had just happened to me. I splashed calming water onto my face. Knowing I was in control again, the therapist asked if I wanted a minute to myself.

'I'll be in my office. Come in when you're ready,' she said before leaving.

As the door closed, I examined the woman staring back at me in the mirror. My face was not quite so ashen, and my lips looked like they would come back to life soon. But I looked tired, I looked old. When did that happen? Fine lines spread from the corners of my eyes. The skin around my jaw had lost some of its elasticity, and I knew, if I didn't dye my hair grey would streak through it.

After cleaning myself up, I walked towards the therapist's office. I could see the receptionist wanted to check on me but stopped himself. I knew that I needed to go inside, sit down with Shauna and say what I came for so then I could get back to work.

But I couldn't.

CHAPTER TWO

Carlson

3.14 p.m.

Ds Howard Carlson turned off his car ignition and stepped out into the cold. The scene before him was hard to read. Two ambulances sat idling, their rear doors open. Three police cars blocked most of the pedestrian walkway, a vain attempt to ward off the gathering crowds of people who wanted to see what was going on. When the call first came in, there was talk of a terror attack, but as the armed unit was scrambled it became apparent it was isolated, albeit like an incident that had happened only three days before. As Carlson pushed his way through the thrum of people, he was horrified, but not surprised to see most had their mobile phones out, trying to video and photograph the scene. Approaching the cordon, he waved at the uniformed officer and slipped under the tape.

'DS Carlson.'

'PC Sommers,' he acknowledged. 'What have we got?'

'Same as the other day. A man approached, disguised, told another to attack the first person he saw.'

'In red?'

'Yep, wearing a red coat. Said he would kill the attacker's dog if he didn't.'

'What? A dog?'

'That's right. The guy – the attacker – is homeless, says his dog is his world.'

Carlson nodded. Three days ago, a woman attacked someone elderly in a red coat. She'd claimed that the person who made her do it had threatened her daughter, had showed her photographs of her daughter at school so she knew the threat was real. The attack was brief, and the elderly lady wasn't seriously hurt. The scene Carlson saw in front of him looked entirely different.

'How's the victim?'

'Looks like he's got several broken bones – and there's lots of blood.'

'Clearly,' Carlson said, looking at the pool of blood on the pavement outside one of the city centre's more upmarket bars. 'Any witnesses?'

'Loads.'

'Anyone get an ID?'

'None so far.'

'None? Let's follow the homeless angle. Get a round-up of our usual suspects from the homeless community. Someone will know who he is. Where is the victim now?'

'In the ambulance, he's off to hospital to get treatment.'

'I mean the other one.'

'The other one?'

'The dog owner.'

Sommers looked confused. 'But sir, he is the attacker.'

'He is, but if we believe his story, he's a victim too. Where is he?'

'Back of the van,' PC Sommers said, pointing behind them.

'Thanks. Keep going, and Jake, if you find anything, shout me.'

'Sir.'

As Sommers turned back to the scene to speak with the few witnesses who claimed they'd watched the attack unfold, Carlson made his way to the van, and opening the back door, he came face to face with Mikey. A man Carlson had run into a few times for petty crimes: shoplifting once, begging a few times. Nothing of huge consequence, nothing so violent as this.

'Where's my dog? Is my dog OK?'

'Mikey, calm down.'

'Where's my fucking dog, he promised he wouldn't hurt him. He promised.'

'Who promised, Mikey, who made you do this?'

'I don't know who he was.'

'What did he say, Mikey?'

'Where's my dog, please? I need to know he's OK.' Mikey started to cry, his face buried in his hands, and Carlson leant in, rubbed his shoulder. Carlson couldn't help but feel for Mikey. He wasn't a violent person, far from it – his small, rat-like stature and painfully thin physique hardly made him a physical threat. Carlson could even recall a few times where Mikey had been assaulted himself. But there was a lot of blood, and Mikey was behind an attack that had left a person seriously injured and on their way to the city hospital.

'Give me a minute, Mikey. I'll look.'

Carlson closed the police van's door; he didn't want the public hearing Mikey's sobs from inside. Grabbing the first police officer that passed he asked them to find out if there was a dog nearby that was missing its owner. Confused, the officer nodded and turned to search for the mutt.

'Have they got him?' Mikey asked between jagged breaths when Carlson opened the van door again.

'An officer is just finding him now. He'll be here.'

'I don't know what I'd do without that dog.' Mikey began to cry once more.

'Mikey! We'll find your dog; you need to tell me what happened.'

'I didn't want to hurt him.'

'Then why did you attack him?'

'He said he'd kill my dog if I didn't.'

'Mikey, I need you to be specific. Who said they would kill your dog?' Carlson asked, suspecting he knew the answer already.

'I don't know, someone else.'

'Someone else' Carlson echoed. 'Did you get a look at him?'

'No, he was wearing a hood, I didn't see his face properly. Tell me about the man in the red coat. Is he OK?'

'He's injured but should make a full recovery. The other man you mentioned wearing a hood, what was his build? Was there anything else you noticed about him?'

'I didn't want to hurt him, I didn't, I'm so sorry.'

Mikey began to cry again. Carlson knew he wasn't going to get anything useful out of him right now. Not until his dog was found and he had calmed down. He closed the van door as Mikey shouted one last time for him to find his dog. Walking away, Carlson took a moment to think. This was the second incident this week that followed the same pattern, but as yet, he didn't know why. Taking out his phone, he scrolled through his contacts to find Karen's number. He wanted nothing more than to ring her, pick her brain, but she was off limits to him due to her suspension.

As he put his phone away and turned to speak to Sommers – who was taking a statement from a teary-eyed teenager – he didn't see that in the crowd someone was enjoying the spectacle. Carlson put his hands on his hips, looked up to the sky, as if begging for answers. The only source who could supply them had slipped away. With the success of the fourth and fifth red coat experiments this week, The Host could now proceed to the next stage.

And the next Game would begin in just four hours' time.

CHAPTER THREE

7.15 p.m.

After my meltdown in the toilet at the therapist's office, I couldn't face getting the train straight away. Instead I walked around Cambridge, along the river, past King's College in all its glory. The rain started to fall, so I nipped into a Starbucks and had two coffees, and watched the world go by. As it started to get dark, I made my way to the train station and after an uneventful journey rattling along the fens arrived back in Peterborough.

Despite the miserable weather, I decided to walk home from the station. My house was only three miles and a brisk walk would clear my head. I always found that walking helped, and I needed those miles to process the day, and try and work out how I would tell Sam about what happened. I found it hard to open up about things, even to her. I didn't know how I would say the day had been a disaster, culminating in a panic attack. My first ever. And hopefully, my last. I couldn't live through that again.

Just over an hour after leaving the station, I walked through my front door, thankful the central heating had clicked on. I took off my coat and wet shoes, peeled off my sodden jeans.

'Sam?' I called out. When she didn't respond, I nipped upstairs to put on a pair of loose-fitting jogging bottoms, assuming she would be in the bath, or working on the bed as she often did. 'You here, love?'

The house was empty. I checked the time, Sam usually went around to her mum's on a Sunday but was never usually this late back. I knew it was nothing, and yet I could feel myself starting to worry. I went into the kitchen and saw a note on the table:

Had to pop back to mum's, forgot some
of her shopping. Don't cook...

Reading the note, I couldn't help but laugh at myself for overreacting. Of course, nothing had happened to Sam, why would it? I was becoming more and more like my mother every day. That reminded me, she sent a text earlier, and I still hadn't replied. I'd get around to it tomorrow when I had worked out what to tell her.

Grabbing a mug from the draining board I made a coffee and grabbed the tin of food for Bob, our black moor goldfish. I watched him drift around his tank, oblivious to struggle. Perhaps that was why people were calmed by watching fish. They didn't have a past, or a future, they just had the present, and they moved weightlessly through it. I watched him until my heart that had threatened to hammer through my chest calmed to a pensive tap. There was something to be said about Bob's life, I supposed.

Sam and I had won Bob at a fair, on a warm spring night two years ago when Sam proposed. That night we drank and laughed, and as we wobbled home, intoxicated on love and cheap gin, Bob hung in a bag from my hand. Neither of us knew the first thing about keeping a fish, and I expected him to die within a week. Two years on, Bob had grown out of his tank twice and was still going strong. We joked about him continuing to grow, year after year, until we'd need a pond in the garden for him.

'Hey, Bob,' I said as I sprinkled fish food into the tank. He sprang to life and started to eat in a frenzy.

Picking up my steaming mug of coffee I turned on the wall-mounted TV to catch the news. I wanted to see if anything was being said about Grayson James. Thankfully, the world had moved on, in the media's eye anyway.

'What do you think, Bob? Think it will be OK?' I asked, seeing he had stopped eating and was now idling around the bottom of the glass bowl once more. 'That's what I thought. Sit on it. Give it time.'

The front door opened, and a cold wind swept through. Sam called my name down the corridor.

'Karen, are you home?'

'I'm in the kitchen.'

Sam walked in, looking like a drowned rat.

'Good look,' I said, teasing her.

'I know, it's really coming down now. Roll on, summer.'

'I hear that.'

Sam was empty-handed, something was missing. She noticed the way I looked at her expectantly, and the penny dropped.

'Oh shit, I totally forgot! I'm sorry, Karen, we'll order online.'

'Not a problem, I'll go.'

'No, we'll get them to deliver, it's miserable out there.'

'Don't know about you, babe, but I'm starving. I'll ring now, it will be ready in fifteen to collect. If we wait for them to deliver, we could be sitting here for an hour. And I'm far too hungry for that.'

'You sure?'

'Yeah. Of course,' I said, pleased that I might actually do something productive with the day.

'Shall I pick up a wine too?'

'Yes, great idea. I could do with a glass. I can't believe the weekend is over and it's back to work tomorrow.'

'Looking forward to it then?'

'Expecting this to be another tough week... Some of my year tens and elevens are being a pain in the arse at the moment.'

'Aren't year tens and elevens a pain in the arse all the time?'

'Usually.' She laughed. 'But this group are pushing against the system, which is fine – we all do it from time to time, test the boundaries – but they're getting carried away.'

'Part of growing up.'

'I guess, but I'll have to come down hard on them. Their parents evening is soon; should make for interesting discussions.'

'Oh God, wouldn't want to be part of *that* chat,' I said, nudging Sam.

'They've had their warnings.' She grimaced. 'But I'm glad I get to meet their parents. This is an important time with their mocks and prep for final exams. A few in particular are bright and could do well.'

'What exactly are they doing wrong?'

'Nothing too serious. It's not like they're fighting or truant-ing. But they're being consistently late for lessons, challenging everything a teacher says.'

'I don't know how you put up with it.'

'Well, we can't nick them, like you.'

'You wouldn't anyway, babe, you're too "glass half full",' I said, grabbing my phone to order on the app. 'Veggie supreme?'

'Of course. And, well, I don't know… ' Sam continued, 'recently, I've struggled with them. I've noticed these last few years, kids just aren't kids anymore. They're like mini adults, streetwise and informed, but still without the ability to make proper judgements.'

'That is why I don't work with children.'

'No, just people who are far, far worse.' Sam smiled then asked, her tone gentle, 'How was this morning?'

I sighed, busying myself confirming the order so I didn't have to meet my wife's eye. 'The therapist insisted that being with her isn't about assessing if I acted lawfully at the time of the arrest. She just wants to support me and make sure I'm fine when I'm allowed back to work.'

'That's good.'

'But really, of course she *is* assessing. Accident or not, the inquest will want to know how I was when I went into Grayson James's house that morning. Whether I was in my right mind, whether I acted lawfully.'

'Of course you acted lawfully.'

'I know that. It's just a game, one I have to play, unfortu-nately,' I said, sounding as if it *was* OK when it was anything but. 'Right. Pizza is ordered, give me your car keys, I'll be back soon.'

'You sure you don't mind going out?'

'Not at all, you look beat.'

'Thanks, babe.'

I knew I looked a state in my faded grey jogging bottoms, but really, on a night like this, I didn't care. I'd only be nipping in to grab the pizza and then next door to the offie to grab a bottle of wine. The likelihood of seeing someone I knew was slim, and after the day I'd had, I wasn't sure I'd care if I did. Throwing on a coat and pushing my feet into trainers, I kissed Sam and headed out the door.

THE FIRST GAME

This was it.

Six months of planning, of researching and waiting was over. The Game was about to begin. As he prepared, he listened to his song, over and over on a loop. There was no doubt in his mind what he was doing was right. And, following the two successful experiments he had conducted this week, both concluding in the same manner, he had no doubt that what he was doing would work. He would host The Game in a way that ensured the people he had chosen would play.

It had started to rain, but he didn't mind if it kept the majority of people from venturing out tonight. He was confident it would be quiet anyway, because it had been quiet every Sunday evening for the last few months. Soon, he would see Timothy Smart approach, cross the road and walk in. He would order two chow meins, one chicken, one tofu, for him and his wife. He would then walk back to his car, parked close to the church and away from the main road, then drive the ten or so minutes home. His kids would be in bed, that was why he came late. Timothy Smart was a hands-on father. The Host had seen him read a bedtime story to his youngest several times.

His Player would order his meal tonight from Michelle Reed, the woman who ran the Chinese for the ageing owners, her parents. She would be alone, because soon she would be closing, and she always sent home the young man who worked Sundays half an hour before they closed. He knew all this, because, like most people, Timothy Smart and Michelle Reed were creatures of habit; Timothy went to the same takeaway at the same time every week, Michelle was always there, alone. And they were so wrapped up in their own lives that neither had noticed him watching.

As The Host waited for his Player to arrive, he took out his notebook and read the page where he had listed the items he would need for The Game. His bag was packed, it had been ready for days. Above his checklist was a statement, one he had read to himself countless times, a truth he wanted everyone to know. Written in capital letters and underlined, the one sentence gave him direction when he was lost.

<u>THERE ARE NO GOOD PEOPLE, ONLY THOSE WHO HAVE YET TO DO WRONG.</u>

Timothy's car drove by, he indicated and parked as usual. A few moments later, a car door slammed shut. His Player was on his way. The Host put the book back in his bag beside the motorbike helmet he would soon wear. Timothy rounded the corner, only metres from where he sat. As he passed, Timothy smiled at him, and he smiled back.

He had no idea.

Timothy crossed the road and entered the Chinese. The Host wanted to follow straight away to begin The Game. He wanted to revel in the glory of it, but he knew, despite the growing excitement for what would come, he had to wait. He watched as his Player ordered, exchanged pleasantries with Michelle Reed, saying something that made her throw her head back laughing, and with a satisfied expression on his face, Timothy Smart sat down on the window ledge, and began to look at his phone. Checking his watch, The Host put on his motorbike helmet, crossed the road, and stepped into the Chinese restaurant.

At first, neither Timothy nor Michelle noticed him, but as he locked the door, the snap caught their attention.

'Excuse me. What are you doing? Unlock my door, please!' Michelle Reed said, angry for the intrusion. 'Could you remove your helmet too.'

The Host didn't move or comment, but watched through the tinted visor. They looked at him quizzically, then, as the seconds passed, their expression changed to looks of worry.

'Come on, mate. Take it off,' Timothy echoed, getting to his feet. He didn't stand to intimidate the stranger, far from it, he stood because he was afraid. And The Host was enjoying every moment.

The Host didn't comply, instead he spoke, the voice distorter inside his helmet hiding his true tones as it bounced off the white cracked tiles.

'Timothy Smart, Michelle Reed.'

Both Timothy and Michelle physically recoiled at hearing their names.

'What is this?' Michelle said.

'This evening, the three of us are going to play a little Game. I am your Host, and you two are The Players.'

CHAPTER FOUR

8.11 p.m.

There was something I loved about driving alone. The freedom of being behind the wheel and by yourself where no one could hear you sing or talk or rant. As I pulled out of our road, I turned the radio up on Sam's Volvo, and changed the station from Radio 2 to Radio 1. To my delight, 'Shake it Off' by Taylor Swift was on. I didn't tell anyone, except for Sam, that this song was a guilty pleasure of mine. However shit the day had been, I was driving – something I'd not done since I had to step down at work and forfeit the car – one of my favourite songs was on the radio, and shortly, I would be tucking into a pizza and having a glass of wine with Sam.

Maybe, just maybe, it would all be OK.

But no sooner had I had that thought, the face of Grayson James came into my mind. I had let my guard down, and my subconscious took advantage. His smile taunted me, the vile words aimed at me and Howard swam around my head, and then, that horrific noise I heard after I took him to the ground.

Fuck.

The traffic in front was drawing to a stop. I only just snapped out of my nightmare to brake in time and avoid running into the back of the car in front. The driver shot me an angry glance in the rear-view mirror.

'Sorry!' I mouthed, holding up my hand to show I was accepting my mistake.

Ahead of me, cars were doing three-point turns and heading back the way they'd come. Beyond them, several police cars blocked the road, and I could see two ambulances with blue lights flashing. It must be a major incident for this response.

As each car in front edged forward, turned and drove away, I drew closer and closer to the cordon. I didn't want to be seen – and I couldn't look. The closed road, police cars, ambulances, it reminded me too much of what had happened with Grayson James. I felt my heart rate increase, my forehead prickle with sweat. I needed to leave. Much to the annoyance of the cars behind, I did my three-point manoeuvre even though it wasn't my turn and drove away.

Looking in my rear-view mirror, I saw Howard walk out from a Chinese takeaway. He pinched the bridge of his nose, something he did when he was stressed, although he didn't stress easily. I watched him put his hands on his hips, look up to the sky, and when he was approached by another officer, he offered a kind hand on the younger copper's shoulder.

Whatever had happened, I got the feeling it wasn't pleasant. If it weren't for Grayson James, I'd be working the scene alongside him. I almost grabbed my phone to dial his number, but I stopped myself. We weren't supposed to be in contact right now while the investigation was ongoing, even less so when he was at the scene of an incident. As hard as it was, I drove away and didn't look back.

CHAPTER FIVE

The Host

10.39 p.m.

His hands were shaking. Adrenaline pulsed through his veins like molten lava, hot and dangerous and beautiful. Soon the world would start to learn what he had done, and what he could do. Soon he would become omnipresent, and his message would be delivered to all. The city, perhaps beyond, would live in fear, their actions and words controlled by it. Soon they would start to realise there was no such thing as good – and he couldn't wait. He would be heard, and he would be understood.

The Game had gone perfectly. It had begun.

He searched on Facebook to see if any of the community pages he was a member of had posted anything. As he scrolled, he fiddled with pipe cleaners that were scattered all over his desk. Their bright yellows, pinks, reds, greens, whites and fluorescent oranges were the only real colour in his whole room, which was mainly shades of black, cream and grey.

Absentminded, as he continued to search online for traces of his Game, he picked up two white ones, and without being consciously aware, bent them into the shape of a person. Only when he had finished did he notice what he had made. One arm was disproportionately longer than the other. He doctored the shoulder, giving it a hunch. It now looked a little like Timothy Smart, after his shoulder had been destroyed.

But it wasn't Timothy at all. The person he held was Michelle, because Timothy was gone. She had survived and would have to live with what had happened. He manipulated the pipe-cleaner person, deforming its hand. Bending its arm to emulate what Timothy had done to hers in The Game. Spinning in his chair, he placed it gently on a shelf, beside another pipe-cleaner figurine that had sat there alone for so long.

Turning his attention back to the computer screen, he closed his Facebook page and looked on the local news websites. So far, there was no mention of what had happened tonight. In a way, he was glad, because he could still enjoy the anticipation of the moment when they began to talk. Right now, nobody knew what he'd started, and he fed on the power that came with that.

He looked at the GoPro mounted on the top of his helmet and knew that uploading the footage from this evening would get everyone talking. The conversation would spread like wildfire throughout the country, globally even. But as much as he wanted to, he wouldn't do it yet. He had to be patient because he knew that timing was everything. And whilst the police were scratching their heads, trying to work out what had happened to Michelle and Timothy, he would strike again.

Unzipping his bag, he pulled out his notebook, a companion to him on this journey. He took a moment to read it. Page after page of details about his Game and his ever-growing list of potential Players. He had been thorough and the level of detail was impressive, even to him. At first, he tried to keep his information locked on his phone. But his phone didn't allow him to deviate, be creative, have revelations. The notebook spoke to him, it shared ideas, it allowed evolution, and even though it came with the added risk of being accidentally left somewhere it could be seen, he wouldn't have it any other way. It was his accomplice, his confidant. In a world that was all but lost to him, his notebook offered companionship.

Picking up a pen, he ticked off Timothy Smart and Michelle Reed. Turning to the next page, he looked at the words concerning tomorrow: thoughts about his entrance into the building, the time he would strike, and his next two Players, of course.

And once that was done, once the Second Game had concluded, only then would he share the truth with the world. And everything would change.

DAY 2

4 February 2019

Emily Curtis > Peterborough Free Discussion

Hey all, does anyone have any idea what happened on Fletton High Street last night? The road is closed, and I could see lots of blue flashing lights? They were there for hours. I've looked on the news, and there are no reports yet…

39 Comments

Amanda Belkin

Emily I was wondering the same thing? Watching this thread now.

Jack Anderson

I saw loads of police wearing those white overalls you see on CSI going in. Weird AF. Think someone died?

Emily Curtis

I wondered the same thing, Jack 😨

Jack Anderson

There is nothing in the news yet…

Marky Markson

Maybe someone killed the owner. One less forenner… 😂

Emily Curtis

Really, **Marky?** 😫

Marky Markson

Yeah, fuck 'em. 😂

Johnny Ormo

I've got a friend who works in the police, he says there was a fight of some kind. And **Marky**, don't be that guy…

Emily Curtis

A fight?

Marky Markson

Well they shood all go back to they're own country.

Johnny Ormo

This is their country, you dickhead. And **Emily**, yes, that's what he told me.

Emily Curtis

Jesus, some fight.

Johnny Ormo

I moved to Peterborough ten years ago because it was quiet. But things like this, fights and racist attacks are becoming commonplace, aren't they?

Emily Curtis

I know what you mean, **Johnny**. It's like the streets aren't safe anymore.

CHAPTER SIX

5.17 a.m.

I felt like I hadn't slept at all, but I must have dozed off at some point as it was nearly dawn. Thankfully, Sam was snoring away to my right and blissfully unaware of my struggle. I couldn't stop thinking about the therapy session, and the panic attack I suffered. I wasn't used to feeling out of control like that. I kept seeing Grayson James flash into my mind's eye, in the same way he had when I was driving – an unexpected and unwelcome visitor. And I couldn't stop thinking about what I had seen in Fletton.

Not because it was a crime scene. I seldom lost sleep over that anymore, and it was none of my concern. It was Howard I thought of, the slumped shoulders, pinching the bridge of his nose. It was unlike him to show something was wrong. He was an ex-soldier and even though he and I didn't talk about his time in the army, I knew he'd served overseas, and I suspected that wherever he'd been posted, he'd seen terrible things. Howard was solid, even when things were really bad. And yet, despite not being able to see his face, I could tell he was shaken.

Howard and I had worked on many cases together, some of which were truly horrific and difficult to forget. We'd been on the scene at bad traffic accidents and first responders to a flat where an occupant hadn't been seen in days but a smell had made someone raise the alarm. We'd been to a house fire once where three people didn't make it out. Even with the horrors we had seen, Howard kept his chin up, remained professional. But now it seemed that something terrible had happened and I couldn't support him through it.

Knowing I wouldn't be able to switch off, I gently got out of bed so as not to disturb Sam and got dressed. I left the bedroom, pausing in the doorway to make sure she hadn't noticed the disturbance, her gentle snoring remained steady and deep. I pulled the bedroom door too and tiptoed downstairs.

As I put on my coat, I realised what I was doing. I was going back to Fletton. I felt compelled to have a look, hoping if I did, I would see there was nothing to worry about. Howard could have just have been having an off day. It was probably a routine crime scene and not the tragic, violent, horror story I had painted in my head. I'd just take a peek, that's all, see it with my own eyes and be reassured it was fine. Besides, an early morning walk as the sun emerged over the horizon would make me feel calmer and hopefully, sleepy.

Grabbing my phone and keys I wrapped up in my thick dark green scarf, donned a hat and some gloves and quietly stepped into the pre-dawn morning. The wind and rain that dominated yesterday had vanished, and today was calm but chilly. Beyond the row of houses on our street, I could just about make out a sliver of sunlight reflecting off the lazy winter clouds.

It reminded me of early in my career, when I was first a PCSO. I joined in the October, which meant the first six months on the job consisted of dark, cold mornings. It was a joke with my sergeant at the time. She used to tell me I looked like death until around 10 a.m. But then, spring came, and I started to notice birdsong, the myriad of colours dawn presented, the stillness of this time of day, and I grew to love it. Howard was the same. We spoke of the stillness, the silence that didn't exist at any other point. Night creatures held on to that silence deftly, as the fragile peace would soon be lost to traffic, and the chatter of children walking to school, radios blaring, dogs barking and the sirens in the distance. The orchestra of day.

What they say about crime is true, it never stops. Never, but more often than not it seemed there was a brief interlude around this time. Howard and I would often sit in our police car with a cup of coffee with the window down, listening to the wind in the trees. We called it our time. No wonder people in the office thought we were having an affair, until, of course, they learned Howard is not my type.

I wondered if he was still there, at the scene, or would he be at the station by now?

It would take me about thirty minutes to walk to where I had seen Howard, and then after a quick look, I'd come home. There and back in just over an hour. Sam wouldn't even know I'd gone. Even if she did, I'd tell her I couldn't sleep and went for a quick walk. She knew I loved this time of day, and I'd not be lying, I'd just omit where I had walked to.

After around twenty-five minutes, I was in Fletton, and up ahead, I could see the road was still closed. I tried not

43

to read into it; if it had happened in the middle of the day, they would have rushed to get the road open and resume the illusion of normality. They could take all night if they wanted. There were several forensic police working, their white suits reflecting off the portable floodlights erected around the shop front.

From inside, I saw the flash of a camera. Outside, uniformed officers stood, quietly talking and drinking from takeaway cups. There was also a suited officer with his back to me. At first I wasn't sure who, but then he turned to speak to one of the uniforms, and I saw it was DI Rawlinson, so I stepped behind a white van, obscuring myself from view. The last person I'd want to see me was him. He was no doubt staking his claim on the scene when he discovered it was a 'juicy one' as he liked to call them, which would have been Howard's cue to leave. After Rawlinson spoke to the uniforms, laughing at his own joke, he stepped under the tape that acted as a barrier to the shop, and closed the door behind him.

I knew I shouldn't be here. I had come to try and ease my racing mind and seeing Rawlinson joking and being his usual self told me it surely wasn't as bad as I'd thought. But now I was here, I might as well try and have a closer look.

Moving casually, like a person who was just on their way home from a night shift, I made my way as close as I could. Thankfully, I was able to nip around a corner to a side road and stand beside a large wall, hiding in its shadow. From my viewpoint, I could see the takeaway door. After a few minutes Rawlinson stepped out, leaving the door wide so he could finish his conversation. In that moment I could see past him into the waiting area. There was blood, lots of it, everywhere. It wasn't a routine crime scene; it was a massacre.

Taking out my phone, I rang Howard. It was an automatic response, something I had done for years without giving it a second thought. Surely he wouldn't be asleep, not after what he'd seen? It rang and rang and clicked into voicemail. When the tone beeped, I hung up. Berating myself for being curious, knowing I shouldn't have called – it would mean crossing a line and I wasn't ready for that – I walked away, not daring to look back. When I reached an underpass beneath the dual carriageway, I stopped and caught my breath.

Something awful had happened. Someone must have seen something. My eye was drawn to where the road above connected with the bridge. In the corner was a raised ledge where several of the city's homeless slept. When I was a PCSO I was called out to this very bridge. It was winter then, too, but colder than now, the temperature barely scraping zero degrees in the middle of the day. A homeless man known to us all as Charlie, a career petty criminal, lay in his sleeping bag. When I tried to rouse him, I discovered he had died in the night. It was the first dead person I'd ever seen. I didn't know what was worse, that I hadn't thought about it for a long time, or that now I had, I didn't feel anything. Pushing Charlie out of my thoughts, I focused on that corner. Cardboard boxes lay in the sheltered space, another Charlie taking residence. I scrambled up the slope, to see if anyone was there. A mound lay perfectly still under a stained and torn sleeping bag, the polyester innards spewing through in multiple places, and my heart skipped a beat. Because I was thirty feet above the ground, I could see the Chinese restaurant and the police officers outside. Slowly I reached forward and gave the mound a nudge, nothing. I tried again, this time a little harder and jumped when a young woman rolled over, dazed and startled.

'What the fuck do you want?' she said, her words cold and hard, like the ground she lay on.

'Sorry, I just wanted to see how you were,' I replied, my heart thumping in my head, mirroring the thrum of early morning lorries only feet above us. The girl barked she was fine until she was woken, and I backed away apologetically. I took in the girl's face. She was young – too young to be having a life that hard. She had good teeth, a strong jaw. She could just as easily be at college or work instead of dishevelled and cold. I wasn't on shift; I couldn't ask her any questions; I shouldn't even be here. Sliding back down the ramp, I knew I needed to go home.

'Karen?'

I jumped, startled to hear a familiar voice. 'Sam? What are you doing here?'

'I should ask the same question – why are you out so early in the morning?'

'I couldn't sleep. So I went for a walk to clear my head. How did you...'

'I woke up, couldn't find you in the house. A coat missing, no note. I was worried. I've been driving around for half an hour. Are you all right?'

I looked behind me, the crime scene was thankfully obscured from view.

'I'm fine.'

'Are you sure?'

'Yes, honestly, I just didn't sleep well, I needed a pre-dawn walk.'

46

'Karen, why didn't you wake me and tell me you were going out?'

'I didn't want to worry you.'

'Well, that plan failed.'

'Sorry.'

'And of course I'm going to worry about you.'

'I'm all right, I just need time, that's all.'

'Sure, time will help, so will talking, opening up. You're so distracted all the time, and clearly you can't sleep. Karen, I want to *do* something.'

'I know you do.'

'Then let me.'

'Sam, I'm, I'm not there yet.'

'OK, I won't push, but when you're ready, I'll be waiting.'

Sam stepped towards me and wrapped her arms around me, and I let myself fold into her, breathing in her strawberry-scented hair.

'Can I take you home now?'

I nodded into her neck, worried if I tried to speak I might sob.

'Good, I'm bloody freezing.'

I laughed and Sam pulled away and we began to walk back towards the car.

As I opened the passenger door, I took one final look back towards the takeaway in the distance, just in case.

CHAPTER SEVEN

The Host

8.49 a.m.

He loaded his bag, ticking off the items from the list in his book as he did, and when he was done, he placed the book with the rest of the tools needed for the next Game. Zipping up his bag, he took one last look at the shelf with the two pipe-cleaner figurines, knowing there would very soon be a third, then he grabbed his helmet and left.

The first Game was a success and the second was in motion. People weren't talking yet, but they would be very soon. And oh, how they would talk.

CHAPTER EIGHT

Carlson

12.52 p.m.

As Carlson entered the Echo Lounge, one of the few remaining nightclubs in Peterborough, it took a moment for his eyes to adjust to the dark. Once they had, he was glad for his tough constitution. Carlson didn't know what to make of the scene in front of him. It was just like what he'd seen in the Chinese restaurant. One dead, one as good as. No motive, no reasoning. No warning. Two people who seemed unlikely to be involved in a crime had committed, or attempted to commit the most heinous of them all. He wanted answers, something that would help him make sense of what he was looking at. Neither Michelle nor the latest to survive, twenty-three-year-old Milly Hallam, was in a fit state to be interviewed. And judging by the scene, and the description of her injuries, he suspected Millie might never be.

Carlson felt overwhelmed. The forensics were busy working around the empty, eerie nightclub, gathering evidence and documenting images to help understand the choreography of the crime – until they did that, he could only watch. As he looked helplessly on, he was approached from behind by PC Sommers, who despite his shift finishing hours ago, said he wanted to help.

'DS Carlson. What's going on?'

'I wish I knew.'

'I mean, two similar incidents in less than twenty-four hours...'

'Don't jump to conclusions, it might just be a coincidence.'

'Some fucked-up coincidence.'

'Yeah.'

'It's weird, isn't it?' Sommers continued.

'Wanna be specific?'

'The club, I've only ever seen it when it's night – loud music, drinks flowing – it's eerie in the day. Spooky, almost. I'd not wanna work here.'

'Yeah,' Carlson said laconically.

'Sir, I know you don't want to hear it. But after last night, and now this, there are a few people outside who want to know something.'

'Who?'

'Local paper.'

'Tell them, as soon as we have information, we will let them know.'

'Will we? Let them know?'

Carlson smiled. 'What do you think?'

Sommers nodded, and headed back the way he'd come to pacify the few who had linked the two scenes together. Carlson liked PC Sommers; he was young, a little naïve, but he was a good copper, and he wanted to be a great one. He reminded Carlson of Karen Holt when they were both starting out. Her progression from being a PCSO, his from his stint in the forces. Despite them starting their policing career at similar times, Karen was a better copper and he knew it. She could read a scene, find the truths that were hidden in plain sight and connect the dots. He had seen it several times before, cracking wide open cases that seemed impenetrable. Like that of Daniel Lynch the year before, the man suspected of killing his ex-wife's new husband and kidnapping her and his son. The whole country had been gunning for him, wanting him arrested, Carlson included. But Karen had seen it from a different perspective, and although she disobeyed the rules, went at it alone when no one would listen, she ended up saving both Lynch and the boy. It nearly cost her her job, the fact she was right saved it, but still, she was busted down from a DCI to a DI for it. He wished she was there with him, showing him what he couldn't see. Just like she did with that case.

'Right, Howard, be like Karen, connect the dots,' he said to himself as he scanned the scene. 'Milly Hallam, the club's PR manager, comes to work for nine, assuming she keeps a nine to five schedule. The owner is in by 9.30 a.m., and by 10.30 a.m., this…'

His eye was drawn to the two items in the middle of the room. A rounders bat, which reminded him of school, but bloodied and chipped, a tooth clearly visible embedded in it. A tooth that should have been in Milly Hallam's head. And a crowbar, a dark mass of hair caught in its claw. On the floor three feet away, the lifeless body of fifty-one-year-old Alexandru Stoica, the nightclub owner.

Blood pooled beside him. It wasn't just confined to that one place. It was on the bar, on the stools in front of it, on the optics behind, everywhere. They had fought like two people who hated each other, not like two people who were employer and employee. Before Milly Hallam passed out, she told the first responder that she didn't want to kill him. What Carlson saw was contradictory – the evidence showed that she did want to kill him, and he wanted to kill her. She had succeeded by caving in his skull, and he had come close, too, by beating her with a rounders bat. But so far, Carlson didn't know why. Nor did he know how it had anything to do with Michelle Reed and Timothy Smart.

Two fights, two men dead. Was there a connection?

He recalled his conversation with homeless Mikey. He had said something similar, that he didn't want to hurt the man in the red coat. He'd been genuinely concerned for the wellbeing of the man he'd attacked.

'Sommers?' Carlson called out, and his young colleague turned, one hand on the door to outside where the small crowd waited hungrily.

'Sir?'

'You remember the homeless chap we arrested last week. Mikey. Is he still in custody?'

'No, the other bloke wasn't as badly hurt as he looked. He didn't want to press charges.'

'He didn't want to press charges?'

'Nope. Said he understood, he had a dog he loved too.'

'So Mikey could be anywhere.'

'Yeah, but he pops up, doesn't he? Want me to find him?'

'No, it's OK. I'll go, you sort out the vultures.'

'Yeah, cheers, boss.' Sommers smiled, and continued on his way.

Carlson nodded, and turned back to face the scene.

'Hey, Georgia!' he called out to a forensic officer photographing an upturned shoe. She lowered her camera, turned and pulled down her face mask.

'What's up, Howard?'

'Have you seen any evidence of a third person?'

'A third person? No, nothing.'

'OK, keep your eyes peeled. If you get anything, can you let me know?'

'Sure.' She sounded curious as to what Carlson was thinking.

Without offering further explanation, Carlson stepped out of the nightclub and back into the blinding daylight. A small crowd had formed, PC Sommers in the middle of them, trying to calm people down. Most were holding out their mobile phones, grabbing a sound bite from the officer about the crimes over the past twenty-four hours. Carlson noted how young some of them looked. Kids wearing suits and shiny shoes, pretending to adult. But then he could say the same about Sommers.

Eyes cast down to avoid soliciting any interest, Carlson stuffed his hands into his pockets and walked towards the city centre. He hoped Mikey was at his usual spot. He wanted to ask a few more questions about the mysterious third man.

CHAPTER NINE

The Host

2.14 p.m.

After the Second Game had been played and the fate of Alexandru Stoica sealed, he had planned to slip away and return home to begin the next phase. But curiosity took over, and as the police arrived on the scene and a small crowd gathered, he couldn't help himself. He wanted to hear what people were saying, see if they had connected any dots, what conclusions they drew. They would have questions, he knew all of the answers, and silently answering them would be exciting. Seeing the police cluelessly move in and out of the nightclub made it nearly impossible to suppress his smile. When the officer came over to the group, standing only five feet away from him, he tingled with excitement. A local journalist fired a barrage of questions: what had happened? Was this connected to the incident last night? Had there been a fatality? These questions were deflected with assurances of a full investigation. He kept quiet, and watched the tennis match rally back and forth between him. It was obvious from the police officer's face that he felt the nightclub and the Chinese killings were connected, but of course he couldn't yet say that. If he did, there would be panic, there would be terror. And The Host was glad, because he wanted the panic and the terror to come from *him* and him alone. As the young officer wrapped up and headed towards the club, he brushed past The Host's shoulder. The rush of adrenaline was like no other and it had lasted the whole journey home.

The Game had taken a not unexpected but still surprising twist with Stoica's defiance. He was glad Milly won. He hoped Milly pulled through. She needed to; The Game needed a victor. Of all the people he had followed, he admired her the most. She was kind, a young carer for her unwell mother, working hard to pay their bills. She was good. She was also a creature of routine, like the others. She always got the same number three bus to and from work. At around the same time each morning – 7.45 a.m. – and then in the afternoon at 5.30 p.m. He often rode the number 3 at those times, so he could build his case for her to be a Player.

Once, on the number 3 bus, she sat next to him, and they exchanged a polite smile. He expected her to sit in silence, as people do, but to his surprise and delight, she struck up a conversation about the book he was reading – ironically, the very book which helped him begin his Game. She asked him about the content, and when he explained it was a debate around the value of life, posing an ethical question about sacrificing one to save many. She commented that she couldn't answer, because she couldn't take a life.

'But what about additional circumstances?' he asked.

'Additional circumstances?'

'What if one of them was terminally ill, or what if one was old, and the other was young?'

'It wouldn't matter, I still couldn't do it,' she replied.

He wished he could believe her; he almost did. But after The Game, it turned out, she was lying to herself.

Now, back at his desk, he watched the footage from that Game, captured in high definition for the audience to enjoy. The violence was spectacular, beautiful. Alexandru Stoica and Milly Hallam played The Game very well indeed. He watched until the end to check it had all been recorded. Then, he saved it for another time and opened the video on his desktop from the Chinese takeaway with Michelle and Timothy. Once he had absorbed it, he put on his motorbike helmet, and picked up his GoPro. He held it in front of him, the dark visor filling most of the screen, and started recording his message.

'*What you are about to see is unedited footage of a game I played on the night of the 3rd of February. A game I will play again.*

'*I am your Host.*

'*I am in your offices, in your restaurants and pubs. I am on your high streets and in your libraries, I watch you at the gym, I sit beside you on your buses. I see you eating popcorn and laughing at the cinema. I observe you on your lunch breaks and follow you on your way home from collecting a takeaway.*

'*I. Watch. You. Sleep.*

'*And I might come to you, and choose you to be a Player.*'

Once recorded, he uploaded it and edited it into the first Game. He wanted to release it there and then, but knew it wasn't quite time.

Good things come to those who wait.

The best things came to those who knew this without anyone needing to tell them.

Reaching forward, he picked up two pipe cleaners and shaped them. Arms, legs, torso, head. This one was called Milly. He bent the side of the head in, caved it towards the centre, just like it looked after The Game. Placing it next to Michelle, and the original – the name he would never say – he sat on his bed, put in his headphones, and pressed play on his iPhone. As he listened to Black, he thought they were right, it really was a wonderful life.

Johnny Ormo posted a picture > Peterborough Free Discussion

Emily Curtis
What on earth? **Johnny**, where is that?

Johnny Ormo
Geneva Street. Outside my work. I heard sirens, looked out, two ambulances, several police cars. Something's happened. And it reminded me of what you were talking about last night.

Emily Curtis
Shit. Do you know what's going on?

Johnny Ormo
Not a clue, but it's clear it's something big. Anyone know what's happening?!?!?

Emily Curtis
😱😱😱

Jack Anderson
I've just found this on the Peterborough Post website...

Police were called to the Echo Lounge nightclub in Peterborough following a disturbance. It's believed there has been a fatality, less than twenty-four hours after a similar incident in another part of the city. The police are yet to comment. Were you involved? Get in touch **here**.

Emily Curtis
Anyone else think this is a little fucked up?

Johnny Ormo
Seriously fucked up…

Jack Anderson
You don't think the two things are linked?

Johnny Ormo
It's a bit of a weird coincidence.

Emily Curtis
Shit, I go to the Echo Lounge. I was there three nights ago.

Jack Anderson
My friend works there. I've messaged him, he has no idea what's happened.

Marky Markson
The owner of the club isn't British…

Emily Curtis
What's your point, **Marky**?

Marky Markson

Nothing, just saying, wouldn't want to offend a bunch of snowflakes.

Johnny Ormo

Prick.

Marky Markson

Fuck you. I'll fuck you up like someone fucking up foreners. Pussy.

Johnny Ormo

Says the guy who hides behind the fake name, **Marky.**

Claire Turner

Foreigners*

Johnny Ormo

😂 😂

Emily Curtis

Is anyone else really worried? Why aren't the police saying anything? I was at the Echo Lounge, only a few days ago. And the Chinese, it's right near my house. It all feels so close to home.

Claire Turner

Hey. I know what you mean, **Emily**. Peterborough is small, and this thing is starting to feel really scary. 💀

CHAPTER TEN

3.18 p.m.

I messaged Sam, eager for her to get home and keep me company, asking her to let me know what time she'd be back so I could whip up one of my world-famous carbonaras. I wanted us to have a good relaxing evening together. I needed to make amends for this morning.

After Sam left for work, I cleaned the house, hoovered, dusted, opened windows to let fresh air circulate, all as my way of saying sorry for how I have been recently. When the therapist's office called to say there had been a cancellation, I confirmed a rescheduled appointment for 10 a.m. tomorrow. I didn't want to go back but I'd said I would, for Sam. With nothing left to do until she got home, I settled on the sofa and put on the TV, and dozed until there was a knock on the front door, making me jump.

Jesus, Karen.

I expected it to be a courier, delivering something Sam had ordered, she probably told me she had bought something, I have a habit of forgetting the little things lately. As I opened the door, I was shocked at who had come to see me.

'Howard.'

I hugged him and he hugged back.

'Whoa – PDA,' he joked.

'Sorry, I've missed you.'

Howard waited for me to invite him in, as I had done a thousand times before, but I hesitated.

'You gonna make me a cuppa?' he asked, feeling uncertain by my reluctance.

'Howard, I don't think you coming in is a good idea.'

'Yeah, I get it. So how are you?' he asked.

'You know.'

'It will be over soon.'

'We hope.'

'It *will*. It's a fucking joke.'

'Does anyone know you're here?' I asked.

'No,' he replied, 'thought it was for the best nobody did.'

'Probably a good thing.'

'It's not a good thing. It's bullshit, we all know you did nothing wrong.'

'The system is the system, no point fighting it.'

'Still, it's wrong. They treat you like a criminal when all you were doing was your job. It's fucking ridiculous.'

'Well, I don't exactly have the best track record for following the rules, they have to take that into account.'

'But even with that, you were right. They shouldn't have reprimanded you then, and they shouldn't now. Sometimes being a copper is a fucking—'

'Howard, have you come here to rant about me not being at work?'

'No, sorry.'

'Are you all right?'

He looked at me, opened his mouth like he was about to say something, and closed it again. 'No. I'm not. Can I come in, please?'

There was something in the way he asked that told me I needed to say yes, despite knowing it was wrong. I showed him in, he closed the door behind him, then we both made our way to the kitchen where I fixed us a cuppa.

Taking it in his hands, Howard nodded his appreciation, and then pinched the bridge of his nose. Stress.

'Howard?'

'Something's happening, and I can't work out what. And you should be on the case. We'd all be in a better place with this if they hadn't suspended you for doing your job.'

'Howard, wanna climb down from your soapbox and fill me in? You say something's happened, and you wanna tell me, so tell me.' I smiled.

'Yes, sorry.' He blushed. 'There was a murder last night.'

'At a Chinese restaurant in Fletton.'

'Yes! How do you know?'

'I saw something online.' I shrugged.

'It's fucked up, seriously fucked up. The murder victim was a guy called Timothy Smart. Forty-three. Married, two kids. Worked for an IT company in Hampton. One of those who minds his own business. No previous, not even as much as a parking ticket.'

'How old are his kids?'

'Thirteen and nine.'

'Shit.'

'It gets worse.'

'Worse? How?'

'The other person involved was Michelle Reed, thirty-seven, manager of the takeaway where it happened. Again, no previous.'

'The Chinese takeaway manager killed a customer?'

'Yep.'

'Why?'

'This is where it gets really fucked up. We don't know why.'

'How did she kill him?'

'Honestly, if I didn't see it, I'd not believe it. The shop was like a scene from *Game of Thrones*.'

I thought about what I saw when Rawlinson held the door open, and I glimpsed inside. 'Did they fight?'

'Yep. To the death.'

'And we don't know why?'

'Nope.'

'How is she, the woman?'

'Alive, but pretty beaten up. She's in Peterborough District Hospital right now.'

'Has anyone spoken to her?'

'Not yet. She had to have quite a bit of emergency surgery. Nearly lost a hand. She's gonna pull through, but we aren't allowed access to her until she's been moved from the HDU.'

'Jesus.'

'Karen, that's not all.'

'Go on,' I said, feeling my heart begin to pump harder. Howard did not scare easily, but right now, he looked terrified.

'This morning a call came – there's been another murder. The circumstances are far too similar to overlook.'

'Who was involved?'

'A nightclub owner, and one of his employees. Both no previous, no clear motive.'

'Shit.'

'Yeah, shit, and going by what I've been told, we'll get nothing out of the survivor, at least not for a while.'

'Who survived?'

'The employee, the club's PR manager.'

'You think the two crimes are connected?'

'I'm sure of it.'

Howard then told me about the previous week, two people had each attacked a stranger in red, a third party making them do it. I couldn't help but feel abandoned for not being included in this. But I pushed the discomfort down – I'd not been included for my own good.

'So someone might have made the two murderers do what they did?'

Howard was solemn. 'It's only a hunch, but yes.'

'Think it will happen again?' I asked. Howard didn't reply. 'If they are connected by the same third person, things are moving fast. And you're saying the only people who might know something and can shed any light on this are two women, both of them in the high dependency unit?'

'Yep.'

'You need answers.'

'Yeah, we do.'

Howard looked at me, a question on his face, he was so easy to read.

I raised my upturned palms in a clear gesture. 'No.'

'Karen—'

'No, Howard, I'm strictly not allowed to be involved in any investigations.'

'Karen, Michelle is conscious and might be ready to talk but we can't get to her right now.'

'So wait.'

'And let it happen again?'

'You don't know it will happen again.'

'Two similar incidences in twenty-four hours... it shouts—'

'I know what it shouts, Howard, but even if I wanted to, I can't.'

'Sorry. It's just you have that way of finding out things, you know, and I'm desperate. I shouldn't have asked.'

'You didn't.'

'You know what I mean.'

Simultaneously, we sipped our drinks.

'I can't wait until you're back.'

'Hopefully, if the IOPC—'

'*When* –' he interrupted – 'when the IOPC state you did nothing wrong.'

'Howard. Stop.'

'Sorry,' he replied before we fell into an uncomfortable silence. I felt awful that I couldn't help. Howard rarely asked for anything. I hated I had to say no. But I had to think of Sam. I had to think of myself.

'How is Jess?' I said, changing the subject.

Howard's face lit up. 'She's great. Doing really well at school. Keeps getting on the star chart thing they have.'

'That's lovely.'

'Becca does a really good job raising her.'

'You are both raising her.'

'Yeah, but I only raise every other weekend and one night in the week. Becca is doing most of it. She's a good mother.'

'Are you two still on good terms?'

He smiled, a shy one out of the corner of his mouth.

'Howard?'

'We've been talking more recently.'

'I see.'

'Trying not to read into it too much, and we don't want to get Jess's hopes up.'

'Well, I hope either way you two continue to talk. I always liked Becca.'

'Yeah, she's a good one.'

Howard's phone rang and, apologising, he answered it. I moved away, not wanting to overhear the conversation and began to rinse out our cups. The phone call was short, and when it ended, I turned back to see that the colour had washed out of his face.

'Howard?'

'I gotta go,' he said, unable to look me in the eye as he went to put on his shoes.

'Howard, what's happened?'

'I...' He couldn't get his words out.

'What?'

'A video has been posted online.'

'A video? Of what?'

He didn't answer but nodded and left, the door banging shut behind him. Running to my phone, I went onto the internet but I couldn't find anything; I didn't know where or how to look. So I went to my Facebook. Scrolling down, a news article leapt out.

Video posted online of a murder in a Chinese restaurant

I clicked the link, but wasn't ready for what I saw.

CHAPTER ELEVEN

5.31 p.m.

Somehow, as Sam and I ate dinner, I managed to disguise the state I was in. The video had shaken me to my core. The level of violence was hard to dismiss. Thankfully, Sam hadn't seen, nor heard it. The video was posted just after school had finished, when she was doing detentions and marking, and she didn't go online all that much anyway. Being a teacher and having Facebook wasn't a good idea. Kids were naturally curious and invasive, and Sam learnt years ago it posed too much of a professional risk. She would see the video, soon enough, but as she told me about her crushing workload, I suspected she'd be buried under a pile of marking tonight and too busy to be browsing online. However, I had no doubt by morning she would know. It would be everywhere by then.

As we sat at the dinner table, I watched Sam greedily tuck into her steaming carbonara. My appetite was all but gone, but I made myself eat some. Each mouthful was hard to swallow, my stomach was tight, not wanting anything in it, and I knew if I tried to force it all down, I'd likely be sick. Sam told me about her day, shared funny things students had said, like reasons for not handing in homework or being late for school. I laughed with her. I hoped she couldn't tell it was faked.

'I swear, these kids don't believe we were ever young,' she said through a mouth full of tagliatelle.

'Well, we are dinosaurs, I guess.'

'Speak for yourself!' she protested. 'We're not even forty-five.'

'Remember when we thought forty-five was ancient.'

She laughed. 'Well, the world has changed since then.'

'Yeah, but not for the young. Anything over forty is still ancient.'

'Oi,' Sam protested, smiling at me. I offered back a smile that was as close to hers as I could manage. I needed to keep her talking, so she wouldn't ask too much about my day: but also, I craved normality. I needed it, because the video was as far from normal as it got. I was happy Sam hadn't seen it yet because if she had, we'd no doubt talk about it, or nothing at all.

'Kids do funny things, don't they?' I said.

'Tell me about it. I had one who was late for school today, said, and I quote, "Sorry I'm late, miss, I lost my hamster."'

'Lost a hamster?'

'Yep. I knew full well he probably didn't have a hamster. But I had to let it slide, it was so original.'

Sam fell into a comfortable silence as she ate. She cleared her plate, but I only managed about half. I tried my best to push away the video I had seen, tried and failed. The violence kept coming back, with each blink it was there, imprinted on the back of my eyelids.

'Karen?'

I snapped my attention back to Sam. She looked concerned.

'Are you all right?'

'Sorry, yes, I'm OK. Sorry. Distracted.'

I blinked away the image of the woman holding a claw-hammer above her head.

'It's OK if you want to talk about anything.'

'No,' I said too quickly. 'No, it's fine.'

'You sure?'

'Yep.'

Blink. The man stabbing her through the hand.

'I've got another counselling session tomorrow.'

'Tomorrow? I thought your next slot was next week?'

'They had a cancellation, asked if I wanted it.'

Blink. The woman sinking her teeth into his cheek.

'Well, that's great. Hopefully it will speed things up.'

'Yeah, hopefully.'

'Karen, look at me.'

Sam reached over and took my hand.

Blink. The man choking her.

'They'll come back and say you did nothing wrong, and when they do, you'll be back to work, and this will all just fade away.'

'I hope so.'

'I promise.'

I smiled, and Sam reciprocated sympathetically. I should have told her there and then about the video, but I didn't. Because despite how fucked up I was, I couldn't sit back and do nothing. Howard needed answers. I needed to help.

'A few of the guys from work are going for a beer – asked if I wanted to come.'

Shit, Karen, what are you doing?

'That's great, are you sure it's all right, with – you know?'

'Howard isn't there, he's on shift, and it's a big group. It will be fine.'

'Good.'

'You don't mind?'

'Why would I mind? I've got a ton of work to do anyway, it'd be good to get you out of my hair. I'm not used to you being at home so much.' She smiled, her right cheek full of pasta she had stolen off my plate. 'Need a lift?'

'No, one of the guys said they'd pick me up at the end of the road,' I lied, again.

After washing up I got ready, kissed Sam goodbye and told her not to wait up.

'Have a good evening,' she called.

'I will, babe.' The guilt I felt made it nearly impossible to smile. As I closed the door, the winter air cooled my cheeks which were flushed from lying to the person I loved.

Head down, I walked towards the bus stop. I almost stopped, I almost turned back and went home where I could climb into bed with Sam and watch Netflix and fall asleep as she stroked my hair. But I didn't because every time I blinked, the video came to me. I knew Sam had no reason to doubt my plans for this evening, but I looked back anyway, just to make sure she wasn't watching. I crossed the main road and waited for a city centre bus. When it arrived I took a corner seat in the back row, and watched the world go by, planning how I would get close enough to Michelle Reed to find out exactly what had happened.

CHAPTER TWELVE

The Host

6.36 p.m.

Staring at his computer screen, he read the responses to his video in a thread on the Peterborough Free Discussion board. The YouTube account he originally posted on using a discreet Belarus VPN company had been closed down, but he'd assumed that would be the case. No matter, there were plenty more accounts he could choose from, plenty more ways to get his video out there without being detected. Before the account was blocked, hundreds of messages had been posted.

He read a few, most written in disbelief at what they were seeing, calling it a cheap-looking slasher movie, poorly edited, badly acted. The same was being conveyed on Facebook. People had posted screen grabs of the video, showing they had 'proof' the video was a deep fake. They said the moment Timothy Smart thrust the chisel into Michelle Reed's hand was obvious, because she didn't scream. They said the hammer crashing down on his shoulder was fake because of how damaged it was afterwards and that the moment he strangled her – nearly to death before she pulled the chisel out of her hand and stuck it in his face – was nothing more than a clever edit.

Reviewing the comments made his cheeks flush. It was too real for them, and so they had to try to rationalise or desensitise it – but soon they wouldn't be able to. When he posted again, they wouldn't be quite so dismissive.

On the news, the police called it a 'clever hoax', no doubt trying to keep the public calm, assuming they would find him before he could do it again, but they never would. Soon the police would have to change their script. Soon, Timothy's wife would speak out, or Michelle Reed's parents. Soon they would have to tell the truth.

And when they did, when everyone knew what another human being was capable of, they would be one step closer to understanding there was no such thing as good.

Logging off, The Host got up. He needed to walk, to enjoy the evening, and see if he could hear any quiet whispers from the public about his Game. There would no doubt be a thousand questions, and one by one, he would answer them all.

CHAPTER THIRTEEN

7.46 p.m.

Peterborough District Hospital seemed quieter than expected for the end of visiting hours. The few people I saw outside as the bus pulled up were mostly patients, wrapped in dressing gowns, some in wheelchairs, IV drips attached to a trolley, who had braved the frigid February air to have a cigarette or chat on the phone. I tried not to look anyone in the eye as I walked into the main entrance. Even now, after countless visits, I couldn't help but be surprised at how warm it felt, how clean it all looked. The huge, light atrium adorned with giant colourful kites in the ceiling was nothing like the old hospital, which had been lifeless and frightening.

I smiled at the older man standing in the reception area, and made my way towards the lifts at the far end. I suspected that Michelle would still be in the high dependency unit, as Howard told me, and reaching the lift, I pressed the button for the first floor and waited for it to come. As the doors opened, a uniformed officer I recognised was on the other side. I dipped my head and stepped past him into the lift. He didn't seem to notice me.

At the first floor, I held the lift open for a young man, late teens at most, and after he thanked me, I walked towards critical care. My phone rang as I approached.

'Howard?'

'Just checking up on you.'

'I'm fine.'

'You sound like you're out?'

'I am.'

'Anywhere nice?'

'Give you one guess.'

'Thank you, Karen.'

'Yeah, yeah, thank me when I find something out, as long as I don't get caught, of course.'

'You don't have to do this.'

'Really? You say this now?'

'I shouldn't have asked today. I was out of line.'

'Out of line?'

'You know what I mean, you've got bigger things to deal with at the moment.'

'To be honest, it's nice to feel useful.'

'Yeah, but ——'

'Howard, I watched the video. I've not seen anything like it in my life.'

'No, me neither. How are you gonna speak to her?' he said, the guilt in his words tangible.

'By blending in. I'll keep you posted.'

I hung up and walked on. After the next corner, there was a copper leaning against the wall, looking vigilant. I suspected

76

someone from the media had turned up, trying to get a statement from Michelle Reed now the case was all over the local news.

I walked past, keeping my head low, pretending to read my phone and made my way towards the seating area, tucked just out of sight of him, opposite the nurses' station. When I got there, a nurse flashed me a glance. I smiled, and it seemed to be enough for her not to ask anything. She kept an eye on me for a while longer, no doubt assuming I was here for a scoop. As she lowered her head, continuing with her paperwork, I looked around for an idea. Somehow, I needed to be in that room, but the officer outside couldn't know who I was.

I sat down, kicked off my shoe and began kneading the arch of my foot, pretending to be another poor soul who was on their feet all day, like her. She glanced my way, gave me a knowing smile and continued with her work. Without saying anything, I had identified myself as yet another overworked, tired woman. She was subconsciously on my side, which would make it easier to get around her.

I just had to wait for the right moment.

Around me, hospital staff moved to and fro, busy, stressed to the limit. Behind the nurse, who was now talking on the phone, I could see a white lab coat slung on a back of a chair. I knew a hospital chart and an air of confidence would likely be enough to slip by the police officer. But a lab coat would guarantee it. The nurse finished her phone conversation, picked up some paperwork from her desk, and flashing me a trusting smile, walked away.

I didn't waste a second, as soon as the nurse was out of

sight, I moved. Stepping behind the counter, I grabbed the coat, slipped it on and picked up a patient's chart. With a purposeful stride, I headed towards the room where Michelle Reed was recovering. I exchanged a polite nod with the police officer, and slipped inside.

Michelle Reed was looking at the ceiling, hooked up to an IV drip and heart rate monitor. Once the door was shut behind me, I took a deep breath and paused, my fingers working over my nails, thumb to little finger, there and back twice, waiting for the police officer outside to recognise me and storm into the room. Nothing happened.

She was a mess. I could see deep purple marks on her neck where she had been strangled. The right side of her face was swollen, her eye clamped shut, the skin stretching over it looked like it would tear at any moment. Both her arms were bandaged up from the defence wounds sustained as she tried to stop Timothy Smart killing her with a chisel. And her left hand, the one Howard said she nearly lost, was braced with several external pins in it. In her other hand was a small button for pain medication. Christ knows she looked like she needed it.

As I examined her, Michelle turned and peered at me.

'How are you feeling?' I said quietly.

'Can I have some water?' Michelle croaked, her voice barely audible from the impact of strangulation.

'Sure, let me help you,' I replied, picking up a cup and placing the straw near her lips.

I had a million questions and didn't know where to start. But I was aware time wasn't on my side. Another nurse might walk in, or a doctor, or the lead investigating officer, whoever it was. I suspected it would be Rawlinson, but hoped I was wrong. He was a brute of a copper, he barked orders at those below and scoffed at those above; he wasn't someone to get on the wrong side of or owe anything to. If Rawlinson walked in now, I would be for the chopping block. He was old school and wasn't much in favour of a woman DI, let alone a gay woman DI. Time was critical.

'Michelle, how are you feeling?'

'I… I hurt.'

'We can get you something for the pain,' I said. She assumed I was a doctor; I wouldn't tell her any different.

'Michelle, lots of people want to talk to you. About what happened.'

'I can't.'

'It's OK, we know you didn't want to do what you did.'

'How? How do you know?'

I wasn't about to tell her that her video had been all over the internet, that she had become infamous.

'When you were coming out of your anaesthetic, you told us.'

'You were there during the operation?'

'Yes,' I lied.

'What did I say?' she asked, her voice distant and weak.

'That you never meant to hurt anyone.'

I watched a tear roll out of the corner of Michelle's eye and trail around the swelling to her cheek and jaw.

'I didn't,' she said, barely audible, her eyes closing, each blink seconds long. I needed to ask quickly, or I'd miss my chance.

'Michelle, you told me about a third person?'

'Did I?'

'Yes. Can you tell me any more? The police want to know, and I want to pass on the message, so they'll leave you in peace.'

'I didn't see a face.'

Outside the door, I heard the officer talking. Although I couldn't distinguish the exact words, I could tell he was asking someone to leave. I held my breath.

'Is someone there?' Michelle asked sleepily.

'The police, they're guarding your room to keep you safe. Michelle, help me. Tell me what you can remember about the third person.'

'I need to sleep.'

Tears began to fill her eyes, and before I could say anything to stop her, she clicked the morphine dispenser in her hand. Soon she would drift again.

'Michelle, quickly. What happened? I need to know.'

'There was a motorbike...'

'A motorbike – helmet? Someone was wearing a motorbike helmet?' I knew this already. I needed more. 'Michelle?'

'A Game.'

'A Game?'

'Four minutes... I didn't know...'

Her words slurred, and before I could ask more, she had drifted into a drug-infused sleep.

Knowing I'd not get any more out of her, I slipped out the door, past the police officer and towards the exit, dropping the white lab coat and clipboard on a chair. It had been a wasted trip. I hadn't learnt anything new. The third person – the one who recorded and released that video – had made them fight.

But I had no idea who or why. Taking out my phone, I sent
Howard a text.

> I've learnt nothing. Sorry. I'm staying out of this now,
> I can't take the risks. You'll get this guy, Howard. But it
> will have to be without me.

CHAPTER FOURTEEN

The Host

8.31 p.m.

If the first Game in the Chinese set the tone, the second shouted it from the rooftops. The violence was magnificent, glorious. And he couldn't wait to share it with the world. The video was ready, waiting to be uploaded. Soon. With the next Game planned, he spent the evening walking around the city. Watching the world that was becoming aware. He sat in McDonald's and listened to conversations about it, he saw it in the way people looked at each other. Fear was spreading.

Checking the time, he knew he could do one more thing before going home and trying to sleep, and after a twenty-minute walk, he found himself standing on a footbridge, looking down at the cars speeding by. Drivers thought they were invincible in their metal bubbles. It was an illusion; at any moment they could lose control, or swerve to miss an animal in the road – at any moment, it could be over. But as they say, ignorance is bliss.

As the cars continued uneventfully, he took out his phone and went on to Facebook. He looked up the Peterborough

Free Discussion group he'd joined. It was full of the same unnecessary ranting of little people moaning about traffic jams caused by roadworks. Parking issues outside local schools. Some people made political statements under fake profiles. There was the occasional missing dog or cat. None of that interested him; he only wanted to see the thread about The Game. When he found it, he stopped; he had read it several times now, and each time was just as exciting.

Johnny Ormo > Peterborough Free Discussion

I can't stop watching the video. It has to be a fake, doesn't it?

116 Comments

He read the replies, mostly a dialogue between a few individuals. He enjoyed their curiosity, their banter, and silently promised they would have their answers soon. Embedded in the thread was an online feature from the city's only newspaper, the *Peterborough Post*. They were just as clueless, but speculative.

Speculative was good.

The thread fizzled out, after lots of likes and stupid fucking emojis of sad faces. The contributor who started the conversation asked the group to stay safe, and to post if anyone saw or heard anything.

Perfect.

He could have read it all over again, drawing the energy from it, but somewhere in the distance he heard a cough. Putting his phone away, he looked ahead, watching the cars speed past thirty feet below. The wide shape of a man appeared in his field of vision, holding onto the rail as he ascended the footbridge, breathing hard. The Host expected him to walk past without comment – it was late, dark; people feared the dark, people feared people. But to The Host's surprise the man stopped.

'Is everything all right?' he asked, clearly thinking that the person in front of him was having a crisis. The Host understood why, because the sight of someone standing alone on a footbridge at night told a certain tale.

'Yes, fine, thank you.'

'Are you sure, it's just…'

'I'm waiting for my girlfriend,' The Host replied.

'Oh, sorry.' The man was embarrassed. The Host told him not to worry, flashing him a smile.

'Well, have a nice evening.'

'You too,' The Host replied, fighting the urge to say his name.

As Jim Weston, the man who would be forced to make the fourth choice in forty-eight hours' time walked over the bridge and disappeared, The Host smiled, pulled out his headphones and cued his song.

CHAPTER FIFTEEN

Carlson

10.22 p.m.

Carlson had been at his desk since leaving Karen's, trying to find some connection between Michelle Reed, Timothy Smart, Milly Hallam and Alexandru Stoica. He had delved as deeply as he could into their personal lives: financial status, home life, friends. They all had their quirks – Michelle had debt, Alexandru, a recreational drug habit – but there was no obvious link between the four of them. They were just four people, chosen, it seemed at random, to fight. Carlson knew violence, he had seen it first-hand. It took a certain character to want to inflict so much destruction on another human being. The four involved were such unlikely suspects.

There had been nothing like this case in his career, and he was desperately searching for a breakthrough before whoever was behind this could strike again.

Rubbing his eyes, Carlson stood and stretched. He had been at work for two days now, opting to push through when sleep wouldn't come. He was supposed to see his daughter but hadn't been able to. He didn't like it, Jess was his world, but those were the demands of the job, and he did it for *her*. He hoped she understood, but suspected, at six, she wouldn't.

He went into the kitchen to make himself another cup of coffee, and was surprised to see Superintendent Bradshaw still at work.

'Sir.'

'Hello, Howard. What are you doing here?'

'Can't sleep, sir.'

'Yeah,' Bradshaw said, giving a sympathetic, knowing smile. 'Coffee?'

'Please.'

Bradshaw started to pour from the instant hot water dispenser on the wall and Carlson leant on the table that had a few empty coffee cups and a scattering of magazines.

'Anything to go on yet, Howard?'

'No, sir. I cannot find anything that links our victims.'

'That's troubling.'

'Yes, sir, it is. From the outside, it looks like they were just in the wrong place at the wrong time.'

Bradshaw handed Carlson his coffee and considered it for a moment. 'No, I struggle to buy that.'

'Me too, sir.'

'We probably also agree that they are linked.'

'Yes, sir.'

'Who's really behind it all? Who is this Host? What's their motivation, their ideology?'

'I don't know, sir.'

'Well, let me know when you do.'

Taking his coffee, Carlson walked back to his desk and sat down, hoping that a few minutes away would give him a fresh perspective. It wasn't going to happen. Not tonight; his eyes stung, and the words on his computer screen blurred. Bradshaw passed on his way back to his office and tapped Carlson on the shoulder.

'Go home soon. Get some sleep.'

'Yes, sir.'

'I mean it, Howard. You're no good to me if you're exhausted. Rawlinson is on tonight.'

'Yes, sir. I'll pack up now.'

As Carlson began to pack up his things, his phone screen lit up as a Facebook notification pinged. Carlson automatically tapped it and when the link loaded, he saw the image of a person in a motorbike helmet staring at him. He thought it was the first video, somehow back in circulation. When he pressed play, it only took a few seconds for him to know it was new.

'Boss, you need to see this.'

THE SECOND GAME

'What you are about to see is unedited footage of a game I played on the morning of the 4th of February in the Echo Lounge nightclub, right in the heart of the city. It's a game I will play again.

'I am your Host.'

'Howard? where has this come from?' Bradshaw asked, unable to peel his eyes from the screen.

'It's just come online.'

'I am in your offices, in your restaurants and pubs. I am on your high streets and in your libraries, I watch you at the gym, I sit beside you on your buses. I see you eating popcorn and laughing at the cinema. I observe you on your lunch breaks and follow you on your way home from collecting a takeaway.

'I. Watch. You. Sleep.

'And I might come to you, and choose you to be my next Player.'

Carlson walked around and stood behind Bradshaw so he could get a better look at the video. He knew what was coming, he had witnessed the aftermath. But still, he couldn't look away. The video faded from the motorbike helmet to inside the empty nightclub. In the shot, both Milly Hallam and Alexandru Stoica stood. They looked terrified. Then, the automated voice spoke.

'Do you both understand the rules?' The image went to the floor between where the man and woman stood. A rounders bat and a crowbar lay waiting.

The camera lifted, framing Milly and Alexandru once more.

'This is a game you have to play, you have no choice in that. You do, however, have the choice as to *how* you play.' There was silence back from both terrified people. 'Good, I'm glad you comprehend. As The Host in this Game, I want to make sure you understand correctly.'

Milly shifted her weight from one foot to the other, Alexandru rubbed his sweaty hands down his jeans leg. His breathing was sharp as the realisation set in. The Host lowered his gaze, to a small clock in his hand. Carlson watched as he wound it to four minutes.

'Tick. Tick. Tick.' As the Host spoke, neither person moved.

'I won't do it. You can't make me do it,' Alexandru said.

'Can't I?'

'Fuck you. Get out of my club.'

'Three minutes forty-two,' the Host replied calmly.

'If you don't leave I'll—' Alexandru stood and picked up the bat.

'I would think about what you are doing, Alexandru. The next few seconds might seal your fate.'

Carlson watched as Alexandru started to come towards The Host, squaring up to him. Behind, Milly began to cry.

Alexandru shoved The Host, shouting at him to get out, waving the bat at him, and for a moment, The Host was complicit.

'Go, fuck off,' Alexandru said, assuming he was scaring The Host away.

'I'm afraid it doesn't work that way,' The Host shot back, stepping towards him.

Alexandru wildly swung the bat, not to hit The Host, but to startle him. As the bat passed the camera, Alexandru could be seen turning away, driven by inertia. The Host stepped forward and with a small baton in his left hand, struck Alexandru on the back of the head, sending him crashing to the floor.

'Please,' Milly screamed. 'Stop.'

Alexandru moaned as he pulled himself to his hands and knees, blood dripping from the wound.

'Three minutes.'

'I won't do it,' Alexandru said from the floor.

'That's your choice,' The Host replied.

'Then get out,' pleaded Alexandru, still unable to get to his feet.

'You know what will happen if I do.'

'Please, why are you doing this?' Milly asked, shifting, looking from the intruder to her employer.

'Two minutes fifty-one,' the voice stated, ignoring the plea.

Milly looked at the terrified Alexandru across from her, fixed her gaze on him until he met her eye.

'I can't,' she said quietly.

'Let me make this clearer, Milly. The only choice you have is whether you live or die. If you refuse, I will leave, go to your beloved mother at 17 Cherry Bloom Close in Gunthorpe, and I will slit her throat.'

'Please, no.'

'And Alexandru, Alexandru – look at me.'

Alexandru managed to pull himself to his knees, his eyes barely able to focus.

'I will then pay a visit to your three-year-old child.'

'I'll give you whatever you want, I have money...'

'Two minutes seven seconds.'

Alexandru tried to get up, but he couldn't – the injury to his head made it impossible to stand. Carlson and Bradshaw watched as Milly picked up the crowbar.

'What are you doing?' Alexandru asked, his voice slurred, his hands raised in front of him protectively.

'I don't want to die,' she repeated, tears beginning to fall. She raised the crowbar above her head and began to shift towards him. Alexandru tried again to get up, but failed. The Host kicked the rounders bat towards him, and he picked it up.

'Please, don't come any closer, Milly,' he begged, and for a moment, Milly did as he asked.

'Less than two minutes,' The Host said, prompting her to move again.

'Stop!' Alexandru shouted, pulling himself up onto one foot before falling.

'Sir, should we stop it?' Carlson asked.

'No, we need to watch.'

'Yes, sir.'

'I'm sorry,' Milly said, tears streaming as she hurled herself towards Alexandru, the crowbar swinging wildly for his head. If she made contact, it would surely be enough force to crush his skull, but she missed – adrenaline and her total inexperience in smashing someone's head with a crowbar meant her aim was off. With her weight thrown forwards, she fell into the wall, hitting her shoulder, knocking herself to the ground.

'Don't do it again,' Alexandru shouted at her as he finally managed to pull himself upright, his legs wobbling like a boxer's after twelve rounds. 'Or – or I'll have to defend myself. Milly, are you listening? Stop.'

She didn't respond and looked at the clock. He did the same.

'One minute forty-one,' The Host said.

'He's fucking enjoying this. Sick bastard,' Carlson said quietly.

'I don't want to do this,' Alexandru said directly into the camera as he backed away from Milly as she rose to her feet.

'Then die,' the automated voice replied, matter-of-fact.

'But…'

'I know what you are trying to do, you are trying to find a different way out of this. There are only three options. You fight and win, and live, you fight and lose and die. Or if you don't fight, you stand to lose it all.'

'Why are you doing…' Alexandru began, but his words were cut short as Milly crashed the crowbar into his ribs. The clatter of bone snapping temporarily paralysed him before he let out a guttural sound and fell to the floor. The colour drained from his face, his eyes hollowing as shock took hold.

The video focused on the impact site; you couldn't see any damage from the outside, but Carlson knew his ribs would have been badly broken with such force. It was confirmed to him when he heard Alexandru start to wheeze. His lung was punctured. Carlson had heard that wheeze before.

Alexandru touched his side, and tried to scream as pain flooded in. Milly stumbled backwards and threw up over herself.

'Oh God,' she said, wiping her mouth. She looked at the camera, crowbar in hand and for a moment it looked as if she would try to attack The Host. The video shook from side to side.

'Not just your mother Milly, think of Christy also.'

'Who is Christy?' Bradshaw asked.

'It's her niece, her older sister's baby.'

'Just over a minute, I'd get a move on if I were you,' The Host said.

Milly turned back to her boss, who had somehow managed to pull himself to his feet once more. He swayed from side to side, like a drunk, his skin washed out, the colour of sea foam. He wheezed the warning that he wasn't going to die before lunging at her. She tried to swing the crowbar again but it was heavy and she only managed to get halfway round when he connected the end of the wooden rounders bat with the side of her head. Her left ear exploded on impact. She crumpled like a house of cards.

Alexandru dropped the bat, stumbled backwards, gasping for air, then turned, assuming Milly wouldn't get back up and staggered towards the bar. By the force with which he hit her, Carlson would have assumed the same. Somehow she got up, staggered side to side, and as Alexandru turned, she hit him around the head with the crowbar.

Carlson knew he was dead before he hit the ground. Milly stumbled backwards and fell. She landed where she was discovered by the first responders.

As Alexandru lay dead, and Milly Hallam dying, the video continued long enough for Carlson and Bradshaw to see the third person behind the camera use Milly's thumbprint to unlock her phone and dial 999 on her behalf.

The screen faded across to the motorbike helmet once more.

'*You cannot stop what I am doing, you cannot bargain with me. If you are picked you have to play.*

'*The Third Game is in motion, and will be played at 8.15 tomorrow night, when the day is done.*'

The video finished and neither Carlson nor Bradshaw spoke for several moments.

'This thing is going to spread like a wildfire,' Bradshaw eventually said. Carlson didn't reply. 'We need everyone in on this. If we are to believe him, we have less than twenty-four hours until he does this again.'

Carlson left the office and ran to his desk, discovering quickly that the video had been posted everywhere. YouTube, Facebook, Twitter. It had already been seen thousands of times, and the view count was quickly rising.

'Shit. This thing has gone viral.'

Without giving it any thought, he dialled Karen's number. He needed her to watch the video, and help in the way only she could. It rang and rang, eventually going to voicemail. He knew he shouldn't, but he left her a message anyway.

DAY 3

5 February 2019

PETERBOROUGH TERRORISED BY THE HOST'S WICKED GAMES

Ross Cooper for the *Peterborough Post*

Shocking footage has appeared online of a violent fight in a nightclub in Peterborough City Centre, which is thought to be orchestrated by 'The Host'.

A video posted online – the second in two days – appears to show another orchestrated fight, filmed by a third party wearing a crash helmet and using a device that alters the wearer's voice.

And in a chilling moment, The Host warns that his 'Game' will be played again.

Millions of people worldwide are thought to have watched the video across social media.

To date, police have denied the first video's authenticity, but have yet to comment officially on the latest development.

Are you involved? Get in touch:
editor@peterboroughpost.co.uk

Emily Curtis > Peterborough Free Discussion

Don't know if anyone is awake, I've just seen there has been another video. I don't think this is fake. What the fuck is happening?

159 Comments

Johnny Ormo
I feel sick, but I can't stop looking at it.

Emily Curtis
Those poor people. I couldn't watch it all.

Claire Turner
It scares the shit out of me.

Johnny Ormo
It's horrific. Can you believe they had to do that?!

Emily Curtis
No, God, could you imagine…

Claire Turner
I don't know what I'd do.

Marky Markson
Isn't it obvious?

Emily Curtis
No one asked you, **Marky**.

Johnny Ormo
Fucking terrifying.

Amanda Belkin
It's like something out of a horror movie.

Jack Anderson
I thought that about the first. But this is real. Do you really think he'll do it again?

Claire Turner
Do it again?

Jack Anderson
At the end of the video he says it will happen tomorrow evening at 8.15 p.m.

Claire Turner.
😱

Emily Curtis
First a Chinese, now a nightclub in the middle of the day. It's like nowhere is safe.

Johnny Ormo
Yeah, I was at work when this happened. Like, 100 feet from it.

Jack Anderson
Shit, that's scary. And you didn't hear anything?

Johnny Ormo
Not a thing. Until the police and paramedics arrived.

Emily Curtis
There is no way I'm going to be out any later than 6 p.m. tomorrow.

Johnny Ormo
Me neither.

Emily Curtis
Stay safe, everyone.

CHAPTER SIXTEEN

7.19 a.m.

I was woken by Sam planting a kiss on my temple and I smiled before I had the chance to open my eyes.

'What time is it?' I asked sleepily.

'Just gone seven.'

'Wow, I slept.'

'Like a baby. That drink with your work colleagues must have been one hell of a drink.'

I sat up, rubbed my eyes and as the room came into focus I saw Sam in the doorway, dressed for work. She smiled at me.

'What?' I asked, half covering my face with the bedding. Even after all these years, she still could make me blush.

'Later, shall we go out for dinner somewhere?' she said.

'Really?'

'Yeah, I realised when you were out last night that all I've done recently is work. And that's not fair on you. Let's go for a bite, and maybe even a drink or two?'

'On a school night?'

Sam approached, sat on the bed beside me and took my head in her hands.

'Yeah, on a school night.' She kissed me and as she headed towards the stairs, she called back that she would book us a table somewhere for eight.

The thought of being out, in a crowded place, made me feel uneasy. At first, I didn't know why. But then it dawned on me that the last time I went out for dinner was with Howard, the night before the Grayson James arrest.

Jumping out of bed, I dashed to the banister and looked down at her.

'Actually, I'd like to cook.'

'Again?' she called up to me.

'Yeah, again.'

'I feel special.' She smiled.

'You are.'

Sam didn't reply but looked at me in that way she had.

'I'll see you later.'

'Yeah, see you later.'

'Will you let me know how your session goes today?' she asked.

'Of course.'

'Love you.'

As the front door closed, I padded back into our room and flopped on the bed, the good night's sleep – the first good night's sleep since it happened – had worked wonders. I ached less, my head felt clearer, and for a while, I just lay looking at the ceiling, imagining a romantic evening ahead. I wish that I could have stayed like this for the whole day, lost in my own thoughts of Sam and me. I wish that I hadn't rolled over and seen my phone, and picked up the voicemail message from Howard. But I did.

'Karen, I know it's late, I know you don't want to be involved in this. There's been a second video from inside the nightclub. It's everywhere. In the video, he tells us we have just over twenty-four hours, and he is going to do it again. Ring me back when you can.'

I wish I hadn't immediately gone online and seen the video posted.

But I did.

I knew I should have stayed in bed, this wasn't my fight, and yet, 8.15 p.m. was just over twelve hours from now, and from how Howard sounded in his message the police didn't know where he would strike.

I shouldn't do anything, I told myself. Legally, I wasn't allowed to investigate anything; personally, I wasn't ready to get back into a case – my pathetic attempt to talk with Michelle Reed last night was evidence enough. And yet… people were dying. And my partner needed me. Howard had been there for me when I asked him to help me off the record last year. It could have cost us our jobs, it nearly cost me mine. He was there without me needing to ask twice. So I needed to try.

Besides, I was a police officer, a detective, but it wasn't *just* a job, it was who I was. Just as much a part of my personality as any other aspect of me. I couldn't be hands-on, but I could, at the very least, be there for my friend.

Rolling out of bed, I went downstairs and watched the video again as I made a coffee. I tried to take in the scene beyond where the eye was naturally drawn. Then I rang Howard – he was busy, he would ring me back. Until then, I would watch the video, and I would write down everything that I saw.

By the time Howard called back, I had seen it six times. I was both transfixed and horrified in equal measure.

'I take it you've seen the footage?' he said as I answered his call.

'Yes. I assume there is going to be a press conference. Who is lead?'

'Rawlinson. No press conference, he told us to keep quiet.'

'Of course he did.'

'Think he's wrong?'

'If he doesn't talk, people will panic. If he does, they'll know we have no idea what's happening. So he's screwed either way. Bradshaw and higher up will make the decision. I think they have to say *some*thing, and as Rawlinson is lead…'

'Yeah, almost feel sorry for the guy – almost.' He sounded like he was trying to smile. 'Have you seen what people are saying on Twitter?'

'I have it, but I don't use it.'

'People are really afraid, saying they won't leave their houses. This thing is gonna cause mass hysteria.'

'Sounds like it has already.'

'And they're talking about whether or not Michelle Reed is a killer or victim.'

'She struck first,' I said, rubbing my eyes that were feeling tired all over again.

'Only because she had to.'

'I agree. But I think she'll be charged regardless.'

'It's really messed up. Karen, I hate that I left that voice message last night. I just wanted to pick your brain, even though I know I shouldn't. I don't know what to make of anything. I mean, good people are hurting each other—'

'Maybe that's the point, though? Maybe that's exactly what this Host wants to happen. It's clear he's not motivated by money, so maybe it's an ideology that inspires him.'

'An ideology?'

'Maybe he wants us to know that good people are capable of doing bad things?'

'Why, though?'

'To make ordinary folk think about what they would do?'

Howard didn't reply. Despite The Host specifying the exact time of the attack, there were no leads, no lines of enquiry, nothing. He could drive around and hope that they got lucky. Peterborough wasn't a huge city, but with a population of just under 200,000 spread over a 132-square mile area, the odds of stumbling upon the scene in time were slim. The Host knew that and was taunting everyone.

'I wish you were here with me on this.'

'Howard, you know we're a team and I want to be there helping you, but I can't be involved. There's too much at stake with the investigation. Going to the hospital last night was a risk I shouldn't have taken. It achieved nothing and I'm not rea—'

I stopped myself, too embarrassed to tell anyone about the panic attacks, to admit I wasn't coping well. 'So what are you going to do?'

'I don't honestly know. We can't find anything that connects the victims. They appear to be random.'

'No, if he is confident enough to state the exact time, there is nothing random about this.'

'I agree. But Karen, we're totally in the dark here.'

'Have any witnesses come forward at all?'

'None, it's like this guy is a ghost.'

I assumed Howard was at the station, as the sound of Rawlinson barking came over the line.

'Shit, I gotta go. I know you're not in on this, and I get it, I really do. I hate that I'm going to ask this. But I need you.'

'Howard, please—'

'You don't have to do anything but let that brilliant mind of yours tick over. If you get any ideas, send me a message, and I'll follow it up. The office today is like the blind leading the blind.'

I hesitated. It wasn't good for me to be thinking of anything other than feeling better, but I owed Howard so much. And if I was honest, after seeing this second video, knowing the sick bastard was going to play his Game again, I knew I'd think of little else.

'OK. I'll message if I get any ideas.'

'Thank you.'

'Hey, Howard. Be careful. This feels…'

'Yeah, it does.'

The line went dead.

Howard said there were no witnesses, but someone must have seen something. Then it came to me, maybe someone *had*.

The girl at the underpass near the Chinese.

I messaged Howard, giving him that lead. He messaged back instantly saying he would get on it.

Putting on the radio and turning the volume up so loud the small speaker rattled, I got myself showered and dressed for my appointment with Shauna.

CHAPTER SEVENTEEN

10.04 a.m.

Eight hours and eleven minutes until the next Game

'Shall we?' Shauna asked as her door swung open. I smiled – or tried to – as I got up and made my way into her office. Forty-eight hours ago, being in this room triggered the first panic attack of my life. I was anxious about it happening again. I closed her office door behind me, and the air felt thinner, each breath difficult and sticky.

'Morning, Karen. Sorry to have kept you waiting. How are you today?' Shauna asked as she moved towards her desk.

'Fine, thank you.'

'Please, take a seat.'

I did as Shauna said, and again examined the space for a moment.

'So where should we start?' I said, jumping straight in.

'You seem eager to talk about this today.'

'I am. It's been two weeks since I've been allowed to work. I'm anxious to get back to it.'

'Anxious?'

Shit, wrong word.

'Keen, I'm keen to get back to work. I love my job and I'm finding it hard being at home so much; I don't know how to fill my time.'

'I guess a lot of your identity is being a police officer?'

'It is.' I nodded, slightly spooked that she had said something I had recently thought.

'But it's not just that, is it? It's more than your identity. You need to be back at work for other reasons.'

I hesitated. 'What other reasons?'

'You tell me.'

She was trying to tease out a confession that I was eager to finish our session, because I couldn't deal with it. That was the irony. I knew deep down that I wasn't ready to go back to work, but until I was *at* work, I didn't think I would feel OK. She also knew I had to prove I was still a good copper. She would have read my file. She would know that twelve months ago, I was a DCI, busted down to a DI after the Daniel Lynch case. That caused enough controversy, some still thinking I was bent for it. Now, since the Grayson James arrest, it looked conclusive that I was. I needed to prove to everyone – to myself – I could still police.

'Nope, I just want to return to duty. I miss my job. I miss my work friends, the camaraderie,' I said, hoping she bought it.

'Have you thought about a holiday, perhaps time away?'

'You mean go away whilst they investigate me?' I smiled wryly. 'My partner works in a school. No chance in term time.'

'I see,' Shauna said, grabbing a folder from the desk behind her. 'So if you want to jump back in… ? As I recall, two days ago we started to discuss the morning of the incident.'

A flash of memory jumped into my mind. The sound when I took Grayson James to the floor. Crack. I pushed it down, cleared my voice.

'On the morning of the 23rd of January, Detective Howard Carlson and I arrived at the residence of Grayson James. We knocked, declaring who we were, and the door opened. The suspect—'

'Karen, could we use his name. It will help.'

'Grayson James tried to run, and we entered the property to arrest him. There was an altercation and force was needed to suppress him. The incident was documented on my bodycam, and as far as I can tell, I followed procedures to the letter, as I had done many times in my career. It should have been a routine arrest.'

Saying the last part felt untrue, if I was honest; I wasn't sure if I had followed procedure. I wasn't sure if I handled him wrongly – the whole situation wrongly.

'Thank you for sharing that, Karen. I really mean that, it mustn't be easy. But as I said, I'm not investigating the incident. I've read the police report, I know what happened. I want to know what you were thinking. How you felt after. These sessions are for you to say what will help you to deal with that day.'

'There isn't anything to deal with. I don't regret the decision to restrain Grayson James,' I said, impressed with how credible I sounded. 'He was attacking my partner; he was trying to get through the property into the kitchen. I had to assume he was going to try to cause further harm.'

'And after?'

I paused. 'After, when we realised what had happened, DS

Carlson began to administer CPR while I called for medical help.'

Shauna didn't reply but waited for me to continue. 'The first responder was on the scene within four minutes and they took over from DS Carlson in trying to resuscitate Grayson James. He was taken to Peterborough District Hospital and pronounced dead shortly after.'

'Yes,' Shauna said sympathetically. 'How did that make you feel?'

I almost blurted out that it made me feel guilty. But wouldn't that be an admission? 'Shit,' I eventually said.

As Shauna began to talk about the grieving process, my phone buzzed in my pocket, distracting me from what she was saying. It might be Howard; it might be important. They might have had a break. I knew I couldn't check. If I made excuses, again, I would only be back here every day and this thing would never end. And I needed it to end. I needed to close this chapter and try and move on: two weeks living like this was two weeks too long.

'I miss work, I miss helping people.'

'I understand that. I'd miss it too if it were me.'

'Have you always worked in this field?' I asked.

'Absolutely, it's all I ever wanted to do.'

'I'm the same, I've only ever wanted to be a copper. Is your job hard?'

'At times, yes.'

'Do you ever have to deal with things you don't want to?'

'Again, at times.'

'As a copper, we get a lot of that. The worst bit, the bit that I lose sleep over, is when a kid is involved. I once attended a car accident where a newborn died.'

'That's awful.'

'It's the worst thing anyone could ever see. I didn't sleep for weeks after that. Like all things, skin gets thicker, the mind gets more robust. A kid's death would haunt me forever, when not much else will.'

'You're referring to Grayson James?'

'What happened was terrible, and obviously, I wish it hadn't ended that way.'

'So you're telling me you're OK?'

'Not yet,' I said honestly. 'But when they determine I didn't do anything wrong, when I can return to work and the shadow of doubt has been lifted, then, *then* I will be OK.'

'You don't feel regret? Guilt?'

'Should I?'

Yes, you should.

'No,' Shauna said, smiling.

'I am sorry that Grayson James died. But I couldn't have handled the situation in any other way,' I said, almost believing myself. It didn't matter what I believed. It mattered what the woman in front of me believed. I needed everyone to believe I did no wrong, because if they did, I might. She held my eye, and just as I almost caved and avoided her stare, she nodded.

'It seems that being at work will help you deal with this.'

'Yes, yes, it will. I need to keep my mind busy.'

'Or bury your head in the sand perhaps?'

I must have looked shocked, as Shauna followed it up with an apology.

'It sounds blunt, I know, but you strike me as a woman who doesn't appreciate nonsense.'

'I'm not burying my head,' I protested.

'Karen, you've worked on some of the most difficult and complex cases this city has ever had. Over the years, you've been involved in some pretty intense stuff. It's going to leave a mark. How do you deal with these cases? Emotionally?'

'It's my job, I just do it.'

'Don't you think it could be seen as unhealthy, to not have a release from it? I know I wouldn't cope. You say your skin has thickened, but that doesn't mean it's impenetrable.'

'You learn to adapt.'

Shauna didn't respond but nodded. 'Karen, in your file I read about the case where you were stripped of your rank.'

'What about it?' I said, feeling defensive.

'It says your judgement was called into question.'

'It was.'

'With evidence of you and the suspect meeting and conversing, when he was wanted for questioning.'

'I thought you weren't investigating me?' I said.

'I'm not, I've read the whole report. I'm trying to make you see that you are not as thick-skinned as you say you are. That man, that case, got to you on a personal level.'

'He was innocent.'

'And yet you still didn't bring him in.'

'Which is why I was stripped of my rank.'

'But I feel that because of that, and now Grayson James, you have developed an unhealthy relationship with work.'

'The only thing that's unhealthy is that I'm not allowed to do my job.'

'I see. In part, I agree, sometimes to work through trauma, you have to be physically moving.'

'I am living under a cloud right now. I need to be back at work, it will help me feel better.'

'OK. Karen, I'm not saying our sessions have finished, there are other things I'd like us to have time to talk about. I will however file my report to the IOPC, stating that, in my opinion, if possible you should be allowed to return back to restricted duty. In the meantime we can regularly meet, and we can re-assess. How does that sound?'

'Thank you,' I replied.

'But it's not up to me. I will voice my opinion that you are physically and psychologically fit to return to work. However...'

'I know, it's in the hands of the IOPC. Do you know how long these things take?' I asked.

'It varies. It can be quite slow. But hopefully it will be over very soon. I understand what a difficult time this must be.'

Thanking Shauna, I got up to leave, and she told me to make an appointment for a week from today, but also reminded me that I could call her whenever, and she would get back to me as soon as she could. I thanked her again and left, messaging Sam, as promised, to tell her what was said. She responded saying she was happy, and I should do a spot of shopping to celebrate. It wasn't the worst idea, so I walked around Cambridge again, taking in its architecture, had some lunch and window-shopped. And for a couple of blissful hours, I was just another shopper, another person going about their day. I wasn't thinking of Grayson James or my failing career – and when I did wobble, and tried to watch those awful videos, thankfully they had been removed.

Feeling better for my leisurely afternoon, I headed for the

train station, and for home. As I walked, I saw a message from Howard sent half an hour earlier, and the good feeling had gone.

Karen, we can't find the girl.

CHAPTER EIGHTEEN

2.14 p.m.
Six hours one minute until the next Game

Back in Peterborough, I began my three-mile walk home. I opted to not put my headphones in, instead I focused on birds calling to each other and traffic that floated on the breeze, and to *think*, like Howard had asked. Halfway home, I stopped at the local supermarket and picked up some things to make a nice dinner, as I promised. Making dinner and helping around the house were small gestures but they gave me a sense of accomplishment.

If I turned left from the shops, I would get home in the next ten minutes or so. Right would take me longer, but it would also take me past the Chinese restaurant in Fletton. I knew I had no business turning right, but I felt, maybe – just maybe – the girl would be there. Several of the homeless people in the community mingled with the public in the mornings, but in the afternoons they retreated to wherever they would be as warm and safe as possible. It was still relatively early in the day, but the sun would be setting in the next couple of hours. She might be back now. So I turned right and took the long way home.

Ten minutes later, and I'd reached the Chinese restaurant where the first Game happened. It had been just under two days since the incident, and already life was back to normal. The police officer posted outside was gone, but the Chinese still wasn't open for business. A crude, hand-drawn sign said it was closed for the foreseeable future. I assumed it might never open again. Blocking the front door at floor level were a few flowers, acting as a makeshift shrine.

Approaching the premises, I cupped my hands and pressed them to the glass to see inside. If you didn't know someone had brutally killed another here you'd just think it was too early in the day for it to be open.

I counted the steps to the spot where I had seen the girl the other night, hoping to see her again. If she was there, I wouldn't confront her but message Howard to let him know she was back so he could come and question her.

Seventy-seven steps later, I was staring at the concrete of the underpass and it occurred to me that probably somewhere around here The Host had disappeared after his crime. It was dark, secluded. It would be easy to slip into the night without being seen. Because if you didn't know that people slept on the ledge, you'd never notice them. Looking up the steep bank to the ledge, I saw the same cardboard boxes I had noticed two nights ago. I scrambled up. The boxes where there, but the girl was gone, as was the sleeping bag. It felt clear to me she had moved on.

'Fuck sake,' I whispered, rubbing my eyes. I tried to picture her again, see if her face was one I would know if I happened to spot it from afar. I could hear her voice telling me to fuck off, but the image was of Charlie, the poor man I'd known at the start of my career. I found it unnerving; I usually didn't forget a face.

I slid down the concrete bank, looking back seventy-seven steps, towards the scene of the crime. Surely, someone had seen *something*. There appeared to be no clear motive, no explanations, no eyewitness accounts. As far as I knew, anyway. The police would have been out, canvassing door-to-door to try to find common threads to pull together. But from the way Howard had spoken this morning, it looked like no one had seen a thing. It seemed random, two innocent people pitted against one another in a gladiatorial battle to the death, and then a second battle in a different part of the city. The crime *wasn't* random, not to him, it meant something, it *had* to.

I'd turned to leave when something caught my eye. It was small, but it stood out amongst the graffiti on the concrete bank of the bridge. Someone had spray-painted an old steam train. Stepping closer, I touched it – it was dry, but definitely more recent than its surrounding designs. Leaning in, I could smell the paint, faint, but there. The train could only be a few days old, at most. It was probably nothing; still, I took my phone out of my coat pocket, and snapped a photograph of it.

CHAPTER NINETEEN

The Host

2.35 p.m.

Five hours and forty minutes until the next Game

Being invisible suited him. Sitting on a long bench, surrounded by people who were deep in conversation, he listened as they discussed the latest attack and barely registered his existence. It was interesting to hear most naïvely state they couldn't take a life as they discussed what they would do if they had to play. They spoke of defiance, but there was the unmistakable sound of fear in their words.

Of course you can kill, we are all capable of killing, if we had to make a choice.

To his surprise and delight, a teenager sitting opposite asked him directly what he would do. He was tempted to say he wouldn't talk to someone with a mouth full of of food, but didn't.

'I don't know,' he replied, and the conversation swept on to the next person and the next and the next. Despite the videos being removed from most online platforms, he could see his Games played out on no fewer than five phones from where he was sitting. Some screens were filled with him speaking mechanically, some were of the first Game, some of the Second. And all who watched did so without blinking. The terror was palpable.

Before he started to play, he did wonder how his videos would be received. Now, it was clear: they were feared. People didn't draw together in good times, they were all too selfish to share – only when the chips were down, when the fear was tangible did people communicate properly and close ranks.

And with what was yet to come, fear would bind them all.

CHAPTER TWENTY

3.51 p.m.

Three hours and twenty-four minutes until the next Game

I was shocked to see Sam's workbag slung over the banister as I walked through the front door. I wasn't expecting her to be home before me.

'Sam?'

'I'm in the kitchen.'

Taking off my coat I walked through and joined her at the breakfast bar. She was seated, a glass of wine in her hand, staring at Bob, who was idly floating in his tank.

'You OK?' I asked, giving her a kiss.

She didn't respond straight away, instead a sad, resigned smile crossed her face. 'Yeah, fine. Are you?' she asked.

'Yeah, I'm assuming you know about the videos?'

'Yeah. Along with hundreds of kids.'

'Is that why you're home earlier than usual?'

'The head thought it would be a good idea if everyone went home before it was dark.'

'Probably best. Has it been a rough day?' I asked, placing my arm around her shoulder. Sam took a long sip of her wine and sighed again, leaning her head against me. 'It's been quite the battle,' she said quietly, before taking another sip. 'All the kids have wanted to do is discuss the videos. We teachers were told explicitly not to talk about it, but when a fourteen-year-old asks you about what they have seen… what am I supposed to do? Ignore their anxiety? Pacify their fear? They're right to be afraid; they are allowed to be anxious, Christ, *I'm* anxious.'

'Hence the wine. Mind if I join you?'

Sam got up and grabbed another glass, pouring me a healthy measure. Sitting down, we clinked glasses, and both took a good mouthful.

'The questions about it have been tough, but that's not what's really troubled me.'

'Sam, you don't have to worry about being safe, I'd not let anything happen to you. You know that, right?'

'It's not that, it's after everyone had seen it, I heard kids talking about what they would do. So many of them said they would kill.'

'I've thought about it too. I guess everyone has. I don't know what I would do.'

'I wouldn't be able to kill; how would you ever be OK with that?'

My stomach did a somersault as Grayson James came into my mind, and Sam saw. 'Oh babe, fuck, I'm so sorry, I wasn't thinking.'

'No, it's fine.'

'No, it's not, I didn't even put it together, I really don't see what happened with you in the same way.'

'I don't either,' I lied. 'So you couldn't do it?'

'No, I don't think I could.'

'But then you'd die?'

'I guess so,' Sam said, another big mouthful of wine following. 'This world…' she murmured.

'Kids will say they would without hesitation. It's a huge question, and difficult to process the ramifications. Don't judge them for it. They shouldn't ever have to consider it,' I said, giving her a reassuring squeeze on the shoulder.

'It doesn't feel real. I mean, how could anything like that happen here? It makes me so sad to think that so many children will lose their innocence seeing those videos.'

'I hadn't thought about that,' I reflected, trying to picture how I would have reacted if something like this had happened when I was young.

'Someone from work must have mentioned it a bit last night when you went for a drink. Is he really going to do it again tonight?'

'I don't know. They are taking it seriously, although we didn't talk about it much. Just established that the police don't have anything to go on.'

'And Howard, have you two spoken about it?'

'A little. He asked me to let him know if anything came to mind but I'm trying to not get involved.' I didn't tell her I went to see one of the victims. I wasn't sure if omitting that detail meant I was lying again; it probably did. It was becoming a habit, one that was too easy to indulge.

'I'm glad you're staying away from this, Karen.'

'I don't want to jeopardise anything with the investigation.'

'I hope they catch him before tonight.'

'Me too.'

'It's so scary, I guess for us it's a little less so. We can lock our doors, close the curtains. Hide. Those poor people who are working until eight o'clock, can you imagine how terrifying it would be going home?'

'Who would be finishing at eight?'

'Loads of people. Anyway, you said in your text Shauna had signed you off. It sounds like the session went well then today? What happens next, do you know when you'll be going back to work?'

Putting down my wine glass, I stood. I could feel a stirring in my chest – not an anxious one, the type I felt at work when I was about to have a breakthrough on a case. Sam had latched onto something without even knowing.

'Karen?'

'Late-night shopping.'

'What?'

'Hang on,' I said. I needed to hear what my thoughts were guiding me to. Tonight is late-night shopping. When the day is done.

'Shit,' I said, turning and running to dig out my phone from my coat pocket.

'Karen, what's happening?' Sam said as she followed, panic on her face at my sudden urgency.

I didn't respond but called Howard. He picked up on the second ring.

'Howard. Where are you?'

'In the city. Loads of us are, hopeful we'll see something, but it's impossible.'

'That's why I've called,' I said, struggling to catch my breath. 'In the second video, what time did he say the next Game would be?'

'Eight fifteen.'

'Precisely, and then he said when the day is done.'

'Yeah, no one can work out what he means…'

'It's a clue. He's leaving a clue. Usually, the day is done at midnight, right?'

'Yes.'

'Unless you're referring to a workday; now, for most, it's what, 5.30, 6 p.m. But tonight is late-night shopping in Queensgate Shopping Centre. The shops shut at eight. If you're cashing up early, able to tidy before the store closes—'

'Your day would finish around quarter past. Shit, that makes sense. It will be quiet, but people will still be around,' Howard said.

'Smaller shops will only have one or two people cashing up at the end of the day.'

'And just like the Chinese, he could trap them in the space, give them no choice. I'm going to call it in,' Howard said. 'I won't say we've spoken and drag you into anything that could get you in trouble. But I can explain the reasoning.'

'Just make sure Rawlinson does this with soft hands. If he brings the whole force in, our guy will only back away. Tell him it's just a hunch, a potential lead, not a foregone conclusion. You know what he's like.'

'Karen, I'd better go, get this across. Well done, mate; this feels like we might be onto something,' he said before hanging up.

Putting the phone down, I slumped onto the bottom step and looked at Sam. 'Sorry.'

'No, don't be. I'm amazed by how your brain works sometimes,' she chortled.

'I hope I'm right.'

'Eight fifteen p.m., when the day is done. Now you've said it, it makes perfect sense.'

'Well, we'll see.'

I really did hope I was right. Because if at 8.20 p.m. a call went through to the 999 switchboard – the person calling to say they had killed someone – the city would go into absolute panic.

CHAPTER TWENTY-ONE

7.28 p.m.

Forty-seven minutes until the next Game

As the evening closed in and darkness descended, I watched my wife draw the curtains, make sure the door was locked and switch off lights in rooms when leaving, something she didn't usually do. She was clearly worried and trying to make the house look empty, like I remembered my mum used to do on Hallowe'en, so the kids didn't egg our windows. I understood, I was anxious too, my attention flicking to my phone every few minutes, hoping for news. I couldn't decide if Howard's silence was a good sign or not. I tried not to think about it – it only made me feel helpless. Howard – the whole force, no doubt – was in the city, looking for this guy, and I was at home, hiding behind locked doors. Yet another reminder that my career was on a downward spiral.

At seven thirty, forty-five minutes until the time stated in the video, I told Sam I was nipping to the loo, and I took my phone. I couldn't bear it anymore. I needed to know something. When I was sure she couldn't hear me, I rang Howard.

'Anything?' I asked when he picked up.

'Nothing so far. We have plainclothes in the centre. We've done all we can to stop him.'

'If we're right about the location,' I whispered, keeping an ear on the stairs in case Sam came up.

'I think so,' he said. 'It fits. Most of the high street shops are shut, the few that are open are being watched closely.'

'God, I hope I'm not wrong.'

'I back you on this a hundred per cent. It *has* to be here. I'm sure of it. Opportunity, time, impact.'

'Impact is his number one priority,' I said, feeling deep in my gut that, despite my anxiety, I was right about his clue.

'And the shopping centre is the biggest target for impact, surely. Right in the heart of the city. Under people's noses. I'd better go. Speak later, yeah?'

'OK. Be safe.'

Going back into the living room, I sat beside Sam, who was curled up on the sofa, flicking through the channels, unable to focus on anything other than the time, like me. She turned over to the news channel, and I wanted her to stop, just in case there was something about the events that were unfolding. But she skipped on, finding an episode of *Friends* we'd seen several times on More 4. I tried to let myself be absorbed into what I was watching, but I couldn't. My mind was fixed on Howard, the time, and The Host. I could feel Sam watching me, but I didn't look at her, just kept my eyes glued to the screen.

Guilt, I guess.

'Karen,' Sam said, taking my hand, 'I know how difficult it must be to not be there with your colleagues, but you're doing the right thing staying out of it. I'm proud of you.'

'Part of me wishes I could be there on the frontline with them,' I said, not telling her that that part of me was becoming more frustrated by the hour. 'Another part knows I'm not ready.'

'Babe, let's just go to bed, watch a movie, forget the world.'

'No, not yet.'

'We can't control anything, other than what we do. I'm going up. I don't want to think about these horrible things anymore. Join me?'

'You go up, I'll come soon. I'm gonna put on the news, see if anything is happening.'

'OK,' Sam sighed, getting to her feet and making her way to the stairs. As she reached the bottom step she looked back into the living room towards me. 'I get this is really hard on you, Karen, I do, and I'm on your side, always. But it's hard on me too.'

She turned and from her slumped posture I could tell she was upset but she'd disappeared upstairs before I could reply.

CHAPTER TWENTY-TWO

The Host

7.55 p.m.
Twenty minutes until the next Game

Standing outside the future crime scene, he watched people come and go, oblivious to him as usual. They always were – but for that one time, when he was seen, that one time he wasn't invisible. At the inquest, it had been determined that they would have only been able to save one. They were all told they'd made the right decision by choosing to save him. But he knew they'd got it wrong.

Behind him, the doors opened and out stepped a middle-aged man in a black jumper and coat. Beside him was a woman, an older lady, with kind eyes, a soft smile and features. Roberta. Widowed, semi-retired, good at reading stories to little ones. She was thanking the man, a local author who had been doing an event. He shook her hand and left for the city centre. To The Host's delight, Roberta then turned to him.

'Hello, are you all right?'

'Yes, fine thank you.'

'I'm sorry, if you wanted to return something we're closed now.'

'No, I'm just waiting for a friend, thank you.' He smiled as she went back inside.

He counted to ten as he watched her disappear upstairs, and once she was gone, he slipped into the building. It was time for kind-hearted Roberta to play.

CHAPTER TWENTY-THREE

Carlson

8.08 p.m.
Seven minutes until the next Game

Carlson struggled to keep his cool: with each minute that went by, doubts crept in that they may have got it wrong. But the clue was there teasing them. 8.15 p.m., when the day is done – it didn't make sense in any other context. And so, Carlson remained diligent, his eyes working over the few people who were still out, although it seemed the public were taking the threat seriously, since the shopping centre was now nearly deserted. Carlson saw a group of kids hanging around by the cut-through to Westgate arcade, a clutch of independent shops branching from the main centre. As he approached they saw him, panicked, and ran away, shouting, 'It's The Host! Leg it!'

'Bloody kids,' Carlson said as he doubled back on himself, making his way towards the bus station and car parks. He radioed the other plainclothes officers in the centre.

'Anything?'

A chorus of 'nothings' and 'no signs' came back. It *had*

to be here. He was sure of it. The only other explanation was that The Host had seen one of the undercover officers and had retreated. Carlson wanted to catch him, but if they had spooked him there would be no Game, no one would die tonight, and it would be a win for the police. It would show they had control of this thing, and people need not be afraid if they listened to advice. And it would be thanks to Karen's brainwave. But if they were wrong and The Host was elsewhere, preparing to play, the loss would be catastrophic.

As Carlson walked by a clothes store in the far corner of the shopping centre, closest to the bus station and multi-storey car park, he saw a man who began to run when he knew he'd been spotted.

'Hey!' Carlson shouted but the person didn't stop. 'Hey, police!'

The man didn't respond, and Carlson gave chase. His training in the army meant he still kept a good cardio routine, and before the man could reach the escalators, Carlson was able to grab him.

'I said, stop. Why are you running?'

'I...'

'Howard, you all right?' a voice called through his earpiece.

'Standby,' Carlson replied.

'So why are you running?'

'You scared me.'

'Did you not hear me call out I was the police?'

'Yeah, but that man, he'd say something like that, wouldn't he?'

'Howard?' the voice in the ear spoke again.

'Where are you going?'

'Home, I just want to go home.'

Carlson saw he was scared, scared almost out of his wits, and he let go of his arm. The man didn't wait to be excused and ran towards the car park.

'*Howard?*'

'It's nothing,' he replied.

Turning around, Carlson paced, looking into each shop as he passed. He started off discreetly, but as the time drew nearer, the more frantic he became until his watch alarm beeped, telling him it was 8.15 p.m. Stopping, he listened for the sound of a struggle, or a cry, but there was nothing. Was The Host not playing after all? Another minute elapsed, and another, and Carlson started to meet the eyes of the other officers milling around. Satisfied as they all concluded they had averted a serious crime with their presence.

But Carlson wasn't convinced, and through his closed-circuit earpiece, he told everyone to stay vigilant. The Host might still be close by; he might still be playing his Game.

THE THIRD GAME

He watched as the young man, barely out of his teens, tried to unlock his phone, but his hands shook too much, hands that were covered in blood that ran from slash wounds on both of his forearms. After three failed attempts to dial 999, The Host stepped in and helped.

'Nine-nine-nine, what's your emergency?' a woman said.

The boy tried to speak, but the words wouldn't form, they were caught somewhere between the place where thought originated and his vocal cords.

'Hello?' the operator called out. The boy didn't respond, just looked at his arms, cuts thrown like ribbon across both, the wounds so deep he could see the white of fat tissue exposed and glistening under the fluorescent lighting. It should have hurt, his nervous system should have been screaming at him, but he couldn't feel any pain.

'Hello?' the operator said again, this time with more urgency. The Host tapped his shoulder. 'You're supposed to speak now,' he said, his voice mechanical. Cold.

'I...' the boy managed to say before the words got trapped again. The Host gave a thumbs-up prompting him to keep going before turning and walking away, stepping over the corpse and descending the stairs.

'Hello?'

The boy didn't know how to articulate what had just happened. It was a typical evening, a local author doing a talk in the main library for a few dozen fans. He had heard on the news about some sort of video that had been posted, but as he had been busy prepping the event he hadn't read or seen much about it.

'Hello? Do you need assistance?' the operator said.

'Yes,' he managed to say before falling silent again. He thought about how he should be on his way home right now, ready to eat a microwaveable lasagne and share with his mother the author event, telling her how wonderful and inspired he felt, as he did after every event he was a part of.

'Can you tell me where you are?'

'I'm…'

He looked at the woman opposite him on the floor; his boss, his friend, his mentor, her unblinking eyes staring back at him.

'Can you tell me where you are?' the operator said again.

'The library.'

'Good, that's good. Which library? Can you tell me the city?'

'Umm… Oh God. This, this wasn't supposed to happen.'

'What was not supposed to happen?'

'It.'

He pictured the motorbike man again, the image he would never shake. And the way he spoke, so calm, so in control.

'What is your name?'

'This wasn't supposed to happen. This wasn't supposed to happen.'

'We've traced your location to Central Library in Peterborough. Is this correct?'

'Uh huh.'

'Help is coming, what is your name?'

He didn't hear the operator. The moment it happened screamed too loud.

'Are you still there?'

'Uh huh.'

'Good, stay with me, all right? What is your name?'

'Umm, Richard.'

'Richard, tell me what happened. I'm sending help now.'

'I – this wasn't supposed to happen.'

'Richard, are you hurt?'

'Yes.'

'Are you bleeding?'

'Yes,' he said again, beginning to sob. 'Yes, a lot, I've got cuts everywhere, I'm covered, but it's not all mine, it's not all mine.'

'What's not all yours, Richard?'

'The blood, it's not all mine. Oh God, it's not all mine.'

'Richard, have you had to hurt someone?' the operator said quietly.

'He made me do it, he made me,' he sobbed.

'Is there someone else with you?' the operator said, getting to her feet to flag down a supervisor in the call centre. 'Richard, are you badly injured? Can you move?'

He looked at his forearms, the blood flow beginning to slow. He assessed his injuries; his face hurt, where he had been hit and there was an ache in his stomach but he couldn't remember what happened to cause it.

'I don't know. My arms are cut up pretty bad. My left is bad.'

'OK, help is on the way. Is the man who made you do it still there?'

'I don't know. I don't think so.' He cried harder; his words barely audible.

'OK, Richard, calm down, take a deep breath so I can help you. Is anyone with you?'

'My boss.'

'Is she injured?' the operator asked, knowing the answer.

Richard looked across the carpeted floor towards the Crime Fiction bookshelves and into the eyes of the kind woman who had been his mentor since he'd started working at the library a year ago. Roberta Richardson was his friend, she felt like family to him, and he had attacked her with a screwdriver. Her body lay at an angle Richard didn't think a person could lay in.

'No.'

There was a pause. 'If you can, find something to apply pressure to your wounds, to slow the bleeding, can you do that?'

'I don't know how.'

'A belt perhaps, do you have a belt, to tie it off?'

'Yes.'

'Great, that's great. Loop it above your wound and pull it really tight. Do it now, I'll hold.'

He put the phone on the floor and took off his belt, and tied off his left arm, which was the more injured of the two.

'I feel sick. I'm going to be sick.'

'You're in shock. Help is coming. Can you tell me what happened?'

'He told us only one of us would get out alive.'

'Can you repeat that?' the operator said, knowing the tape would be listened to again by the police. She couldn't help poor Richard, nor his boss, but there might be something in the tape the police could use, if it was clear.

'We only had four minutes, or he would hurt my mum.'

'Is your mum there, Richard?'

'No, he knows where I live, he told me he would go and hurt her.'

Beside the operator, stood the manager, who was on his mobile to the police. He wrote something down in capitals on a piece of paper and held it up.

GET A DESCRIPTION.

'Who did, Richard? Can you describe him?'

'I didn't want to do it, I didn't.'

'Richard. Take a breath, breathe with me, OK? What did he look like?'

'A helmet,' Richard replied. His body started to convulse as the numbness subsided and the shock kicked in.

Another scripted sign from the manager as he emphatically fed the information to the police on the other line.

GET MORE DETAILS.

'What did he say?'

'I don't know, oh God. Oh God. Am I going to die?'

The supervisor tapped the note again and mouthed, 'Details.'

'Take a deep breath, Richard, you need to help us. The paramedics are coming.'

There was another pause, as Richard fought to control his breathing. The operator covered her mouthpiece and told her supervisor they wouldn't get much more out of him. He nodded and continued talking fervently into his phone; it seemed the whole floor was watching, waiting. The manager nodded and scribbled again.

WHERE DID HE GO?

'Richard, are you sure the man isn't still there?'

'No, I mean, yes. He's gone, I'm sure.'

'How long ago?'

'He helped me dial 999.'

'Do you know where he went?'

'No. I don't know.'

'And he told you to kill your boss?'

'She attacked me first. I didn't mean to kill her. I've murdered my friend. God, I've murdered my friend.'

CHAPTER TWENTY-FOUR

The Host

8.23 p.m.

He knew it was time to leave the area, go home, prepare the next video for the world to see, but in the distance, he could make out police cars. One vehicle he would dismiss as a coincidence, two would raise an eyebrow. But *four*? It had to be related. Parking his motorbike behind the cathedral, he slipped off the helmet, locked it to the back of the bike, and confident he would go completely unnoticed, put in his headphones and walked into the city centre through the cathedral grounds. The way the cathedral was lit with upturned orange lights, capturing each and every detail carved into the limestone, was both beautiful and intimidating. The early English gothic west front was imposing in its size. The song he listened to told him there was no need to run, or hide; the lyrics couldn't be more appropriate. As ever, it truly was a wonderful life.

Stopping in the middle of the deserted grounds, he let the music sweep over him, the synthesised keyboards and melodic vocals transcendent. The rhythm surged through him and raising his arms he swayed, arms outstretched to the heavens, his head thrown back, entirely immersed in the song. As it ended, he saw atop the cathedral were goblins, cherubs and knights that looked down on him, their eyes hollow and black. He wondered if perhaps they were judging him, but knew they couldn't be, for they knew more than anyone that God was the ultimate killer. He took when He desired without explanation, or reason. He caused earthquakes and famines and forest fires. He made cars skid off roads into water. He watched as people died, he watched and did nothing. 'God's way' – he hated that phrase. It left no choice. At least what he was doing gave people a choice.

Playing the song again, he left the cathedral behind and walked through the central archway that separated the holy and sanctimonious grounds from the less virtuous shops and bars of the city centre. Two worlds separated by one large gate. By the time he approached the Queensgate Shopping Centre, it seemed that word had got out: several men and women were running from inside, back to their cars. Some ignored the cars and began sprinting up the road, towards the Central Library. The police were there in force, most of them plainclothes. They'd been only half a mile away when he'd made the librarians become The Players.

A tall black man came out of the shopping centre, a phone glued to his ear. Even in the streetlight, The Host could see a large bruise on his jaw. The police officer looked over, caught his eye, but didn't hold it for long as a helicopter flew over. He ran in the same direction it was flying. He was fast, strong, The Host knew if he was instructed to play The Game, he'd win every time. Thankfully, because of his demeanour, and the world's preconceptions, The Host could hide in plain sight, and the strong-looking officer didn't give him a second thought. They would never suspect it could be someone like him.

CHAPTER TWENTY-FIVE

8.27 p.m.

I waited and waited for the phone to ring, but the call didn't come. Either Howard hadn't called because he was arresting a suspect or because we were wrong about the location. I went online; lots of people were talking about The Host, but no one mentioned any details about the Third Game of his. Sam was right, I couldn't control this, so I turned off the TV, put my phone in my pocket and went upstairs. Sam was sitting up in bed, a small pile of exercise books on my side. I sat down on the edge, tentatively.

'Sam, I...' I began, but she waved me off.

'I think we should go on holiday at Easter. What do you think?'

'We can't go then, it will cost a fortune.'

'We've both been so stressed lately. I think we deserve it.'

Her words caught me off guard, and I smiled. 'I must admit, the idea of getting away for a bit is more than tempting. A break from it all would be good for us.'

'Yeah, it would. Where do you fancy?' Sam smiled back, scooting closer so we could both look at holiday locations on her phone. It was nice to be thinking ahead for a change, and the more we looked at hotels in the Canaries with sprawling beaches and year-round sunshine, the more I felt like we needed it. Sam was truly amazing, and I felt very lucky. She had every right to be upset with me but she chose not to. She chose to see the world from where I stood. I leant in and kissed her.

'What was that for?'

'Just because.'

As we flicked through travel agent websites, comparing prices, I felt myself begin to relax, then my phone started buzzing in my pocket. It was Howard. For a moment, I didn't pick it up. I was too scared about what he might say.

'Babe? You don't have to answer that,' Sam said.

'But it's Howard. What if he's ringing to tell me they caught him?'

'What if he isn't? You've done more than you should, so much more. Let them handle it now.'

'I'm sorry. I can't ignore him. It's Howard.'

'OK,' Sam conceded, resigned.

'OK,' I echoed, taking a deep breath before answering the call. 'Howard, tell me it's good news.'

'I'm afraid not.'

After Howard filled me in, I hung up. Dropping my phone on the bed I sat quietly beside it. We had got it wrong; *I* had got it wrong, and now, someone else was dead. Sam knew something had happened, and rather than asking, she sat closer, so I could put my forehead on her shoulder. I took a few deep breaths, forcing the anxiety that bubbled inside to stay contained. As I rocked forward, putting my head in my hands, Sam rubbed my back, knowing better than to ask how I was. I was convinced I had got it right, the time matched, the opportunity was there. But I focused on one location, without offering any alternatives, as I should have done. The person responsible had even mentioned a library in the first two videos and I hadn't seen it.

'Fuck.'

'Karen?'

'I was so sure he was going to attack in the Queensgate. I was *so sure*.'

'Love, there was no way you could have known.'

'But that's my job, it's my job to know.'

'You're not even at work.'

'Someone is dead.'

'And the police will deal with it. They'll find him.'

'I *am* the police, Sam.'

'No, Karen, right now, you're not, you're a woman who isn't sleeping, who needs some time to process what happened with…' She trailed off.

'I'm fine about that, and we don't have time. He's going to do it again.'

'You're clearly not fine, and right now this isn't your responsibility.'

I stood up, left the bedroom and walked downstairs, grabbing my shoes. Sam followed.

'Where are you going?'

I put on my coat and opened the front door. 'I need to get some air.'

'Karen, stop, *Karen!*' Sam shouted, ensnaring my attention. Sam never shouted. 'Don't go, stay with me. Please don't go out, it's not safe. I'm worried for you. I know you're strug-gling. But he could be out there. You know it's dangerous.'

'It's not. He has a pattern, he won't be out now. He's done what he needed to do and for now he'll be lying low, waiting to strike again.'

'Maybe, but you don't know when.'

'We all will soon, when he posts the video, and there is fuck all anyone can do about it. Sam, I need some air. Please.'

I walked towards Sam and gave her a kiss.

'Go to bed, I'll be back soon,' I said before grabbing my keys and walking out of the front door.

CHAPTER TWENTY-SIX

9.17 p.m.

I knew I shouldn't have left, but I needed a moment to think, to collect my thoughts. The night was clear, cold, the stars were out in full force. I loved the stars, and as I reached the end of my road, I paused to look at them. They were so big, most of them bigger than our own sun, and yet, so far away they were just a pinprick in the black. It made me feel small, and with it, my problems were small too. As I walked, I became aware that the streets were quieter than usual, eerily quiet. Very few cars were out on the road and even fewer people.

From where I stood, the Chinese was only two miles away, the nightclub and the library another mile beyond. A stone's throw. I suspected most of the people in Peterborough knew how close to home the threat really was. The latest attack would likely filter to the national news, and I would put money on Facebook being a frenzy of thoughts, theories and panic. People would be terrified that they could be next, but that wasn't my biggest fear. The uniqueness of these crimes was what scared me. Usually, the reasons for murder are obvious: rage, passion, revenge. The majority of murder victims are killed by people they know. This was the first time in my career I had come across a situation where anyone could be a murderer, or a victim.

I couldn't change what had happened. I could, however, step up my response. I *should* have seen the library as a potential location. Foolishly, I'd assumed it would close at 5 p.m., forgetting tonight was its late-night trading. I should have checked. The fact he had mentioned libraries was salt in the wound. I was wrong about the location, but right about the thought process behind the clue. I had touched on his mindset, if only skimming it.

I was so caught up in my thoughts, I had completely zoned out of my surroundings. Now, taking them in, I felt sickened. Without realising it, I had walked to the address where we had arrested Grayson James. The door that was damaged when we entered had a board in the glass, and the single bunch of flowers on the doorstep had turned brown. I walked away quickly, before anyone saw me there.

Rounding the corner, I found a bus shelter and sat down on the metal bench; it was so cold it felt wet through my jeans. Sam was right: I wasn't doing very well. I'd tried to hide it from everyone, but Sam could see it, and I knew it too. It was clear, I hadn't dealt with what I had done. I took out my phone as I began walking away. I should have emailed Shauna there and then, asking to speak, like she said I could if I needed her. But I couldn't. Going to my call log, I hovered over Howard's number for a moment, then tapped on Sam's number underneath.

'Karen, is everything all right?'

'No,' I said, struggling to catch my breath.

'Where are you?'

'I'm outside his house.' I didn't need to say whose house, she knew. 'Sam, will you please come and get me?'

CHAPTER TWENTY-SEVEN

Carlson

9.26 p.m.

It was a fucking mess, both figuratively and literally. Blood was everywhere, and every copper they had, including Carlson, had been looking the wrong way while it had happened. In front of him, the paramedics were still working on the young man who was seriously injured. Carlson knew he wouldn't die; he had seen what the human body could endure if it had to. Besides, someone had to live, right, that was The Host's modus operandi.

Carlson wanted desperately to talk to him, to try and coax something out, but Rawlinson was already there, barking at him, pushing him to get some answers, until the boy passed out from shock. He must have only been twenty at a push. What kind of life would he have going forwards with another person's blood on his hands?

Knowing he would have to wait to speak to the kid, he continued to process the scene before him. The other victim had been identified as Roberta Richardson. She had worked at the library for over fifteen years. Carlson was sure he had met her once, when he and Jess came to summer reading club last August. She read classic fables to a group of young children in the open reading space only thirty feet from where he stood. If he was right, and it was her, she was too lovely to end up lying with a screwdriver sticking out of her chest.

'This is so fucked up,' he said out loud to no one in particular, before being asked to stand aside so the crime scene photographer could get closer to her body. He wondered what Karen would do if she were here: would she insist on trying to talk to the boy? He doubted it. She would step back, look at the problem from afar. Come at it from a different angle. She would be interested in The Host's journey before and after he forced the librarians to play. Walk in his shoes, so to speak.

So Carlson wondered: when the staff locked up the library, where did The Host wait? The boy, or perhaps the deceased, would have said a farewell to the last of the guests and author before locking the door. Carlson assumed the fire exits would have been closed and the doors alarmed, which meant The Host was already inside the building. Carlson guessed he would have been up here, on this floor. Waiting patiently. But where would he wait?

Three backward steps and he was level with an aisle labelled HISTORICAL FICTION. He wandered down it, trying to gauge where The Host might have stood. Karen would know where to look. Her ability to know how people were thinking unnerved him and impressed him in equal measure. Once again he resolved he had to be more like Karen.

Ignoring the scene, the carnage, the violence in front of him in the middle of the main artery of the library floor, he walked, turning down narrower aisles walled with books. He didn't know what he was looking for, but hoped something, anything was out of place.

Outside, people were gathering. He expected it to happen, the whole city was waiting for the next crime, and as soon as the police came rushing, they would know it was because of The Game. But still, so many people were there, media and morbidly curious alike. The Host wanted that, didn't he? He wanted recognition; he liked the spectacle. Carlson wondered if he had waited in the True Crime or Crime Fiction aisle. After all, true crime was all about recognition. The killers more famous than infamous. Would he have enjoyed reading their names, identifying with them, before playing his Game?

Carlson couldn't hide his disappointment that nowhere was there any obvious sign of disturbance. Stepping into the central area, close to the boy who was being strapped to a gurney to travel to hospital, he looked across into the Ethics and Philosophy aisle. Towards the back, near a wall, he could see something was awry. The spot felt right. A solid wall behind, a clear line of sight in front to where the attack happened. It was a perfect ambush point; if The Host had kept still, he would have been difficult to spot in the low light. Along the wall of books, one was pulled out, precariously balanced on the edge in an otherwise neat aisle, like it had been placed there intentionally. Carlson approached it, and taking a glove from his back pocket, he put it on, stretching it over his wide hand. He picked up the book and turned it over: *The Death of Altruism in the Modern Mind* by H. J. Card.

Carlson turned it over and read the back, having no idea what the title was supposed to mean. It didn't take long to understand he had found something left for them, if they cared to look. The blurb discussed how society, because of technological advancements, had desensitised humanity, and how the sense of self was more important than anything in the history of time. Carlson wasn't much of a philosopher but could understand the gist; the book argued people didn't care about other people or right or wrong anymore, only themselves. At the bottom of the back cover was a quote from another author stating it was 'the most accurate and terrifying description of the future of our planet'. Beside the barcode was a small picture – it wasn't supposed to be there, it had been drawn on.

From the clearing, where the deceased lay, Rawlinson shouted his name, and Carlson began to approach. He knew he should present the book, let Rawlinson take it and process it, but just before he turned the corner, he pulled out his mobile, took photographs of its front and back covers and the picture beside the barcode. What he had found meant something, it had to, but he didn't know where to start in discovering what. He doubted Rawlinson would either. Only Karen might understand.

Putting his phone away, he reminded himself that he shouldn't ask any more of her. He knew he had already asked too much when he told her about Michelle Reed in hospital. Looking at the boy on the gurney, desperately crying over his dead work colleague, Carlson knew he needed help. He would *have* to ask Karen to take a look, to see if she could make sense of any of it, because he couldn't let any more people – good people, kind people – get hurt.

CHAPTER TWENTY-EIGHT

The Host

11.47 p.m.

He was delighted with the outcome of the Third Game. He'd been surprised that it was she who'd struck first. He assumed that the boy would have felt he had more to live for. Yet she was the one who was prepared to fight – even to kill. The battle that ensued wasn't as glorious as the first two, but it was the best for the legacy. When The Players' identities were announced, a semi-retired, doting woman and a mild-mannered, shy young man, it would show anyone could play, and therefore, anyone would. The Game was like cancer: it didn't care if you were old or young, it didn't care if you were a family person or single, it took who it wanted. People were beginning to know this, and that knowledge – and the fear it inspired – would latch onto healthy cells in everyone and kill from within.

Magnificent.

He knew that the coming days would be the toughest. The adrenaline surges with each Game were taking their toll, and fatigue was setting in. It could be rectified with sleep, but first, he needed to prepare for the morning.

Removing the GoPro from the helmet, he plugged it into the USB cable attached to his computer, opened his video-editing software, and began the import. He picked up two pipe cleaners and bent them into the shape of Richard, and placed it with the others. Four now sat there, silently. Each one knowing. Michelle, Milly, Richard. And the original. For a moment he considered the first pipe-cleaner figure – a kid he once knew, but now a stranger to him.

Knowing he couldn't settle until the video was downloaded, he took his phone, put on his song, and as he hummed along, the sensation he'd felt in the cathedral grounds swept over him. A weightlessness, a peace. Feeling calmer, he went online, eager to see the latest reaction to his exploits. The Facebook group was awash with speculation and people posting photos of the emergency services gathered outside of the library. A few asked unanswered questions about what they would do if they had to play. It made him curious to know. Closing Facebook, he opened Twitter with the intention of creating a poll, posing the simple question. It delighted him to see that one already existed.

If you had to be a #Player would you...

Kill (68%)

Let yourself be killed (27%)

Don't know (5%)

The results were disappointing, but he knew the ratio would change over the next few days. Soon, people would be more honest with themselves and admit that they would all kill if they had to play. And until they all did, he would continue with his work. He would Host game after game after game until everyone knew. It would likely cost him everything, a part of him hoped it would.

An alert chimed, telling him the footage was imported. He picked up his helmet, put it on, and prepared to record his next message.

'*What you are about to see is unedited footage of the Third Game. A Game I will play again.*

'*I am your Host.*

'*I am in your offices, in your restaurants and pubs. I am on your high streets and in your libraries, I watch you at the gym, I sit beside you on your buses. I see you eating popcorn and laughing at the cinema. I observe you on your lunch breaks and follow you on your way home from collecting a takeaway.*

'*I. Watch. You. Sleep.*

'*And I might choose you to be my next Player.*

'*As you watch this video now, the Fourth Game is in motion, and my new Players will play at 8.30 p.m.*'

ARRESTS MADE IN CONNECTION
WITH PETERBOROUGH MURDERS

Ross Cooper for the *Peterborough Post*

Arrests are thought to have been made in connection with a series of brutal murders in Peterborough.

However, according to local sources, none of those arrested are thought to be the orchestrator of the 'Games' that have gripped the city in fear, but the surviving individuals who were forced to play.

Police have yet to make a statement on the arrests.

This breaking news story is being updated and more details will be published shortly.

If you are living in Peterborough and have been affected by the events, get in touch **here**.

Johnny Ormo > Peterborough Free Discussion

Have you seen what's on the Peterborough Post website? WTF?!?

Emily Curtis
What? They have arrested the survivors.

Claire Turner
Jesus!

Marky Markson
Well they did kill sumone. They should be arrested.

Claire Turner
Someone*

Johnny Ormo
Only because they had no choice, **Marky**.

Emily Curtis
I think it's disgusting; they are victims in this.

Jack Anderson
I agree. They should be helped, not made to be the bad guy.

Claire Turner
Can you imagine how they are feeling, the guilt would be enough, without being arrested for it?

Marky Markson
Slap them cuffs on those bitches.

Johnny Ormo
Does anyone know how we can block this dickhead?

Marky Markson
Who you calling a dickhead?!

Jack Anderson
Marky, stop being that guy. No one cares or wants to hear about your far-right bullshit.

Marky Markson
FUCK YOU! You fucking diesece

Claire Turner
Disease*

Claire Turner
Did you go to school?

Jack Anderson
I've blocked him.

Emily Curtis
Thank you, this thing's scary enough without someone trying to incite more hate.

Jack Anderson

Guys, it's just pinged on to my phone. There has been another murder. He did it, The Host did it again.

Emily Curtis

What? How do you know? I can't see anything on the Peterborough Post website. Where is it?

Jack Anderson

It just pinged through on the BBC News app.

Emily Curtis

THE BBC?????

Jack Anderson

Yeah, it's all over there, and on Sky News too.

Emily Curtis

God, this is getting out of control.

Jack Anderson

Literally the whole country is talking about this now.

Johnny Ormo

I've just seen it too. It says the crime happened at the stated time, at the Central Library.

Claire Turner

The Library? I go there with my kids all the time.

Amanda Belkin
What does it say **Johnny**, **Jack**?

Jack Anderson
Not a lot, just that there has been an incident at the library, widely believed to be the Third Game. It says that an older woman has died. Someone who had worked at the library for fifteen years.

Claire Turner
Oh God. I know who they mean. . . I know who has died 😨

DAY 4

6 February 2019

CHAPTER TWENTY-NINE

6.24 a.m.

The Host monopolised the space in my head. He was there as I drifted off to sleep, he was there in my dreams, and he was there when I woke. He was taunting me, teasing me with his clues. Even though I knew it wasn't healthy I was hooked on it. As a kid, I loved reading Point Horror books, and I'd take notes as I read, trying to work out the twist before it came. I remember my mum telling me that I was too smart for my own good, and that there wasn't a single mystery I couldn't work out. I hope she was right. As much as I knew this wasn't my fight – that being involved would hurt me professionally and personally – I needed to do *something*; people were dying, and more would die unless The Host was found.

With Sam still asleep beside me, exhausted after rescuing me and staying up half the night to make sure I was OK, I slowly rolled onto my side to grab my phone and find out what was being said about The Host. The media had come to life now a third murder had been reported. They were being a little unkind, but I understood, people were afraid.

POLICE CLUELESS AS ANOTHER PERSON DIES. FACEBOOK, YOUTUBE AND TWITTER STRUGGLE TO CONTAIN THE SPREAD

Patricia Blakemore, *BBC correspondent*

Police are yet to apprehend whoever is responsible for commissioning the murders that occurred in Peterborough on 4, 5 and 6 February. Despite the suspected perpetrator stating the exact time of the crimes, the authorities have so far been powerless to stop him.

The two videos posted online, showing the horrific crimes, had over 100,000 retweets respectively before Twitter could remove the content. Since then, the videos have been copied and shared by other users. The YouTube accounts accredited for the original upload have been removed by their owner. The company is working with the police and using a combination of technology and reports from other social media users to remove other accounts attempting to publicise the video.

'We are taking every measure to remove the content from our platform,' a spokeswoman for YouTube said. 'Our goal is to take action as soon as possible – meanwhile, our thoughts go out to those affected by these horrific events.'

Tributes have been pouring in for all those involved. The condition of the first and second survivors, Michelle Reed and Milly Hallam, and the third survivor, yet to be named, is not known.

A spokesman for the police, Detective Inspector Paul

Rawlinson, said, 'The police are working at full capacity to apprehend those responsible.' He explained the force would be 'exploring all possible leads'. The public should be vigilant, stay safe, and where possible, stay inside, he warned.

The report was concise but Rawlinson's comment wouldn't do anything to reassure the public. I didn't doubt there would be more panic, more questions raised, following this article.

Unable to lay awake in bed any longer, I got up, careful not to disturb Sam. Using my phone screen to light the way I went downstairs. I opened the living-room window and let the cold winter air sweep in, carrying the sound of early morning birdsong, robins and blackbirds mainly. For them, it was just another day: find food, make nests, avoid predators. Such a simple existence, if only. I sat there for half an hour, doing nothing but listening to those birds, until, at just after seven, Howard messaged.

Are you awake?

Yes. Where are you?

Outside.

Going to my front door, I looked into the street and could see Howard's car.

'Babe?' Sam called from the top of the stairs, her voice thick with sleep.

'It's fine, it's Howard.'

'What time is it?'

'Go back to bed, honey, I'll bring up a cuppa soon, OK?'

'Karen—'

'He's had a rough night; he needs a friend.'

Sam didn't reply, just wandered back to bed. Once I heard the bedroom door close, I grabbed the first coat from the pegs, one of Sam's work jackets, and scuttled quickly to Howard's car, my hands going straight to the vent to warm them.

'Shit, it's cold,' I said.

'Did I wake you?'

'No, I couldn't sleep. Are you all right?'

Howard launched into a blow-by-blow account of the night before: the chaos when they discovered the true location was the library, the scene itself, the poor boy and the dead librarian. He didn't miss anything. He told me about the book he found.

'What did Rawlinson say about it?'

'Not much, you know what he's like. I doubt he can even read. But he filed it. We'll see if anything comes from it.'

'I wish I could have been on the scene – there might have been more clues there like there are in the videos.'

'What makes you think that?' Howard asked.

'I just think it's his way. He tells us when the crime will take place. He'd even said he was in our libraries in previous videos. I think he's taunting.'

'Why, though?'

'To prove he's smarter than anyone.'

Howard pulled out his phone, unlocked it and showed me a picture of a book cover.

'What's this?'

'You talk about clues and taunting? This book looked staged to me. You think it's relevant?'

I took out my phone, went onto Amazon and typed in the title so I could see more about the book. On her Amazon page the author, H. J. Card, had a colour picture. She was younger than I expected, perhaps mid-thirties. She stared out knowingly, her assertive gaze softened by her long dyed red hair and glasses.

'Yeah, not what I was expecting either,' he said. 'Very pretty.'

'Future conquest?' I joked, tapping the *read me* icon on top of the cover page, so I could look inside the book.

He shook his head. 'Not me. Not now.'

I smiled. 'I think you and Becca are gonna be all right.'

'You know what, I do too,' he said.

'Tell me about the book.'

'I only got a quick look, but the gist is, the world is becoming more self-centred. It's arguing how we, as a species, are becoming less concerned with others, to the point of not caring.'

'And our killer is trying to make us see this? Why?'

'I don't know.'

I spent the next twenty minutes skimming what I could find out about the book and its contents, offering observations when they struck me. The author linked a lot of her work back to something called 'the trolley problem'. Howard asked me to explain it.

'I know this one. We looked at it in uni. It's an ethical debate. There are five people tied to a track, and a train is coming towards them. You are standing at a lever which will divert the train onto a secondary track. But on that track is one person. What would you do?'

'I'd throw the switch.'

'And kill a person.'

'Better than doing nothing and killing five.'

'The author here says most would do the same, but she goes on to propose that instead of having the opportunity to throw the lever, saving five people but killing one, imagine you are standing on a bridge above the track and you have the ability to save the five people if a large object fell down into the path of the train. Beside you is a really large man.'

'So you'd have to push the man in front of the train.'

'Yeah.'

'That changes things.'

'Yeah it does: same outcome, but the morality is different.'

'So if this is a clue, what is The Host saying?'

'I don't know,' I replied quietly. As I started to think I had exhausted the discussion, something leapt out. I had seen a train recently, and he had left a book which discussed the trolley problem. Going into my photo gallery, I scrolled until I found the train picture graffitied at the underpass.

'Karen?'

'Near the Chinese, I found this.'

I showed Howard the picture and watched as his mouth dropped open.

'Howard, are you all right?'

Howard scrolled through his picture gallery, until the screen featured the back cover of H. J. Card's book. He narrowed in on a hand-drawn doodle in the corner. A steam train.

The two pictures were almost identical.

'Shit, Howard, you need—'

'Yeah, I know, the nightclub. I'll go right now, see if this image is there.'

'And if it is, we'll have learnt he's leaving calling cards.'

'But why?' Howard asked. 'He's making a spectacle. Why the need to leave another mark?'

My phone buzzed in my hand, and I was shocked to read the message:

> Karen, it's DCI Bradshaw. When you get this, could you call in?

'Shit.'

'What is it?'

I showed Howard the screen.

'I'm gonna call, be quiet. He can't know you're with me.'

Howard nodded as I dialled Bradshaw's number. He picked up on the second ring.

'Karen, how are you?'

'I'm fine thank you, sir.' I almost added 'and you?' but stopped myself.

'Thank you for getting back to me. I didn't wake you, did I?'

'No, sir.'

'Good. Are you able to come to the station?'

'Yes, sir. Of course.'

'I'm assuming I don't need to tell you about what's going on?'

'No, sir. I've seen the news.'

'It's a disaster. And with the surviving victims being arrested, it's only going to get worse.'

'When were they arrested, sir?'

'Last night. Obviously, we tried to keep it quiet but it's already all over the news.'

I hesitated, looked at Howard who was trying to listen in.

'And the third, from last night?'

'You know, huh? Well, I guess everyone knows. No such thing as discreet police work anymore. The survivor, a kid really, no older than my own son...'

He trailed off for a moment, then cleared his throat and continued.

'They will all be released, I'm sure of it. But the law is the law. They did commit a serious crime, and it needs to be processed properly.'

'Yes, sir.'

'Even saying that makes me feel like an arsehole.' He sighed. 'Anyway, we need to talk about your review. Can you be here in thirty minutes?'

'Yes, sir. Thirty minutes.'

I hung up the phone and exhaled loudly, relieved he hadn't mentioned anything about Howard and me talking.

'He wants you in?'

'Yeah.'

'Are you coming back to work?'

'I don't know.'

'Maybe it's all done,' Howard continued, excitement in his voice. 'Maybe you're finally cleared to return.'

'Maybe,' I agreed, trying not to get too excited. 'But just in case, find the train in the nightclub, and then get back to the office. If we know anything about this guy, we know he is going to post the video at some point today.'

CHAPTER THIRTY

8.04 a.m.

Arriving at Thorpe Wood Police Station I wasn't sure what to think. Thorpe Wood had been my home for many years, and I used to feel welcome in it, safe. The security of these four walls protected me in some of the darker times in my career. And yet, now I was here, I felt like I was trespassing. An imposter, a criminal. I thought being back would make me happy. It didn't, I was scared. My chest felt tight, and I could feel pins and needles start to tingle in my fingertips. I forced myself to take deep, measured breaths. Each one became harder to draw than the last as I approached Bradshaw's office. Once there, I took one more for luck, and knocked lightly on his door.

'Come in.' His voice beckoned from within.

'Morning, sir. I'm not disturbing?' I said formally, at attention, hoping he couldn't hear that I was struggling to control my breathing.

'Not at all,' he replied, but I could sense he was frayed.

'You wanted to see me, sir.'

Talk about stating the obvious, Karen.

He was usually a sensitive boss, placing the wellbeing of his staff before most things. *Most* things. The Host was one of those things.

'Let me get right to it,' he said. 'People are panicking, we are inundated with calls about what's happened. Dozens of comments about seeing men in motorcycle helmets, like they didn't exist before. We are on the brink of chaos. And we need to put a lid on it, reassure the public we have this under control.'

'Do we have it under control, sir?'

'Of course we bloody don't,' he said, rubbing his hands through his thinning hair. It was the first time I had ever heard him lose his composure. 'Sorry. I'm tired.'

'Nothing to be sorry for, sir.'

'We have to make it look like we have it under control until we do.'

'How can I help?' I asked, preparing myself to return to active duty, roll up my sleeves and find The Host.

'I need you out there.'

'Thank you, sir.' I'd rehearsed my gratitude to look unexpected. 'Thank you. I'm ready to get involved and find him, and I'm happy to act under the guidance of Rawlinson to do so.' The last part was a lie.

'Karen—'

'I have some theories I'd like to explore, with your permission. I would like to go to the—'

'DI Holt,' he said, cutting me off mid-sentence. 'I need you out there with the public. Being visible, in uniform.'

'Sir, I—'

'Some of the schools in the city have reached out, asking for help to keep students calm in this situation. I need you there.'

'No...'

'No?' he echoed, his voice losing its soft edge, the boss in him taking over.

'Sir, I mean no disrespect but I'm better on the case; going into schools, it's important, but a waste of what I can bring.'

'I totally agree with you.'

'But...' I waited.

'But until the IOPC state you can return to full active duty, my hands are tied. At least you get to do something.'

'Sir.'

'And I had to fight for the suspension to be lifted.'

'Thank you, sir,' I said, defeated. I'd hoped that if I was allowed back to work, and I was with Howard, I could distract myself, bury the past. Being a uniform wasn't what I'd planned. On my own, I wasn't sure I'd cope.

'I don't like it any more than you. I need you back, any way I can have you. We need everyone available on this. We all have to do our bit.'

'I understand, sir.'

'Thank you,' he said, slumping back into his chair, beat.

'Sir, are you OK?' It was unlike him to appear as anything other than a pillar of strength.

'Honestly, no. I've been doing this job for a long time. Christ, you were probably only a baby when I started. I've not seen anything like this before. Who could do something like this?'

'I don't know, sir, but we'll stop him.'

He looked up at me, smiled. 'I hope you're right.'

I wasn't happy that I was on restricted duty, having to don a uniform for the first time in years. But in that moment,

I swallowed my pride. My guilt. Bradshaw looked defeated. If I could do even a little, I would. This was bigger than just me.

'Where would you like me to go first, sir?' I asked. My question was greeted with a smile.

'Thank you, Karen. In the wake of the murders, the City Academy have had a lot of issues with students. They need answers, someone to reassure them, so start there?'

I was taken back; the City Academy was where Sam worked. She had mentioned it was rough, but it appeared to be much more than that. Hadn't she told me how bad it really was? Or had I been so wrapped up in myself I'd not listened?

'Yes, sir, right away.'

I turned to leave, and as I opened the door, Bradshaw stopped me.

'Oh, Karen—'

'Sir.'

'I'm really sorry about what happened. You know, I just want to make it clear. I know I speak for everyone here when I say we don't believe you did anything wrong.'

'Thank you, sir.'

'With what's going on, I've insisted the inquest be bumped up the list, so expect to hear something soon.'

'How soon, sir?'

'A few days, a few weeks – who knows with that lot? But the sooner the better.'

'Yes, the sooner the better,' I said, turning and leaving his office.

I made my way to the changing rooms to dust off my unworn uniform. I was aware of the stares given by colleagues, of the sympathetic smiles when I locked eyes with the few who didn't divert fast enough. As I readied myself to leave, grabbing a notepad from my desk drawer, I couldn't help but feel Rawlinson giving me a stare. When I met his gaze, he held it. Even though Bradshaw said everyone was on my side with regard to Grayson James, it was clear 'everyone' didn't include DI Paul Rawlinson.

I was only gone for ten minutes, but in the short time that I was in the belly of the station, changing into my uniform, everything changed.

In that short ten minutes, he had posted again.

Stopping just before the situation room that was no longer sedate but buzzing, I took out my phone. It didn't take long to find it on the internet.

'... *As you watch this video now, the Fourth Game is in motion, and my new Players will play tonight, this time, at 8.30 p.m.*'

I sat transfixed as the library came onto the screen. I saw the victims. I saw the weapons, and before I locked the screen, I saw the violence. As did thousands of others. A number that was likely to rise. I felt myself begin to hyperventilate again, and despite wanting to get moving, I couldn't. I was paralysed.

And then, from nowhere, Grayson James came into my head.

Calming my breathing, I walked into the bustle, locking eyes with Rawlinson, who was standing over a computer analyst, a kid, barking for him to get YouTube to remove the content. I could hear the young man say it was challenging, because before YouTube could respond, the video had been downloaded onto personal hard drives, and then reposted.

'I don't know what that means. Just get them to turn off

the switch,' Rawlinson shouted before giving me a look and storming away and up a flight of stairs. I approached the young technician; he was clearly shaken up.

'I'm trying, it's not as easy as turning—' he started defensively.

'Don't worry about him, he's a dickhead. You're doing a great job.' I tapped him on the shoulder and headed after Rawlinson.

I didn't know what to do: technically I shouldn't be there, so I stood still, lost, like I was a rookie in the station. Then I spotted Howard across the room, who beckoned me with a nod. I followed and found him in the kitchen area, where we couldn't be seen.

'Hey,' he said.

'Hey.'

'Nice costume,' he smiled, referring to my uniform. An attempt to lighten the mood, perhaps keep us both calm. It didn't work.

'I'll take whatever work I can get.'

'I hear that.'

'Did you find the train symbol?'

'It was there.'

Howard handed me his phone: on the screen was a picture taken inside the men's bathroom at the nightclub. I could see a sink, three urinals, and a mirror. The walls were covered in a paper that made it look like a bookcase – the club's desperate attempt to make the shit-hole, pun intended, look respectable. Really, it was a place where men pissed and did coke and got laid if they were lucky. But at least it tried. At first, I didn't know why Howard had taken the picture, but then, right in the middle of the wall was a familiar shape. Pinching the screen, I zoomed in, and there it was, a train.

'Can you see it?' Howard asked.

'Yep. I see it.'

'You were right, Karen. He is leaving clues.'

'Let's piece it out,' I said, the experienced detective in me taking over from the awkward and anxious woman. Sitting at a table and zoning into the middle distance, I let myself think out loud. 'At first he was measuring the blunt impact, with no prior warning, no clues. Then, he left his calling card and in the video he mentioned the library as a clue. He did it knowing we would hate ourselves for not seeing it in plain sight.'

'Why would he do that? What if we'd worked it out?'

'He knew we wouldn't; it was amongst other things.'

'So why say it at all?'

'He likes to play. To him, this is all just a game. I've not had a chance to look at what he said in the latest video. Did he mention anywhere new?'

Howard took out his phone and replayed the latest video, noting down the locations he stated. Offices, restaurants, pubs, high streets, libraries, cinemas, gyms.

Nothing new.

I banged the table in disappointment.

'Maybe he hasn't left a clue this time?' Howard said.

'No, he has, he definitely has. It's part of his Game.'

'Sick Game,' Howard whispered.

'If it's not in the video, it will be something to do with that book, and the train symbols. Let's talk it through. He leaves a recording, stating the location and the time. Then at that location, we find the book and...' I stopped. 'Shit, the toilet walls. The train was on a bookcase.'

'Oh God,' Howard said, catching on. 'Show me the photo from the underpass.'

'Already ahead of you,' I replied. I tapped the image on the camera roll and pinched the glass to zoom in. The train centred on the screen. I didn't see anything, but Howard did.

'Look, top corner.'

Howard reached over me and moved the image; there was a graffitied word, blended with the many other tags on the wall. *Echo*.

'The nightclub, it's called the Echo Lounge,' I whispered.

'Shit, he's leaving the locations right under our noses.'

'So he leaves the train next to the word "echo" at the Chinese, then he leaves it on the bookcase wallpaper at the Echo Lounge.'

'And the latest is on the back of a book in the library,' Howard said.

'Yeah. It must tell us the next location. The train problem is about the lever being thrown, right? But remember, this book adds the detail that instead of just throwing a switch, you have to push a man in front of the train. Same problem, same solution, different moral outcome.'

'Yeah, but what is he saying?'

'What if he's trying to say it will be on a bridge?' I said off-hand.

'What was that?'

'Nothing.'

'No, finish the thought.'

'What if he's telling us it will be on a bridge? He didn't

disguise the library, he just said it. The word "echo" was clear to see, if you knew where to look.'

'You're right, he didn't hide it, he just said it plainly.'

'And the book focuses on the train problem, but not the bit about throwing a switch – instead of pushing someone from a bridge.'

'What if that's it,' Howard said, 'what if in the Fourth Game he will make someone push another from a bridge?'

From outside the kitchen, I saw Rawlinson look in, before turning on his heels and marching away.

'Shit. We've been busted, Howard. I better go before we both end up on the chopping block. Tell Bradshaw what we've discussed. Find that bridge. Stop this bastard.'

'We'll get the son of a bitch. I can feel it.'

CHAPTER THIRTY-ONE

Carlson

4.46 p.m.
Three hours and forty-four minutes until the next Game

After Karen left the station, Carlson went straight to Bradshaw and told him their thoughts. He didn't let slip that he and Karen had spoken, but Bradshaw knew. There would likely be consequences, for both of them, but now was not the time.

Bradshaw agreed it made sense, congratulated Carlson on a job well done, and mobilised the team in the incident room to hand out tasks to his officers. They were to index and prioritise bridges in the city, and once that was done, they would hit the streets in the hope of catching The Host when he started to play.

As Bradshaw briefed and prepared the team to head out, Carlson could feel the apprehension in the air.

'Remember, people,' Bradshaw said, getting everyone's attention. 'If you see anything suspicious out there, wait, watch; we need to catch this guy in the act. I don't need to remind you that there have been several calls to the 999 switchboard today, reporting people wearing a motorbike helmet, like it's a bloody Hallowe'en costume. And I don't want some poor sod who happens to be wearing a helmet pounced on because a motorbike happens to be his mode of transportation. The Host takes his time, sets up each Game. Wait until you are sure.'

'Really think it's a bridge?' Rawlinson asked, a hint of annoyance on his face that Karen Holt was still influencing police operations.

'No, we can't be a hundred per cent sure. That's why I'm not sending the whole force out. DI Rawlinson, Michelle Reed is out of the HDU. Go and speak to her, find out something new. PC Sommers, go see the families of The Players. There must be something connecting them.'

'Yes, boss,' Sommers said nervously. It was the first time he had been singled out in a briefing. Carlson nodded in his direction, offering reassurance that he would do a good job.

'DS Carlson, when we have the bridges indexed I want your thoughts on which is most likely to be the target.'

As the team got to work, it quickly became apparent there were literally hundreds of bridges in and around the city. Carlson thought it would be impossible to state which was most likely as a location. But as soon as he saw the crescent bridge – a bright blue one that ran over the railway line close to the city centre – he felt sure it would be the one. It was one of the few that ran over the railway lines. Bradshaw agreed, and the eight bridges that crossed the railway line became the primary focus. He messaged Karen, telling her they were focusing on the bridges, but she didn't respond. He wanted to call but thought better of it. She had done enough.

Despite it being hours until The Game's appointed time Carlson headed for the crescent bridge where he found a quiet spot and waited. From his position he could see both sides of the road. The footpaths were busy with people walking into and out of the city centre, but as the hours ticked by, he saw fewer and fewer people. Darkness descended, the shops started to close, and the streets became all but deserted. At various points in the city, other officers sat in wait, and periodically, they would check in, stating there was no sign of him yet. But The Host would come, Carlson could feel it.

THE FOURTH GAME

The Host tapped on the metal railing of the overpass that connected one side of the A15 with the other, waiting. Behind, the streetlamp that lit the footbridge was out, it had been for a while. It made The Host invisible.

Within a few minutes the laboured breathing of Jim Weston would come up the steep incline of the footbridge ramp. He always locked up last, always took his time. Always came over the bridge.

Ten minutes passed, and still no sign of him. The Host began to twitch. Maybe Jim Weston wasn't at work today? If The Game failed to be delivered as promised, what then?

Just as panic began to set in that the plan had failed, footsteps approached. Then, a shape crested the footbridge and The Host breathed a sigh of relief. The target had arrived. It was time. Lying on the ground, careful to mask the motorbike helmet from view, The Host waited, heart thumping, for the target to close in. Jim Weston wasn't a man to ignore someone injured. He was kind. Caring. To him people mattered. And that was why he had to play.

It was so dark; Jim Weston didn't see The Host until he was a few feet away, and sure enough, as soon as he did, he dropped to his knees, both cracking as he hit the asphalt, to see if The Host was OK.

'Hello. Are you all right? Do you need help?' he asked, worried. He shook The Host's shoulder. 'What's your name? Hello?'

He shook The Host's shoulder again, and saw the motor-bike helmet. At first, he didn't do anything. When he realised who it was lying underneath him Jim began to heave himself up to try and run, but The Host was quicker, nimbler and before Jim could stand, The Host was above him, something in his right hand that reflected the headlights of the cars speeding underneath.

'Don't move,' The Host said, mechanically through the voice filter, twitching from foot to foot. The man was big; if he went for it, if he threw some weight in, maybe The Host would lose. Thankfully, he was too mild-mannered to try.

'OK, OK,' Jim Weston said, his hands held up in defence, his head lowered like a subordinate dog. 'Please. Don't hurt me.'

'I won't. That will be for someone else.'

At that moment, The Host heard voices. Someone else was coming onto the bridge, more than one person. As a car drove past, The Host could see his Player's forehead glisten with sweat, despite it being only two degrees. The Host was sweating too. This wasn't going to plan.

The voices grew louder, and two teenagers holding hands came into view.

'Please, they're just kids,' Jim said, shocking The Host at how brave he sounded. But Jim Weston need not worry, The Host didn't want two more Players, just one.

'If you say anything, I'll kill them,' The Host said, thankful that the voice-altering device masked the mounting anxiety. Jim nodded, agreeing.

The Host turned and faced the road below, elbows resting on the barrier, head low to hide the helmet from view. 'If they see me, they, they have to die,' The Host stammered.

Jim nodded, too scared to pick up on the indecision, and rounded the other side of The Host, masking him with his wider frame. As the young people passed, they barely gave Jim a look, and seemed not to notice the smaller, narrower person beside him. To be sure, Jim rounded The Host again, so that they couldn't look back and see the person in the motorbike helmet. The Host and Jim Weston each let out the breath they were holding as the teens disappeared out of sight. Then, the knife was out, pointing at Jim Weston again.

'You're braver than you look.'

'They're just kids.'

'We all have to die at some point.'

Jim looked at The Host and weighed up his chances. The man before him was shorter, slighter, he wondered if he could disarm him, ring the police. The thought didn't last long – he wasn't a hero, far from it. He had actively avoided conflict his entire life. Even seeing violence made him feel sick.

'Do you want to die, Jim?'

'How do you know my name?'

'Jim Weston, forty-six, married to Susan Weston. No kids, but a seventeen-year-old stepdaughter, April. Named after her nan. She'll be at home, just around the corner. Upstairs in her bedroom, the front left window.'

'Leave her alone.'

'Well, that's entirely up to you now, isn't it?'

Jim felt his legs give way and he had to grab the railing to stop himself falling over.

'You think this meeting is a coincidence. There is no such thing. It's been planned for some time. You have been watched for months.'

'Why me?' he quietly asked, defeated. 'I've not done anything wrong.'

'Why not you? What makes you so special?'

He didn't have an answer, and dropping to his knees he began to beg, but his pleading was cut short when another figure approached. Jim looked; it was the boy who had walked past only moments ago with his girlfriend. He must have been fifteen or sixteen, at most.

'If you say anything, if you do anything, I'll chase him down and I'll kill him, and then I'll go to your stepdaughter,' The Host said, dragging Jim onto his feet. Fear crippled Jim's vocal cords and he could only nod.

The Host pulled out a small wind-up alarm clock and turned it. It was happening, it was going to be all right. The boy approached, oblivious to what was ahead of him. In the low light, Jim could make out him smiling, reflecting no doubt on young love. When the boy was only a few paces away, The Host stepped into his path.

'If you run...' The Host's voice snagged. 'If you run, I will kill you.'

The boy froze to the spot, a rabbit in headlights.

'Against the rail, stand against the rail.'

The boy didn't move.

'I said, stand. Now.' The Host approached, the knife out, pointing at his chest.

The boy stumbled backwards into the railing, bumping into Jim beside him. Underneath them, cars sped past, ignorant of what was unfolding; in the distance, there was a siren, and The Host froze. A small glimmer of hope unfurled in Jim's stomach, but the sirens became quieter, they were moving away, not towards. And The Host laughed, anxiety spilling over, then reached up and pressed record on the GoPro.

The Host took off the rucksack, placed it on the ground, unzipped it and rummaged through, disregarding the butcher's knife, saw and rope but instead removing a small metal stake a foot in length, the end a corkscrew for digging holes in soil, and a long, heavy chain. Once they were set in place on the floor in front of the pair, The Host explained the rules to the newest Players.

CHAPTER THIRTY-TWO

8.42 p.m.

As I sat watching the crap eighties comedy that was on Gold, I was looking at the time on my phone – twelve minutes since The Game should have been played. I'd been distracted all afternoon thinking about it. After leaving the station, I'd intended to go in to Sam's school but in the car, driving towards the City Academy, I had to pull over as I couldn't catch my breath, again. Without any cool water to run over my wrists I had to ride it out. The panic attack wasn't as severe as the first, but it was still enough to tell me I couldn't face anyone, so I came home instead.

Sam got back just after five. She told me the video went live when they were all in the hall, the head trying to calm the students. I couldn't imagine how hard it would have been to calm so many young people. I felt guilty for not being there, as I should have been. I was deflated, Sam was defeated. I cooked us a meal neither of us had the appetite to eat. Dinner was awkward, we didn't speak, but both rolled our food around the plate, nibbling every now and then, lost in our own thoughts. Sam had two large glasses of wine.

Now we were sitting here in silence, neither of us wanting to speak, until my phone started ringing.

'It's Howard.'

'Karen, please. Not tonight,' Sam pleaded.

'Sam, I—'

'It's too much. Can we not have it at home? It's hard enough at school.'

'Sam, I have to,' I replied, knowing full well I didn't. If I ignored the call, Howard would understand. Probably tell me I was being responsible. Still, he was ringing. I had to answer.

'No, Karen, you don't. You are not investigating this. You know that, right?'

'I know.'

'Then turn it off, please.'

I couldn't do it; I couldn't ignore Howard. So, even knowing it would upset Sam, I picked up the phone.

'Tell me we were right?' I started before he could speak. 'Tell me we got him.'

Sam stood abruptly, snatching her glass of wine. 'I give up,' she said, walking out of the kitchen.

'We were right, it was a bridge. But we were monitoring the wrong ones.'

'Fuck,' I said, watching Sam mount the stairs.

'Yeah, fuck.'

'Do we know much about the victims?'

'A little. Jim Weston, forty-six. Worked at the local M&S, and a kid.'

'A kid? How old?' I asked, my voice shrill as panic squeezed my vocal cords. This thing was a mess, but involving kids made it different somehow. Sam heard, and stopped midway up the stairs, looking over the banister back at me.

'Fifteen. Lucas Mathews.'

'Dare I ask?' I said, holding my breath.

'The kid is fine. Well, he's alive, I wouldn't say he was fine.'

I looked at Sam and mouthed that the kid was OK. She sighed and continued upstairs.

'This one, it wasn't like the others,' Howard continued.

'What do you mean?'

'They didn't fight.'

'So what happened?'

'Jim Weston jumped off the bridge.'

I didn't respond. Instead I pictured the scene. The Host with his motorbike helmet. The fearful pair, looking from each other to the weapons that would have been laid before them. I wondered how The Host felt about them not playing by the rules.

'Karen?' Howard said, breaking my thoughts.

'I'm here.'

'Jim Weston isn't dead.'

'What?'

'He's in a bad way, but he didn't die from the fall.'

Both had survived, and I knew I should be elated. Not only had we foreseen it would happen on a bridge, but no one died tonight. It should have felt like a victory, and yet I couldn't ignore the churning in my stomach. Jim Weston had broken the rules of The Game. There would be repercussions.

'We need to speak to the kid,' I said, after a pause.

'He's being treated by paramedics. He's happy to talk once the all-clear has been given. I've just spoken to his parents, who are here. They agree that Lucas might have vital information.'

'Good, that's good. Have you found the train yet?'

'No, not yet. Forensics are on the bridge.'

'CCTV cameras?'

'One, we are getting the footage now.'

'OK, with the others the train wasn't at the scene. The first was on the underpass 200 yards away, the second in a loo…'

'The third in a different part of the library,' Howard added.

'The train won't be on the bridge, but somewhere nearby.'

'I'm on it,' Howard said.

I expected him to hang up, but he didn't, and I listened to muffled conversations and his footsteps. Rawlinson's voice came over the line, barking, as usual, but in triumph rather than indignation. I could hear him congratulating people on a job well done. No doubt assuming that because no one died, The Host was cornered, on the ropes, about to throw in the towel. I agreed in part; The Host would feel like he was in a corner. But he wasn't a boxer ready to quit, he was a cobra. In a corner he would be far more dangerous, far more unpredictable. Rawlinson's voice faded into the background, as did the other voices, other noises. I listened as Howard mumbled to himself, trying to piece together where the train might be. I didn't interrupt.

'I wouldn't go right, it becomes too lit up, too close to the main road, the traffic would have stopped, he would have been seen. Left it is…' he said to himself before moving again. I smiled. He sounded a lot like me these days. The line went quiet, before muffled sounds and a thud, like the phone had been dropped.

'Shit, sorry,' Howard said. 'I've got you on loudspeaker. Needed both my hands, I think I've found something.'

'What can you see?'

'There's one of those fire hydrant signs. You know – the concrete posts – there's definitely something on it. I'm just grabbing my torch.'

I waited again, I heard a switch click on, then Howard mumbled under his breath.

'Found it.'

'Brilliant. Anything new, any clues?'

'No. Just the train.'

'And the hydrant. I assume it's one of those yellow ones with numbers on it?'

'Yep, capital H, top number is a hundred. Bottom is twenty-two.'

'Mean anything to you?'

'Not a thing.'

'Me neither,' I admitted. 'OK. So let's focus on what he's telling us. The new location is linked to water. A fire station perhaps?'

'A fire station would be tricky. He wouldn't have access to one. And as far as I know, it's not often there are just two firefighters in a station. Some kind of waterway, then. A lake perhaps?'

'Possibly,' I said.

'We were right about the bridge,' Howard said, sensing my unease.

'Yeah,' I responded, desperately thinking about possible places he would go. Ferry Meadows, Hampton Lakes? If the clue was even water at all.

'I'll send you a picture of this.'

'Thank you, Howard.'

'I'll head back to the station; I want to be there when Lucas comes in.'

'Good idea. Rawlinson will no doubt freak him out more.'

I heard the grimace in his voice. 'No doubt.'

'How badly injured is Jim Weston?'

'He's pretty banged up. He was slipping in and out of consciousness when they got to him.'

'Do you think The Host saw he was still alive?'

'He must have, but I doubt we'll have a chance of finding out anything from him.'

'None. It's all on the kid,' I agreed. 'We have learnt something else, though, haven't we?'

'What's that?' Howard asked.

'Well, he would have seen Jim Weston wasn't dead, and he would have still had the kid next to him. Both alive. But in his Game, someone must die.'

'But no one did.'

'He's a sick bastard, but he himself isn't able to kill.'

Howard let out a long breath. 'It's so fucked up.'

I pressed on. 'Hypothetically, do you reckon you can get hold of the CCTV footage from any of the other scenes, including this one?'

'Hypothetically, yes, of course.'

'I wouldn't mind taking a look at it.'

'Karen, I know I keep ringing you, it's my failing. And I'm sorry. But you should walk away, you shouldn't be looking at any CCTV.'

'Howard, between me and you, I'm not ready to come back to work. I want to be – part of me *needs* it – but I've got stuff I need to sort out. You know?'

'Yeah, I get you.'

'But this Host isn't leaving us any choice, is he? And I feel like I'm getting in his head.'

'You are. No one else would have connected the train symbols and the clues.'

I tried once more. 'If you can, send over the CCTV, and keep me posted on what the kid says, OK?'

CHAPTER THIRTY-THREE

The Host

9.57 p.m.

Sitting at his desk, The Host looked at the Facebook group. The panic was real, tangible, he could almost taste it in every word written. They spoke of locking windows, going to bed with kitchen implements under their pillows, sleeping in the same room as their children. He loved that. Their fear was the voice that spoke loudest now. And interestingly, that fear said indirectly that they would kill. Hiding the truth by declaring they had to protect their kids, or they were too young to die, or their survival instinct would kick in, and they wouldn't be able to stop it.

It was perfect. People were beginning to understand.

Twitter was the same. #theHost was trending, as was #theGame and #thePlayers. All three about *him*. It made him feel a sense of pride.

But the pride he felt in his ideology coming to life, imprinting on people far and wide, was short-lived as he looked at the news on his phone. He expected to see a headline about another death, but both Jim Weston and the kid had survived. The Game had been compromised. The person he had entrusted to act on his behalf, the one who begged to be The Host to show their loyalty had failed him. His message would be diluted for it. He wanted to kill them for their mistake.

Grabbing a pillow, he screamed into it. Tonight, his message would be muddied. There was no evil on the bridge, no irrefutable proof that people were selfish, and he needed the night to show the darkness in humanity.

He needed to rest, he desperately needed to sleep. But it was more important to restore his message. How would he be able to stop Jim Weston dominating the news? The answer was clear. To stop Jim Weston being a hero in the media, to stop hope worming its way into his ideology, tonight's Game needed to be finished with someone else.

CHAPTER THIRTY-FOUR

10.04 p.m.

I could hear Sam moving above me, brushing her teeth, getting ready for bed. None of this was her fault, and yet, I was pusing her away, like she was responsible for how I was feeling. I didn't want to go to sleep with this energy between us. Making my way upstairs, I saw the bedroom door was shut. I decided to knock to be on the safe side. If Sam told me to go away, I would. She'd had an awful day, and instead of giving her my time, my ear to bend, my shoulder to cry on, instead of going to bed with her, cuddling her and telling her it would be OK, I'd chosen to answer the phone. I had got involved in something that Sam had asked me not to – for my own good. I had chosen my work over my wife. I should have been solely focused on trying to deal with what had happened, but The Host and his crimes had forced their way in and taken over. Without him, and his Game, I'd be beside Sam now.

I raised my hand to tap, but hesitated. If Sam asked me to stop taking an interest in the case, would I be able to? I couldn't make a promise that I knew I would break. I shouldn't even *try*. So, I backed away and went downstairs. Sam and I would be all right, we were solid as a couple, resilient, we'd had tough times, but who doesn't?

Instead of telling my wife I was sorry, and that I loved her, I paced, drank coffee, checked my phone every two minutes for an email, or text, and I looked at the image of the train stencilled by the Chinese takeaway a thousand times. There was nothing new to gain from it. The CCTV from the bridge would take time to filter to Howard, and eventually to me, if he decided to share it. And I knew that interviewing the boy would be a lengthy process as well. The shock, time of day, and the fact he was a minor would all impact on how it was handled.

But I needed something to do. I tried to kill time by looking at bodies of water in and around Peterborough. It didn't help, there were too many, and with nothing else to go on, it would be just like the bridge. We knew it would be connected to water, but there was no way we'd ever know where.

'Karen.' Sam's voice made me jump and I tried to not look guilty as I locked my phone screen. 'Come to bed.'

'I'll be up soon.'

'It's late, we both need a good night's sleep.'

'Just a few more minutes, I promise.'

'Why can't you stay away from this?' Sam asked, crossing her arms in the living-room doorway. 'You don't have to prove yourself, Karen.'

'Prove myself?'

'His death wasn't your fault.'

I knew what she was saying, but it *was* my fault. If someone else had been arresting, maybe they wouldn't have fallen. Maybe they could have arrested him without it ending in tragedy. Over the past decade, I had been involved in more arrests than I could count. I had helped so many, stopped murderers and thieves. I had caught serial rapists and helped those trapped in the grip of domestic violence. I had pulled people out of car wrecks. I'd even sacrificed promotions in order to help someone who was truly innocent. But my entire career would now be defined by one arrest, one fall.

'Karen, you don't need to stop this Host person to make amends. You don't need to make anything right.'

I could feel a cold sweat begin to break out on my forehead, my hands began to tingle.

Shit, not now.

'Sam, I...'

'Come to bed, please? I think we'll both feel better after a good night's sleep.'

I couldn't go to bed now, I just couldn't. Sam had just hit a nerve, *the* nerve. I didn't want Sam to see me have a panic attack. I didn't want her to know what a bad state I was in. As my breathing began to catch I mumbled an apology and headed to the front door.

'Karen, where are you going?'

'I need to get some air,' I said as I wrestled on my shoes, the simple task harder than it should be as my hands were going numb.

Keep it together, just for one more minute.

'Please don't go out walking, Karen. Last night you went out, and I had to come and rescue you. Stay with me, let me help you.'

'Sam, I need some air, I'll take the car around the block,' I said, struggling to get my words out.

'Karen? What's wrong?'

'Nothing, I need to get some air, that's all.'

'No, you are not OK.'

'I'm fine,' I said, fighting to put my coat on.

'Please, let me in, let me help—'

'I just need some bloody air! Will you give me a minute?' I shouted, regretting it instantly, unable to take it back.

I expected Sam to say something, but she didn't, she just watched, shocked by my outburst. I could barely look at her as I mumbled an apology for shouting at her and stepped into the night. Thankfully, I managed to get to the car, unlock and climb in. Starting the engine, I opened the front windows, and the cold night air helped me regulate my breathing. I gagged three times. I'd never been like this before, it scared me.

At first, I thought I would drive for ten or so minutes, with the windows down and the radio volume up, but instead I found myself heading in the direction of the city centre. I didn't know why, or where I would end up. I just needed to move, to not look back, and as the miles started to fall behind, I felt myself calm.

I drove through the city centre, a steady 30 mph on the quiet roads. It wasn't until I was close that I realised I was on the A15, driving towards the footbridge. I assumed I wouldn't get near, as they would still be processing the scene. But to see it with my own eyes – to walk the way he would have walked – would hopefully trigger something that would help.

Eventually, artificial floodlights from the scene came into view, and approaching from the south, close to a cluster of houses, I was confident I wouldn't be noticed. The crime scene was taped up, the road below closed. I didn't realise that it wasn't just one footbridge that ran over the road, but several intersecting over the huge roundabout.

Parking Sam's car in a side road, near an Indian takeaway, I climbed out and began walking. This simple action and the sense of control it provided stalled the sick feeling in my gut. Investigating a scene was familiar and comforting, and I could pretend the last few weeks hadn't happened. As soon as I started to think like a detective again, the panic I had been feeling subsided.

Keeping my head down, I walked past the ramp to the overpass where it happened, taking note of the small train stencil Howard had discovered, and the lone CCTV camera above. I crossed the road at the roundabout and scurried to the next footbridge to the north of where the forensics were, confident the handful of officers still working wouldn't see me. From where I stood, I could see across to the bridge to where Jim Weston jumped.

To my right, there was someone like me, watching the police work. They were a fair distance away, and obscured from view by several trees. The police beneath the artificial lights would have no idea they were there. I was curious, and began to cross to the other side of my bridge, to draw closer. Then I saw it. In the hand of the person was a motorbike helmet.

The man turned, catching sight of me and, for a moment, neither of us moved. I couldn't see his face, it was too dark, but I knew he was staring at me, and the way he stood, startled and alert, left no doubt in my mind. It was him, it was The Host, and he had come back to where he failed. It was either brazen, or stupid. His first mistake.

The stand-off lasted for just a moment before he began to run.

'Stop, police!' I shouted, knowing that it would do nothing. I didn't call out again; instead, I saved my breath and forced the oxygen into my legs to power me down the ramp, arms wheeling to keep me upright.

I managed to flash a look across as he reached the bottom of the incline and was on the footpath that ran alongside the road. If he turned right, he would run closer to the working police officers, surely drawing their attention. Left would be towards me and beyond. He turned my way, and I upped my pace to intercept. As I hit the level ground, he was three steps ahead. Pushing myself as hard as I could, my lungs screamed as I fought to get enough air, I chased. I was helpless to stop the space between us growing.

Ahead the footpath hit a wall. If I could keep up, I could apprehend him when he had to slow down to turn or climb over it. He was bigger than me, several inches taller, but I knew I could use his own speed against him to stop him. If I could get him to the floor, I could hold him there until help arrived. The wall approached, fifty feet, forty, thirty. I could feel my muscles begin to tighten and slow me down. Twenty more feet, that was all I needed to push for. Ten. He began to slow. A few feet away, he jumped, his hand landing with a slap on the top of the cold wall. One leg went over, if the second met it, I would lose him. Lunging, I grabbed his left foot, and began to pull back with all my might. He tried to kick me off, but I held firm. As I began to yank him backwards with both hands, he swung the motorbike helmet, hitting me on the temple, knocking me to the ground.

Just before I blacked out, I saw the blurred image of his face look back and then he disappeared.

CHAPTER THIRTY-FIVE

11.12 p.m.

From somewhere, I could hear humming. It sounded for a short time, and then stopped, then started again. I couldn't work out what it was, or where it was coming from. My eyes began to open and focus on the shapes created by the branches of an overhead tree. My vision was blurred, something was wrong, but I couldn't tell what. Then the pain came, a throbbing in my left eye and cheek. I touched the locus and felt blood, not a lot, but some, and some serious swelling to my cheekbone and eye socket – my eye was partially closed, restricting what I could see. I hoped it wouldn't close entirely.

Rolling onto my side, I gingerly sat up, and for a moment, my head swam from the movement. The humming began once more, and realising it was my phone, I reached into my coat pocket and pulled it out. The bright display hurt my one working eye.

'I've got CCTV footage. Both from the bridge, and from a small camera inside the Chinese,' Howard leapt in as soon as I answered. 'There's also footage from the library, but as I tried to get it, Rawlinson approached.'

'I'm glad you didn't get caught. Anything from inside the nightclub?' I said wearily.

'Nope, the cameras were off. Sorry, I've not woken you, have I?' Howard said, noticing I sounded foggy.

'Not quite. I couldn't rest, so I went out.'

'Where are you now?'

'By the footbridge. Howard, he came back, The Host came back to the scene.'

'What? You saw him?'

'I had him, Howard, I had him, in my hands and I couldn't hold him.'

'Jesus, Karen. What were you thinking? You could have got yourself killed.'

'No,' I groaned as I pulled myself to my feet and leant my full weight against the wall. 'Our man isn't a killer.'

'We speculated he isn't a killer because he didn't hurt the kid. But we don't know that.'

'Howard, he is a planner, he isn't impulsive.'

'But your being there meant he would have had to act on impulse. It was a stupid risk.'

'Well, I'm not dead.'

'Not for the lack of trying. Sit tight, I'll call it in.'

'No, don't. Bradshaw will know I've been out.'

'But we can get him…'

'He's long gone by now.'

'Did you get a good look at him?'

I thought about the moment he'd been close enough for me to see his face, just before I slipped unconscious. I focused to recall his features or a distinguishing mark, but as I tried, the dark eyes and high cheekbones of Grayson James projected onto the memory.

'No, I didn't get a proper look.'

'OK, we'll get the bastard. I'm coming to get you. Sit tight.'

Despite the ground being cold, I slid down and sat, my back pressed into the wall. The blow to my head had left me rattled, combined with the lack of sleep and dropping adrenaline I was sure I wouldn't be able to walk far unaided.

As I sat waiting for Howard, I thought about the reasons The Host had come back. His rules had been broken, but to return on the same evening to the scene was blind arrogance or wild petulance. He responded like someone lacking any self-control, and if The Host had shown anything it was that he was disciplined. The risks were huge and he must have known that. If I had to speculate, I would say he came back to play again. I just didn't understand why.

Possible motives were racing through my head when a torch shone towards me.

'Jesus, you look like you've just done twelve rounds with A. J.,' Howard said, helping me up onto my feet.

'Charming,' I said, flashing a tired smile.

'Do we need to get you to a doctor?'

'You need to get me to somewhere serving coffee. Did you bring the CCTV footage with you?'

'Yeah, I've downloaded it onto my phone, but it can wait.'

'No, I want to see it now.'

'You're the boss,' he said, helping me back to his car, before driving a few hundred yards up the A15 to a twenty-four-hour McDonald's.

'Now who says I'm not classy?' he joked as he parked as close as he could to the front door and grabbed a small first aid kit from the glove box.

'I bet you bring all your dates here.' I smiled, then winced, the pain in my face sharp and hot. 'Don't worry,' I added. 'It's nothing a coffee and a few painkillers can't fix.'

'You're tougher than me,' he said, handing me the kit.

We walked inside, the hot air blowing down from the overhead heater stopping me in my tracks. For a moment I let it warm me before Howard told me to go to the toilet and clean up my face. Seeing the person staring back at me in the bathroom mirror with a badly swollen eye was a shock. It looked horrific. Opening my mouth was painful, but I did so as wide as I could, to make sure my teeth were still firmly intact. Thankfully, they were, but my cheekbone wasn't looking great, and as I touched it, I winced again. I was lucky it hadn't been broken. As I started to clean myself up, there was a gentle knock on the door.

'Karen, everything all right?'

'I think so.'

Howard came into the bathroom and closed the door behind him. I looked at him in the mirror.

I tried to smile. 'You shouldn't be in here.'

'Yeah, well,' he replied, running the cold tap and opening the first aid kit, retrieving some antiseptic wipes. As he cleaned the small cut by my eye, I took a sharp intake of breath.

'You're gonna be sore for a few days,' he said quietly, cracking a cool pack that soothed as soon as it was applied. 'Hold this here, go out grab a seat, I'll get you a coffee.'

'Thanks, mate.'

Howard left, and after taking one more look at myself, I followed, and took a booth near the door. There were only a handful of people inside, two in high visibility jackets, either just starting or finishing a shift for Highways England. Behind them, tucked in the furthest corner was a young couple – teenagers whispering to one another, looking at a phone, partially obscured behind their milkshakes. I looked at my watch and saw it was close to midnight. I wondered if anyone was worried for them. I thought about approaching, saying something, but stopped myself. I was beginning to show my age; it had snuck up on me. The young couple must have felt my gaze on them, since they looked up, and seeing my face – the cold compress half covering it, like an odd homage to *Phantom of the Opera* – they looked away quickly. Moments later they stood, threw their milkshakes in the bin and left. I tried to flash a disarming smile, but it didn't work, as they looked back disgusted. With a sigh, I slumped back against the chair. Then my phone pinged, and I pulled it out to see a message from Sam.

Are you OK? When are you coming home?

I'm fine, I've popped to see Howard, I'm safe, don't worry, go to sleep, I'll be home soon. X

I waited for her to message back a kiss or an *OK, see you later*, but it didn't come. Howard returned with the drinks.

'Let me see it,' he said, sitting opposite. I moved the cold compress and he made a face.

'Could at least try and pretend it's not all that bad.'

'It looks bloody sore.'

'Yeah, it smarts a little.' I smiled, taking a sip of my drink. 'I have no idea how I'm gonna explain this to Sam. I'm already in the doghouse.'

'Sorry, mate.'

'What for?'

'I feel like I've dragged you into this.'

'Don't be sorry, Howard, I think I was always going to end up involved.'

'No, Karen, I dragged you—'

'Howard.' I cut him off. 'I'm grateful you asked me. I needed you to need my help. What happened with Grayson James, it's…' I hesitated. 'I, I have to prove I am still a good copper.'

'Karen, of course you are a good copper. Everyone knows that.'

'Yeah, but I don't.'

Howard nodded towards me.

'So, shall we have a look at this footage?'

'Sure.'

'Scoot over,' I said, getting up and sitting beside him. I rested my head on his shoulder as he loaded the PGN file on his phone.

'You all right? Not feeling sick, or dizzy?'

'No, I'm just tired.'

'Perhaps we should get you checked out.'

'Howard, honestly, it hurts like hell, but I'm fine.'

'OK. If anyone finds out I've downloaded this…' He didn't need to say any more, we both knew the risks we were taking.

'Thank you.'

The footage rendered, and a grainy image of the bottom of the footbridge came into view. We could see up the ramp, a little of the top of the bridge, and in the very bottom left corner, the concrete fire hydrant on which Howard had discovered the train image. The A15 ran beside it. We both stared at the video – for a while nothing happened, then Howard tapped the screen, bringing up the timeline at the bottom, and he began to fast forward. The video revealed little beside the odd flicker of tree branches in the wind and headlights from a few cars. Then as the timestamp said 8.21 p.m., I spotted something.

'Wait. Go back.'

Howard cautiously rewound the footage and allowed it to play. We watched as the shape of The Host's motorbike helmet came into view. The image was poor quality, and it was impossible to make him out correctly. However, I could see he took out a phone, looked at the screen for a moment and put it back in his pocket.

'A message?' Howard asked.

'Or maybe he was checking the time?'

He walked onto the ramp and ascended the bridge. When he reached the top, we could just about make out that he was pacing. Several minutes passed with nothing, and then, Jim Weston wandered into the frame and The Host lay down.

'What the fuck?'

Weston ascended the ramp slowly, the image staccato and disjointed in the low light. He saw the figure of The Host on the ground and ran to his side, stepping out of frame.

'Shit,' Howard said, still watching, despite not being able to see anything. After a few moments, a young couple walked past the screen. A minute later, the boy returned on his own.

'That must be Lucas,' I said.

He stopped at the top of the frame, his hands going up in defence.

'I wish there was a camera on the bridge.'

'It's like he knew exactly where he could stand, doesn't it?' Howard added.

'Yeah,' I replied. He was smart, he had planned it well. But it didn't explain why he came back. It was contradictory, and it didn't fit the profile of the man I was compiling in my head.

In the video, Lucas, Jim and The Host came back into shot. Lucas stood against the railings beside Jim Weston. The Host knelt down, took off his rucksack, and removed various items from it.

'Don't you think he's leaving himself vulnerable?' Howard asked.

'Yeah,' I agreed.

'That seems a bit odd to me. Complacent maybe?'

'Maybe,' I echoed, but I wasn't sure.

It was impossible to see exactly what The Host was doing. He was crouched down, his back to the camera, the low light making it difficult to focus on him. But the way Lucas and Jim reacted – the big step back, hands going up in defence – it was likely The Host had pulled out the weapons ready for The Game.

A few moments later, Jim Weston fell. His body bounced off the tarmac. I looked away, Howard didn't.

'Karen, look,' Howard urged, so I did, and saw The Host run down the ramp. At the bottom he looked at Jim on the ground, and then bolted.

'No drawing,' I said.

'No,' Howard agreed, rewinding the footage to the first point the Host came into shot. We watched again; at no point did he lower himself to stencil the train.

'He drew the train picture *before The Game*?' I said.

'He's really organised.'

'But it doesn't make sense…'

'What?'

'Going back tonight. He has planned this well, probably for months, if not years. Why would he jeopardise it?'

'Maybe he likes a risk?'

'No. I don't think that's it. He has planned this in every detail. He has really done his homework, location, person, time, the videos linking it all together, the stencils and clues. He's worked hard to be smarter than us. He's not a risk-taker.'

'But tonight he failed.'

'Yeah, and tomorrow, Jim will be a hero.' I paused. 'That's it! He's worried Jim will detract from what he is trying to make us see. That's why he went back.'

'But what is it? What does he need us to see?'

'I don't know,' I replied. 'Do you have the CCTV from the first Game?'

Howard nodded and loaded up the video from inside the Chinese takeaway. He fast-forwarded to when The Host stepped in. The camera was almost directly above him, making it difficult to get a sense of how tall he was. What was obvious though was he was still, calm, controlled. 'It's weird, he looks less nervous the first time than he did tonight.'

'Yeah, he does.'

'Howard, could you send me these?'

'I'll get into so much shit if—'

'No one will know.'

'It wasn't gonna stop me, I just wanted to point it out,' he smiled, before sending them to my phone. 'I don't know why you want them; the videos don't bring us any closer to finding the bastard.'

'Maybe not, but we have learnt one thing. He leaves the train before he commits the crime.'

'We also know the next one will be near water.'

'Exactly. We're trying to get to him. But if we find that train image, The Host will come to us.'

7 February 2019

Jack Anderson > Peterborough Free Discussion

Have you seen that a guy jumped from the A15 last night? It was around the time The Host said the next Game would be played. You think it's connected?

381 Comments

Emily Curtis

I know, it's awful. From what I've read on the BBC, he's very lucky to be alive.

Johnny Ormo

I still can't believe this thing is on the BBC.

Emily Curtis

And **Jack,** I have been thinking the same thing as you. There are no reports of The Host's latest attack. The jumper has to be connected. Maybe he was pushed? Maybe that was The Game?

Jack Anderson

I hate that the police are keeping the information from us. We have a right to know.

Johnny Ormo

I suspect they don't want to cause panic.

Jack Anderson

But I am panicking. Aren't you? If that poor man jumped from the bridge, or like **Emily** said, was pushed, because of The Game, we should know. This thing affects all of us. He's a psycho terrorising our city, we're at risk.

Amanda Belkin
Guys, has anyone heard from **Claire**? I've been really worried about her.

Jack Anderson
Nope. We're friends on here, doesn't look like she's been online since she found out about Roberta.

Johnny Ormo
Who?

Jack Anderson
She was the librarian.

Amanda Belkin
Maybe she needed to have a break from being online. I feel like I'm becoming obsessed. It's not healthy.

Johnny Ormo
I've not slept properly since I saw the ambulances and police opposite my work. And I agree. I can't find anything about The Game. I think that poor man was a Player.

Jack Anderson
I'm not sleeping great either. I don't blame **Claire** for backing away. This thing is fucking terrifying, and I don't know anyone directly involved.

Michaela Balfour

I normally don't jump in on these threads. But that man, Jim Weston, I work with him.

Emily Curtis

Oh God, **Michaela.** I'm so sorry.

Michaela Balfour

Jim is a lovely guy, kind, sweet. Happy. There is no way he would have jumped of his own volition.

Johnny Ormo

Are you saying you think he was playing?

Michaela Balfour

I don't know how else to explain it. Jim was looking forward to going home. There is no way he wanted to take his own life. Either he was pushed, or he jumped to save someone else. Jim doesn't like violence, not one bit.

Jack Anderson

😨 😢 If he had to jump to save someone, he is a hero. I hope he makes a full recovery.

Michaela Balfour

He didn't deserve this. He didn't deserve this one bit. If he can be forced to be a player, anyone can.

CHAPTER THIRTY-SIX

7.47 a.m.

I woke with a start when I heard Sam getting into the shower upstairs. It had been just before 2 a.m. when I got in and not wanting to wake Sam, who had another tough day at school ahead of her, I'd grabbed a throw and slept downstairs on the sofa. I should have got up, made a coffee, said good morning to my wife, but instead I reached for my phone and scrolled through social media. Both my Twitter and Facebook feeds were dominated by the crimes happening in the city. Both #theHost and #thePlayers sat at the top of the trend list, and in the online papers, there were several articles discussing each person involved, and what was known about the incident. There was no update on Jim Weston on the local *Peterborough Post* website. So far, the only thing I could see that was connected was a short article suggesting someone may have fallen or tried to end their life over the A15. I was confident The Host would not like that.

Another two hashtags were being fiercely contested. One side argued The Players were innocent, and should be #protectednotarrested, the other suggested the opposite

– #murderismurder being both crude and direct. I read a few of the comments under each; people were opinionated, and the arguments quickly became ugly and personal. Strangers attacking strangers over the safety of the internet, trying to hurt one another. It frightened me because it was so similar to what The Host was doing, and yet no one seemed to mind the online character assassinations.

I wanted people to be discussing how they could find him, stop him. I wanted the world to mirror my thoughts. Really, people were just afraid, and more worryingly, as I looked at the Facebook timelines of the 134 people I was 'friends' with, most were openly admitting what they would do if they had to play The Game – and most said they would kill. It felt hopeless.

Sitting up made my eye throb, but I knew it wasn't anything to worry about, and the swelling had receded a little. Gingerly, I got to my feet, went into the kitchen, and flicked on the kettle to make Sam a cup of coffee, hoping it would be a peace offering against the argument that no doubt was brewing.

Upstairs, I heard Sam get out of the shower and walk back into the bedroom. I tried to work out what I would say to her, how would I explain the state of my face without upsetting her. I racked my brain as to what I could say to justify the bruising around my eye. But I couldn't. I hadn't intended to see The Host, but I was at the scene, and I did give chase. So really, there wasn't anything I could say, was there?

As I heard Sam coming downstairs, I turned my back so I was facing away from her, and scooped coffee into two cups.

'What time did you come home last night?' Sam asked.

'About midnight?' Again, another lie to add to the ever-growing list I had told my wife. What sort of person had I become?

'I stayed awake until after one.'

'It was after one then, I lost track of time. I'm sorry.'

'Is Howard OK?'

'Yeah, he's fine. It's just a tough time.'

'Why didn't you come to bed?' Sam asked, her voice low and sleepy.

'I didn't want to wake you,' I replied, pouring a splash of milk in both our cups.

'Babe?' Sam asked, knowing something was wrong. 'Are you all right?'

'Don't fly off, OK? It's not as bad as it looks,' I said, turning to face her.

'Shit, Karen!' Sam snapped, stepping towards me. 'How did you get that?'

I took a breath, ready to spill a lie, but I knew she wouldn't let me get away with it, not this time, so I told Sam what happened and could see her look slowly morph from tender and caring to one full of rage. I only got as far as chasing The Host before Sam cut me off, slamming her cup down, spilling coffee all over the side.

'Never mind that you went out in the middle of the night to do something you have been specifically told you are not allowed to do. Something that if your bosses found out would probably get you sacked.'

'Please, let's not argue, I didn't know he was going to be there.'

'Never mind that you lied to me, again.'

'Sam—'

'Let's talk about how you tried to grab a psychopath on your own. What the bloody hell were you thinking?'

'I had to try; he was there. He was right there.'

'He could have killed you.'

'No, I—'

'You can't explain this one away. It was a stupid and reckless thing to do. Look at the state of you!'

Sam trailed off, it was too much, and she started to cry. I'd been carrying guilt with me since the Grayson James incident and it had been getting worse with each white lie I'd told Sam. But none of that guilt compared to the guilt of making my own wife cry.

'Sam, I'm so sorry. Honestly, I wasn't expecting to see him. When I did, I had no choice.'

'Because you're a police officer?'

'Yes. Imagine if you saw one of your students out of school and they needed help – would you just ignore them?'

'No, of course not,' Sam replied between sniffles.

'It's the same thing,' I said quietly.

'Karen, don't you see what you're doing?'

'I'm trying to catch a killer.'

'You're sneaking around, doing work that isn't yours to do. I understand this is huge, maybe the biggest thing to happen to this city. But you catching The Host doesn't change what happened.'

'I don't know what you mean. The public are at risk and it's my job to protect them.'

'You're hell-bent on getting this guy.'

'Of course I am,' I said, my voice on the turn from defeated to defiant.

'But look at the risks. Look at your face. Look what he did to you.' Sam took my face in her hands, gently touching my still tender eye. She looked at me and I could see her hurting for me. 'You need to stop. I can't help you get through what happened if you're not gonna help yourself,' Sam murmured. 'And I *want* to help. Please don't push me away, we can deal with this together.' She wrapped her arms around me. I hugged as tight as I could.

'You're taking risks, both for your career and your life,' she whispered.

'People are dying...'

'You don't have to prove you are good at your job.'

'What?'

Sam stepped back, her hands moving from my back to rest on the tops of my arms, like she was going to try and shake some sense into me. 'Karen, I know you. I know how you think. Last year you were dropped a rank.'

'I prefer being a DI.'

'And now, with Grayson James, you feel like you're spiralling.'

I opened my mouth to tell her that wasn't true, that I was fine, in control, not worried. But the words wouldn't come.

'You aren't dealing with what happened before,' Sam continued, taking my hand. 'Instead you're pushing all of those feelings into this case, but you're not thinking properly. I know you trust your instincts about work things, but I think your instincts are jaded at the moment.'

'Sam, I'm in this guy's head, I'm starting to see how he thinks...'

'Look at your face, Karen. He could have killed you.'

'Sam, I…'

'You didn't kill Grayson James. Do you understand? You didn't kill that man.'

'But…'

'But *nothing*. It was an accident. Everyone knows it, everyone. And the IOPC will say so soon.'

'They might.' I looked away, to Bob, floating happily in his tank.

'They will. And you need to understand how it's affecting you; you've not been OK since that day. You need to talk about it, open up about how you are feeling. That day was awful for you, I understand that, I *do*. Talk to me. Let me help you get through this.'

'Sam, I—'

'And I hate asking, I've wanted you to come to me when you're ready, but sometimes you have to force yourself to be ready. You can't keep hiding from it, you need to confront it.'

'I need more time,' I said, stepping away to pick up my coffee.

'Karen, love. I know it's scary to open up, but look at you, all you're doing is hurting yourself. Be brave, darling, I'm here, I want to help.'

'Fine! Fine!' I said, my voice rising. 'Sam, a man died in my arms. A man died in my arms because of something I had done,' I said, my words snagging.

'Yes, he did die in your arms,' Sam agreed quietly. 'But his death was his doing, not yours.'

'How do you know that?'

'Because, you wouldn't—'

'How can you possibly know, when I don't?' I confessed.

'Karen—'

'Stop, just stop.' I said, walking out of the kitchen and back into the living room.

Sitting down, I took a breath and realised that Sam was right, I relied on my instincts for everything, and they seemed to be failing. Although I was right about a bridge, I'd chosen the one wrong, and before, I was wrong about the shopping centre. I thought about when The Host swung for me: did he swing with the force to try and kill, even though I said that he wasn't a killer? I didn't know anymore.

'Karen,' Sam said quietly from the doorway. 'I really want you to be able to talk to me about this, but I think you need to talk to Shauna too. Have you tried speaking to her?'

'Not yet.'

'People want to help you process this, so let them help.'

'I will.'

'Good. I don't understand what you must be feeling, but I empathise. I really do. I suspect everyone does. What happened, it's shit, but it's not your shit to carry. Not anymore.'

'I'm trying,' I admitted after a deep breath.

'Let the people who can help take control. Then you can get back to being great at what you do. When the time is right and you're ready.'

'*If* I ever get back to where I was. I'm such a mess.'

'You are right now, but it will pass.'

'I don't like it. The doubt, the worrying. '

'I understand.' Sam said, sitting next to me. 'But it's OK to be a mess. You need to know and accept that you didn't do anything wrong, and you will come through this.'

I nodded, grateful that I had Sam. 'I hope you're right.'

Sam kissed me, and I took out my phone to ring Shauna, leaving a message saying that I'd like to book another appointment. It was time to confront my demons.

CHAPTER THIRTY-SEVEN

The Host

8.26 a.m.

It had been a disastrous night for his message and the moment he nearly got caught played heavily on his mind all night. He had attempted to sleep it off, but after three hours of restlessness, he knew he needed to carry on with his work, and so, as the sun began to break over the horizon, he left to prepare his next location.

When he arrived it was quiet, and confident no one would be around, he took a can of black spray-paint and the stencil from his bag. Then he pulled out the rock he would spray it on. A rock from somewhere else. It was discreet, maybe it wouldn't be found. Unless someone was like him and enjoyed the details too. Someone like the police officer from last night. He didn't know who she was, but he'd seen her face. If he saw it again, he would recognise her instantly.

As he finished and zipped up his bag, a man ran past with his dog attached on a lead to his waist. The man nodded, and he smiled back, watching him until he had run out of sight.

Walking away from the location of his Fifth Game, he

headed in the direction of the city, and home. Despite the muddied message from the night before, he had another statement to record, and another video to prepare for the world to see, after which the clock would begin again. This time he would directly ask those who watched to think about how much they valued life. He would challenge them to consider what they would do. He had always planned to ask them directly once they had started to question themselves. Despite the failed fourth game, he was still on track, but he hadn't accounted for the woman who so nearly caught him. The only thing he could do was draw her in closer to find out who she was and make sure she didn't interfere with his plans.

CHAPTER THIRTY-EIGHT

10.20 a.m.

Sam went to work at her normal time, bracing herself for a tough day to come. Although the school was still open, we both suspected that lots of kids would stay at home. Before she left, she kissed me goodbye. I could see she was still worried for me.

'You gonna be OK today?' she had asked, looking at my battered eye.

'Yeah, I'm gonna sleep, binge-watch something on Netflix. I'll be fine.'

'OK, I'll keep you posted on what time I'll be home.'

Sam then kissed me again, before walking to the car. I wasn't sure if she bought it. I'm not sure if I did either. She was angry with me for my recklessness, and now that the adrenaline had passed, I was too. What had I been thinking? I wondered was I doing this because I wanted to stop The Host, or was Sam right and was I doing this to make up for what I did to Grayson James? It was likely a bit of both. I kept thinking about the voicemail I'd left for Shauna, regretting it. If I could have spoken with her there and then, I might have said it

232

all. But now, in the cold light of day, I could feel the wall of self-preservation going up. In a bid to distract myself I went on my phone, watching and re-watching the two CCTV videos Howard had sent me. The first few times, I looked at the surrounding area, trying to see if a clue had been left by mistake. Then I started to watch The Host himself, hoping I would spot something. In the first video CCTV from the Chinese takeaway, The Host was calm. He locked the door slowly, centred himself, and by the time The Game began – as Michelle and Timothy started to attack one another in the most horrific way – he was completely at ease with the violence. But in the second CCTV video, at the foot of the overpass, and the failed Fourth Game, he looked less ready, less able somehow. Although the image quality was poor, I could see him shaking his hands, as if they were tingling, similar to when I have a panic attack. He didn't come across as someone who was in charge. If I had to call it, he looked afraid.

It didn't make sense.

I wanted to switch off, so I put an eighties playlist on Alexa. I was young in the 1980s, just a kid, and people like Phil Collins, Michael Jackson and Bananarama reminded me of car journeys with my mum and dad, on the way to France on our annual holiday to the same place in Lyon. I almost succeeded in allowing myself to be entirely wrapped up in a different time – a better time – until I was snapped out of it when Alexa finished playing a Rick Astley hit that my dad used to croon along to, and another song began. One that made me think of The Host. I hadn't thought about it before, but it was one that played in the background to one of his videos. 'Wonderful Life' by Black. Was he being ironic, or was there something more?

Then a fresh wave of guilt came. The Host was out there, planning, preparing himself to make another innocent person kill. And here I was, taking a trip down memory lane. Whether I liked it or not, I'd got myself involved in this case now, and until it was over, until he was caught, I'd not be able to walk away. I was in The Host's head, partly at least, I had seen him in the flesh, and if I stopped trying, I would be responsible for anyone who died, like I was culpable for Grayson. I knew being involved was my way of trying to absolve my guilt, but so be it. So I stopped Alexa, picked up my phone and got myself as up to date as I could without Howard linking me in.

I checked BBC News and saw that Jim Weston had been mentioned in their latest bulletin. The time of the incident on the bridge had matched the time The Host had stated in the third video. The article also speculated that he had jumped because he wouldn't fight – and I couldn't help but take solace from the fact that when he recovered from his injuries, if he recovered from his injuries, Jim Weston would be seen as a hero. Of course, The Host wouldn't like the article, just as he wouldn't like the fact I had nearly caught him. I hated that I had to wait to see the outcome.

I also searched for an update on the fate of Michelle Reed, Richard Mullis and Milly Hallam. The last update had been two days ago when they had been arrested and charged with murder, but all three remained under police guard in hospital. There was still no indication that poor Milly would even pull through as she remained in a critical condition. In a statement, the police had warned that anyone caught sharing The Host's videos would face criminal prosecution. The threat wouldn't work, of course, but only fuel the fire. I had read everything there was in the news but I needed to know more. I dialled Howard's number.

'Morning. How's the eye?' he said quietly.

'Fine.'

'That's good.'

'How's the investigation going?'

Howard sighed before he spoke. 'Rawlinson is being a total prick,' he whispered, ensuring no one in the office could hear him, despite them all probably agreeing with the sentiment.

'Shocker.'

'More so than usual; he's got the top brass breathing down his neck for results. He's way out of his depth, and they are starting to see it.'

'Did you talk to him about the water idea?'

'I've tried, he's not having it. There are hundreds of lakes, ponds, dykes, streams – Christ, it could even be a bathtub for all we know, without more. He isn't listening.'

'So go above him.'

'I'm seeing the gaffer soon. He looks like he's got people breathing down his neck too.'

'Howard, I've been watching the CCTV videos again. Something about The Host doesn't make sense. If I didn't know, I'd say the sequence of the killings is wrong. In the Chinese he is so calm, but on the bridge he's a mess.'

'Yeah. I've watched them again too. I had a chat with Jenny in profiling. I asked her about what she thought when she saw the CCTV footage,' Howard continued. 'She said something interesting.'

'Go on.'

'She said that the discrepancy could be one of two things.

The panic on the footbridge could be because there –' Howard paused, and when he continued, he did so like he was reading from his notebook – 'has been a shift in his ideology, perhaps he doesn't trust his agenda.'

'Why though?'

'I asked the same question. Jenny suggested it could be public perception influencing him.'

It made sense as when the first Game was played no one knew, no one cared who he was, and by the fourth, the whole country was starting to talk about him. He must have read what was being said; he must have listened to the news. It could impact on his belief system.

'She said "There could be two sides to this man",' Howard continued. '"One who knows what he is doing is right, and another that is unsure. Perhaps it's due to the environment no longer being controlled. Before it was just him, his thoughts, his opinions."'

'And now the world has a say in all this?'

'Exactly, maybe the massive reaction to his crimes has made him unsure.'

'No, I don't think that's it,' I said. 'He has planned this, possibly for a very long time. If he had doubts, he would have felt them before people started to talk. Our boy likes the attention, the spectacle; he loves the fear that's spreading, or else why would he film it? Why would he call himself the Host, and the victims his Players?'

'Good point.'

'What's the second idea Jenny had?'

'That he might well actually have two sides to him.'

'I don't follow.'

'He could have some kind of detached personality disorder.'

'Detached personality disorder?' I said.

'A Jekyll and Hyde sort of thing,' Jenny said. 'It's worth considering.'

'Yeah.' I agreed, it made more sense. But if that was the case, I couldn't see how it would help us. 'Is there any update on Jim Weston?'

'They say he is responding well. Sounds like he was very lucky to not have been more seriously injured from the fall.'

'That's really good news that he's going to fully recover. Does that mean he might be well enough to talk soon?'

'That's the impression I got.'

'Great, that's really great – and the kid?'

'He's home again, but we didn't get much from him. He said that The Host had a robotic voice, and he didn't see his face. He was lucky too.'

'What about the other survivors?'

'It's a total mess, everyone agrees they are victims, but until the investigation is concluded, they are still under arrest.'

'And Milly Hallam?'

'Too soon to say, she's still critical.'

'It's not fair,' I said.

He sighed, 'No, it isn't.'

'You sound stressed.'

'It's chaos here. So much of our time is being wasted with prank calls. People can be arseholes.'

'Prank calls?'

'Yep, we're getting fake leads with people claiming they are The Host, or know The Host, each lead a dead end.'

'Why would anyone do that?'

'It seems like it's a joke to some.'

'Jesus.'

'Not just that, the force is stretched beyond belief, and we can't be everywhere. Some poor man was attacked in the early hours of this morning in a petrol station, because he was wearing a motorbike helmet.'

'We have to find this guy.'

In the background I heard Rawlinson shout something. I couldn't make out what, but he sounded alarmed.

'Howard?' I asked, but he didn't immediately respond. I tried again. 'Howard, what's going on?'

'Hang on.'

I listened, trying to pick out some of the words people were shouting to one another in the background. It sounded chaotic but then I could make out Bradshaw's booming voice. He didn't raise his voice often, but when he did, people listened. The chatter had been silenced.

'I gotta go,' Howard said in a hushed tone.

'What's happened?'

'He's posted,' he whispered. Then the line went dead. I quickly opened my Twitter account and it didn't take long to find the video which was already being shared.

It looked identical to the first three, the same helmet – but with a small crack in the bottom corner of the visor from where it had connected with my face – and behind, the same white walls. I turned up the volume on my phone. I needed to hear his words as clearly as I could.

'... *You are standing next to a switch that controls the line. If you pull the switch, you save five people. However, there is a single person lying on the side-track. A single life... Most* of you would do nothing. That way you are not responsible for taking a life. Inaction being your defence, allowing you to sleep at night.

'What if you had no choice?

'What you are about to see is unedited footage of the Fourth Game I played on the night of the 6th of February. The Players didn't abide by the rules, and so, in my next Game I will ensure that cannot happen again.

'The Fifth Game is in motion, and my new Players will play at 9 p.m. tonight. I may have been tricked into life being spared but tonight life will end where life began.'

CHAPTER THIRTY-NINE

The Host

4.51 p.m.
Four hours and nine minutes until the next Game

He knew he needed to be planning, preparing for the evening's entertainment, knowing the Fifth Game would correct the error of the previous night. In the aftermath of Jim Weston, the Twitter poll asking if you would kill, be killed or didn't know, had added a fourth option: kill yourself. Kill was still the most popular, but the overall percentage had dropped from 68 per cent down to 57 per cent, with the newest option taking most of those votes. He needed it to go back the other way. Only when it was 100 per cent would he stop. Only when everyone knew they would kill would The Games end. And he would play until that happened.

Tonight, there would be no heroes who challenged The Game. Tonight, they would play and someone would die. The outcome would be the most interesting of all The Games he had played so far, because of who he had picked to be The Players. But as much as he tried to concentrate and walk through his plan in his mind's eye, he kept thinking about the woman, the police officer, who had got too close. He needed to know who she was. He needed to know how much she knew about him. He wouldn't be able to focus until he at least knew her name, so he started to search. Beginning with DI Paul Rawlinson, the officer who had given a quote for the BBC. Through his foolishly unguarded Facebook page he found a picture that featured the man he had seen near the library, DS Howard Carlson. And then, without much work, he found her, the woman who nearly caught him.

Bingo. Now he had a name, he could dig and find out more. The fact she was a copper meant finding things would be harder, but not impossible. Going onto his secure VPN provider, he began his search, knowing, within the next hour or two, he would know more about her than she did about him.

And he would weave her into his Game.

One day soon, DI Karen Holt would be one of his Players.

CHAPTER FORTY

6.58 p.m.
Two hours and two minutes until the next Game

With Sam being out of the house all day, I couldn't rest, and so had spent the afternoon walking, lost in my own thoughts – thoughts about The Host and his latest video, about Grayson James. I visited the Chinese again, read cards left by well-meaning people, and as the afternoon drew on, I noticed there was more activity in the media. The wife of Jim Weston had been interviewed. She asked for people's prayers for her husband's recovery, she asked for people's kindness to one another, and she begged The Host to stop. The interview was not only hard to watch but also a big mistake. It would only fuel The Host further. He was rocked because of Jim Weston and the Fourth Game not going to plan. But this interview would give him power again. I doubted anyone in the police knew about the interview until it was on the TV. I suspected Rawlinson would be oblivious to the potential damage it would do.

After wandering for several hours, I made my way to a pub one mile from the city centre, right on the bank of the River

Nene. I should have gone home, but going home would mean I was admitting defeat, and I wasn't ready for that. I messaged Howard, telling him where I was going for a drink if he happened to be nearby; we shouldn't be meeting, but still.

When I entered, I noticed that besides a few older people drinking, the pub was deserted, deathly quiet for a Saturday night. I smiled at a nervous-looking young lady behind the bar and ordered a pint. I paid, feeling sorry for her that she had to be out at work, probably fearful The Host might walk through the door.

I sat down at a table, and as I sipped my pint my phone pinged.

Hey, just got home, you're not here. Is everything OK?

Shit. I didn't message Sam. I couldn't tell her I was out in the city, walking around. Nor could I tell her I was drinking alone. Both would make her worry, so, I had to lie, again.

Work called me in to help with back-office stuff.

Why didn't you message? I was worried.

Sorry, love, I forgot, it happened quickly.

OK. Are you going to be home at a decent time this evening? Want some dinner?

I paused, my thumb resting over the keypad for a moment. I typed a reply, the words not coming easy.

> Probably not, it's so busy here, they need all the help they can get.

Sam replied a few seconds later.

> I understand, I'm glad they want you back at work. Even if it's doing the boring bits. X.

I locked my screen and as I looked up, Howard came up the stairs into the pub. He looked tired as he sat down opposite, I searched his face for a sign of anything.

'Hey.'

'Hey.'

'Want a pint?'

'Please.'

I got up, ordered another pint from the bar girl and put it in front of him.

'Are you still on shift?' I asked after we'd both taken a mouthful of lager.

'No, the boss sent me home. Not slept in a few days.'

'How's it going?'

'I managed to explain to the gaffer we needed to be looking at water, but Rawlinson is convinced it would be close to the city centre, so he argued we need to focus on the facts at hand, with the four previous incidents all happening within a one-mile radius of the city centre – not wild speculation, as he called it.'

'He's doing my head in and I'm not even there!' I laughed.

'Honestly, Karen, if you were, you'd be climbing the walls.'

'Is he doing his usual walk around like he's in charge?'

'You guessed it.'

'What a dickhead.'

'And as usual with Rawlinson, the size of the case alters the size of his ego, so you can imagine, with something like this…'

'Oh God, is he being a bigger prick than ever?'

'If only you could see him,' Howard laughed. 'I tried to explain that we were right about the bridge, and he countered with saying that the force was out searching bridges on the fringe of the city, and the incident happened close to the centre.'

'How were we supposed to know which fucking bridge? He's so blind – doesn't he see that we got inside his head, we understand how The Host is thinking?'

'You know Rawlinson can't see past his own self-righteousness. However, Bradshaw agrees, although he would never say it. So he sanctioned a dozen officers to look around the city's lakes and river for a train symbol.'

'A dozen, that's nowhere near enough.'

'You know how it is, though – the paradox of a growing city but a shrinking force because of budget cuts. And he says there isn't any proof.'

'What about the "take life where life began" line, surely he must agree it's a good fit?'

'Is it?'

'Civilised life began on the banks of rivers, we stopped being hunter-gatherers and settled because of them. We grew crops, herded cattle, starting with Mesopotamia – Christ, even Peterborough exists because of the river. He's telling us it's the river, life where life began.'

I stopped; Howard just stared at me. I frowned back. 'What?'

'How do you know all this stuff?'

'I wasn't very popular at school.'

Howard smiled, sipped his pint. 'I'm guessing we aren't here – in a pub close to the river – for a social drink, are we?'

'No.'

'I figured.'

'Let's hope it's not a waste of your time.'

'If we can work out just one piece of this puzzle together, it won't be.'

'Christ, gushy.' I smiled. 'Come on.'

Draining our pints, we left and began to walk along the river's edge, the path lit with soft blue floor LEDs that made it seem peaceful and safe. Romantic, even.

Neither of us spoke as we moved. We scanned the edges of the path, searching for any sign of disturbance, the train stencil, or even better, The Host himself lying in wait. On the opposite side of the river, a man walked by, hands in his pockets, lost in his own thoughts. We both considered him, but he was too broad to be our guy. He moved like he was in a different world, not like someone who was about to commit a horrendous crime. Once the man was gone, we kept looking, but as far as we could see, there was nothing else to draw our eye.

After a mile I stopped and asked if we should turn back. Howard shook his head. 'No, let's keep walking.'

With the pub far behind us, and the soft lighting of the path having faded out a hundred feet back, we came across a thick line of trees hugging a bend in the river. We both froze when we heard something from within. At first, I thought it was an animal, but as it moved once more, I knew it was something bigger. A twig snapped close by and Howard stepped to my side and reached for his Maglite.

'Who's there?' Howard asked. 'It's the police – step out of the treeline.'

A person cleared the trees and raised their hands as they were blinded by the torch. We both sighed; it wasn't him but a homeless person, who was taking shelter in the quiet refuge of the riverbed. I knew lots of the city's homeless slept down here, but in the moment, I had completely forgotten. The Karen Holt from before Grayson James would have made that link instantly. Sam was right after all. I wasn't thinking clearly. Apologising to the girl, Howard lowered his torch, but told her she needed to keep a low profile as there was a bad person on the loose. She nodded, still very much startled.

'Have you got anywhere to go?' he asked, and the girl shook her head.

'I'm fine here,' she said quietly.

'OK, be careful.'

'Thank you.'

As we watched the girl slip back into the treeline, she gave me a look, a flash. I couldn't work out what the look meant. Leaving the girl behind, we continued to walk. I couldn't help dwell on the fact of how sad it was that people ended up alone like her. The girl was just a kid. Just like the kid from the Chinese. I turned back to try to see her. She had gone, lost in the trees that she no doubt knew her way around.

'You OK?'

'Yeah, yeah, I'm fine.' I didn't say my thoughts aloud. The girl might just look similar, and at the moment, I couldn't trust my memory to serve me properly, not when it imprinted the face of Grayson James on most things…

We continued looking in vain for something to indicate he was along this stretch of the river, and with each passing minute my dread that I had got it wrong intensified. I stopped to check my watch; it was four minutes to nine. The Host was about to strike again, and we had failed to stop him.

THE FIFTH GAME

As soon as the figure approached, they knew. Perhaps, with their age and their bodies slowing, their minds had also slowed. He had assumed the sight of him would cause panic but instead, they seemed to calmly assess the situation, the flight or fight instinct inside them already dying. The Host didn't need to say much. He instructed them to tie up their dog, and there was a quiet resignation as he informed them of the rules. Then they exchanged a look, a weight hanging in the space between the unsaid words. They understood. He ushered them into the water and wound the clock. It was the easiest Game yet to set, but the one that would probably create the most devastating impact. If one killed the other, then everything good would be dead. The proof would be irrefutable thanks to the GoPro mounted on his helmet to capture it all. No one would be able to deny that they were all capable of wrong, given the opportunity. No one.

'The clock is ticking,' he said, as the pair stood, motionless in the knee-deep freezing water.

'I won't do it,' the woman said, but not to The Host, she said it looking into the eyes of her husband.

'I can't do it,' her husband said, his attention towards The Host.

'Then I will be forced to go after those you love,' The Host said quietly, turning to walk away.

'No, wait!' the man shouted. 'Wait.'

The Host paused. His bluff was working. Turning to face the pair, he nodded towards the clock. 'Tick tock.'

'Maggie, we have a daughter, we have grandchildren. They need one of us.'

'John?'

'Christie needs you. Our daughter isn't like you, she is like me, she needs help, she needs support, if you go, she will be lost, because I will be lost.'

'She will—'

John took his wife by the shoulders and squeezed her tight. She fell into his embrace and he stroked her hair and whispered in her ear. The Host stepped forward, hoping to capture the words on the GoPro microphone so that he might enhance the sound later. Neither noticed him approach the water's edge, neither cared.

The Host checked the clock.

Two minutes thirty-one seconds.

John leant back from Maggie's embrace, kissed her tenderly on her head. Both had tears in their eyes. John nodded, Maggie didn't. John lowered himself into the water, struggling to catch his breath as the lake enclosed his chest and squeezed his lungs. The Host looked away – for a moment John Stroud reminded him of his mother when they went into the dyke in their car. The cold snapping at their breath, his mother unable to speak clearly because of it. He heard her try to tell him to open his door and escape, he heard her try to reassure him when she knew it was impossible. He remembered the song that had started on the radio, his song, telling them there was no need to run and hide. They listened, accepted, and he held her hand for the last time as the water engulfed them.

He shook it off, now was not the time, he had to be present to honour her. He turned back to face his Players and watched the water line draw level with John Stroud's chin.

'Maggie, it's going to be all right.'

'John, I don't want to do this.'

'Maggie, you have to. You're stronger than me, you need to be the one that stays. You can look after our girl, help her raise our beautiful grandchildren.'

Maggie didn't move, so John reached forward and took her hands. He kissed her palms, told her he loved her and placed them on the top of his head, before submerging himself under the water.

CHAPTER FORTY-ONE

9.11 p.m.

As Howard's phone rang, both of us knew what the call would be about before he answered.

'DS Howard Carlson. Hello, guv.'

I watched Howard, desperate to hear what was being said. He looked at me, shook his head.

'Where did she call from?' he asked, and I watched his expression change from something accepting and sad to something charged, ready for a fight. He didn't say anything, nor did he say goodbye when he hung up his phone, but instead he ran in the direction we had been walking for the past hour. I sprang into a run to catch up, but his years of service as a soldier threw a switch in his head, and it was hard for me to draw level.

'Howard, what is it?' I shouted between breaths. He turned and slowed so I could catch up. 'The call came in from the rowing lake.'

He didn't need to say any more. The lake was only about half a mile from where we were, running parallel to the river. He might still be in the area. Watching the aftermath. I found that on the rest of the run, I could keep up just fine.

As we cleared the narrow tree-lined path into the huge expanse of the rowing lake and its nearby club, I struggled to see anyone, victims or Host. All I could hear was the incessant whimpering of a dog somewhere. However, Howard spotted someone straight away.

'There—' He pointed to the far side of the black water and then I could just about discern a figure on the edge, sitting down. As we approached, I could see it was a woman, one I placed at around my mother's age, sitting perfectly still, her hands resting on her lap, both feet in the freezing water. Behind, the dog barked a threat, wanting desperately to protect their owner. Sensing I should take the lead, Howard stopped a few feet back. I dropped onto one knee, my breathing heavy.

'Are you all right?' I asked delicately, taking off my coat and wrapping it around the woman, who was clearly in shock. The woman didn't respond. 'Do you mind if I sit down?' Again, no response. The woman didn't even blink, just stared out into the frigid blackness. I followed her gaze but couldn't see anything. 'My name is Karen. Can you tell me your name?'

Again, the woman didn't reply.

'Are you the one who called 999?'

The woman nodded.

'Can you tell me where the other person is?'

The woman lowered her head and began to sob.

'Please, we want to help you, where is the other person? Or the man who made you do it, is he still around?'

'No,' the woman managed between sobs.

'OK, that's OK. Are you hurt at all?'

'No.'

'Good, that's good.'

'Karen,' Howard said from behind, and when I looked, he was pointing out across the water. In the distance, there was a shape. The woman began to wail. Before I could say anything, Howard barrelled in, wading chest-deep to grab the man who was floating face down. Dragging him back to the edge, he heaved him onto the concrete and began to administer CPR. I asked the woman to move her legs from the water, worried that hypothermia would kick in, and when she didn't respond, I scooped under her arms and dragged her back. Howard needed space to work, and I wanted to avert her gaze, in case he wasn't successful. Sitting her down, the sound of sirens descended on our ears. Howard told me to go, not breaking his rhythm as he administered chest compressions.

'No, I'm not leaving her.'

'She will be fine. You'll get into trouble.'

'No, Howard. I'm not leaving her.'

With thirty compressions done, Howard blew air into the man's mouth, so his chest expanded. There was no sign of him coming back, but he didn't stop and began another thirty compressions. I did all I could to warm the woman, who was shivering violently as the police cars screamed to a halt around us. Several officers charged in, one removing a foil blanket to wrap around the woman. Another two ran to help Howard. I stepped back, allowing people to do their work, and as I did, I bumped into Rawlinson.

'What are you doing here?'

'Trying to help,' I said, not backing down.

Rawlinson opened his mouth to say something, but before he could spill an unpleasant syllable, Bradshaw approached.

'DI Holt, Surprised to see you here,' he said, eyeing me closely.

'Sir, I was walking along the river.'

'You're not supposed to be involved in this investigation.'

'I was with Howard when he got the call. We'd been for a drink and were only half a mile away.'

'Half a mile?'

'Yes, sir. When you called Howard, we both just ran, on instinct. I had to help.'

'Of course, I'd do the same.'

'Thank you, sir. I'm sorry.'

Rawlinson started to mobilise a cordon area. 'The bastard might still be here, so split off into pairs and find him,' he shouted, but still he hadn't moved, an eye firmly fixed on me. 'Sir, I want her off this now.'

'DI Rawlinson, do not forget your place,' Bradshaw said, shutting him down.

Nodding, Rawlinson began to move towards the shaking woman, charging in for answers, even though it was obvious she had completely slipped into shock and would likely not be able to give them.

Once he was gone, Bradshaw turned back to me. 'Karen, you're not allowed to be here, we have lots of people. I need you to go.'

'But, sir?'

'Be in my office at nine tomorrow, is that understood?'

'Yes, sir.'

'Good. Now go home, Karen, you look terrible,' he said softly, examining my eye.

'But, sir, I could help work the scene.'

'Go home. That's an order. And for God's sake, don't let anyone see you, you're in enough shit as it is.'

'Sir, I…'

'Just go.'

I was angry – at being reprimanded for wanting to do my job, at the IOPC investigation for taking so long and leaving this black cloud over my head. I was angry at Grayson James for resisting arrest. I was furious with myself, too. I wanted to help, and because of what I had done, I couldn't. As I walked away I saw Howard watching the paramedics work on the man he had dragged out of the lake. He caught my eye and he shook his head.

We had got there too late.

CHAPTER FORTY-TWO

The Host

10.52 p.m.

The Host plugged the GoPro into the cable to upload the footage. What he had captured and what the world would soon see was definitive proof there was no good anymore, that anyone could kill. People clung to the idea that everyone was special, that life was special, but it was all bullshit. All of it. And after people saw this video, they would know the truth. If a woman could kill her husband of thirty-one years. . .

After he released the video, with the details of the next Game, he would create a new Twitter poll to see what they were thinking. If it came back with the truth, everyone would kill, he wouldn't play the next Game, he would disappear, knowing the world forever be changed. As he waited for the upload to complete, he picked up two more pipe cleaners, lined them up, folded them in half, twisted the top and the middle, fashioned arms and legs, and introduced Maggie to the others on the shelf. There were now four friends for the original.

Behind him, the door opened, and in stepped the girl. She was late.

'Well?' he asked.

'Yeah, she was there.'

'And you're sure it was the same woman who spoke to you outside the Chinese?'

'Pretty sure.'

'How sure?'

'I'm sure,' she said.

The Host sat back, sighed. He suspected he knew exactly who the woman was. 'Did you get a good look at her face?'

'Yes.'

'Was there anything noticeable about it?' he asked, not wanting to guide her answer.

'She had a really bad bruise on her left eye.'

'It's her,' he said quietly, as an image sprang to life on his computer behind him – showing the video frame from the moment he pressed record before tonight's Game.

'It's who?'

'It's the woman I saw on the bridge last night. The one who nearly caught me. It's a police officer, a detective.'

'A copper! Shit, do you think she knows who we are?' the girl said, panicking.

'Calm down, of course she doesn't know who we are.'

He smiled. She didn't have a clue who they were, but he knew everything about her. Her full name, address, police record, bank details. Her private life. It seemed he was closer to DI Karen Holt than he'd first thought.

'What if she recognises me from the Chinese?'

'You were posing as a homeless girl. She wouldn't have seen you, no one sees the homeless.'

'How can you be sure?'

'I just am.'

'But…'

'Stop panicking. You know it does no good,' he said quietly, turning his attention to his screen to begin editing.

The girl watched over his shoulder as he worked, editing the footage to present a clean, shortened version of the events. She was expecting to see unadulterated animal violence, like in the first, second and third videos. What she saw was something entirely different. It was heartbreaking, the way the man whispered in the ear of his wife as he held her, the way her hands were gently placed on the top of his head, her cries as she held him under. She had to look away, her attention fixed on The Host's face. She wanted him to be as moved as she was, she wanted there to be a flicker of regret. But he remained neutral.

She empathised with what he was doing, and why he was doing it, she agreed with his message, understood the costs. He had confided in her what had happened to him, and how those who'd saved him from the car were labelled heroes, despite their actions ensuring his mother drowned. She understood his grief, his pain, and how isolated he now was in a world that hid from the truth. She had even agreed to pose as The Host to show that she was a believer in his message. He had doubted her, said she would eventually go to the police if he let her in, he had called her weak. And although she'd failed to execute as he'd instructed, she'd still worn the helmet, walked onto that bridge and tried to make them play his Game. She'd still done it, and because she had, she'd proved she was committed to his cause.

But there was nothing about this latest Game she was

watching that she understood. It didn't show evil but sacrifice for love. She felt her faith waver.

'I'm gonna go home,' she said quietly, and he replied by waving at her with the back of his hand. Hurt by the dismissal, she turned to leave. Just then, the shelf with the pipe-cleaner people caught her eye, so she approached and reached out to pick one up.

'Don't touch them,' The Host snapped.

'I'm sorry.'

'You never touch them. Understand?'

'Yes.'

'Never.'

'OK, I'm sorry, I won't.'

The Host looked at her and couldn't hide his disappointment. She said she understood, but really, she never would. She looked at the pipe-cleaners as if they were little toys, models crafted for fun or distraction. She would never understand who they really were. She would never understand why they were so important. As she left the room, apologising again, he turned and picked up his motorbike helmet. The girl watched through the crack in the door as he pressed record on the webcam and began to speak.

'*What you are about to see is unedited footage of a game I played on the night of the 7th of February...*'

DAY 6

8 February 2019

MAN PLUNGED FROM BRIDGE
TO SAVE BOY'S LIFE

Patricia Blakemore, *BBC correspondent*

A local Peterborough man has been hailed a hero after plunging from a bridge rather than killing a teenage boy.

The man, who has been named as Jim Weston, forty-six, is thought to have been ordered by serial killer The Host to fight to the death with the unnamed fifteen-year-old on a footbridge north of the city centre.

Instead, Mr Weston jumped from the bridge and suffered serious injuries as a result. His condition at Peterborough District Hospital is not yet known.

A police spokesperson said that the investigation is ongoing, but warned social media users, 'Those who share the video posted online may face criminal charges.'

To date, the video has been streamed and viewed over three million times, a number that is expected to rise.

DI Rawlinson, who is in charge of the investigation, urged the public not to interfere with inquiries and to report suspicious activities rather than act directly.

'We ask you to let us do our work,' he said. 'Acts of vigilantism have occurred across the city, and dealing with these incidents is taking focus away from what we need to do, which is to stop the instigator of these horrific crimes.'

Police have been inundated with calls since the first

incident which occurred in a Chinese takeaway on 3 February and which saw manager Michelle Reed being forced to kill Timothy Smart.

The apparently random targeting of individuals who are forced to 'play' The Games has also affected local businesses as many employees have been too frightened to go to work.

Police have refused to comment on The Host's latest threat to play his last Game on the evening of 7 February. However, several police cars and two ambulances were seen racing through the city, in the direction of Ferry Meadows last night.

When asked if the police thought there would be another attack, DI Rawlinson stated: 'I have no further comment about an ongoing investigation,' but later stressed, 'Our advice remains the same – to stay vigilant and stay indoors.'

Police are urging anyone with any information to contact 111.

If you live in the Peterborough area, and have been affected by this, get in touch **here**.

Emily Curtis > Peterborough Free Discussion

Is anyone watching BBC breakfast? They are talking about
The Host. 😨 Can't believe it's now on national TV!

587 Comments

Johnny Ormo

I've just switched it on. This is surreal. I can't think about
anything else. I'm scared to go outside in case I'm next.

Emily Curtis

I know what you mean, I have been up all night, I felt
sick at 9 p.m. thinking about The Game he was playing
somewhere.

Johnny Ormo

Me too. Have you seen anything online about it?

Emily Curtis

Only what was on the news. Reports of police and ambulance near Ferry Meadows.

Amanda Belkin

Did you all see the video? What Jim Weston had to do?

Emily Curtis

Yes.

Amanda Belkin

It's insane. The man jumped off the bridge, so he didn't
have to fight.

Emily Curtis
Michaela was right. He was involved.

Johnny Ormo
It's so sad. I really hope he is OK.

Emily Curtis
He's a hero.

Claire Turner
Hi, guys. Sorry I've been quiet; it's been a bit tough.

Emily Curtis
It's totally understandable, are you all right?

Claire Turner
I've been struggling. This thing is scaring me so much, I'm barely sleeping, and when I do, I'm having terrible dreams. I still can't get over that Roberta was killed. She was such a lovely lady.

Johnny Ormo
I'm so sorry for your loss. 😥

Claire Turner
I feel like a hypocrite, I barely knew her really, we just exchanged pleasantries when I went in with my kids. But still…

Michaela Balfour

Hi, **Claire**. I understand how you feel. I'm sorry for your loss too.

Emily Curtis

Michaela, are you OK? Any news?

Michaela Balfour

None yet. 😷

Claire Turner

Has there been another video released?

Emily Curtis

No.

Johnny Ormo

It's coming though. The Jim Weston one broke my heart. He is so brave to do what he did, but we are all so powerless in this thing.

Emily Curtis

I hate saying this, but I don't think the police will be able to stop this guy. I'm terrified.

CHAPTER FORTY-THREE

6.15 a.m.

I was back by the rowing lake, but it was different today. In the warmth of the early morning sun I could hear birds chirping. In my hands was a camcorder, a large and heavy one from the mid-1990s, the tape rolling, the grainy image capturing Sam stood beside Howard. 'Smile, you two,' I said. Sam waved. Howard said I didn't have to record it, as it was boring, but I insisted. 'It will be great to look back on in years to come.' He shook his head dismissively, but the hint of a smile crept onto his face.

'Shall I do it now?' Sam asked.

'Ready? *Annnnnnd* – action.'

Sam waded into the water, and Howard followed. I moved too, close to the edge. Sam pushed Howard under the water, held him there, smiling to the camera throughout, talking about how easy it was to hold him. She lifted one hand and waved at the camera again. Howard waved too, his head fully submerged in the murky lake. Then he stopped waving, his arms falling limp. Sam let go, and he drifted away. I cheered as she joined me on the edge of the water. She took a mock bow towards the camera before stepping out of shot. I zoomed in on Howard, his body floating face up and lifeless. As I closed in on his face, it wasn't his face I saw. It was the dark eyes and high cheekbones of Grayson James.

It jolted me awake and I opened my eyes. I swung my legs over the side of the bed and sat up, my elbows resting on my knees. Sam stirred beside me.

'Whassup?' Sam asked sleepily.

'Just a weird dream. Go back to sleep, babe.'

Sam stretched, yawned and rolled onto her side.

'No, I've got to get up soon.' She waited for a response, but I said nothing. 'Are you sure you're all right? You look like you've seen a ghost.'

I turned and faced her, smiled, but knew I wasn't fooling anyone. 'Yeah, I'm fine.'

'Karen…' Sam started, but stopped as I got up and walked out of the bedroom, heading downstairs. In the kitchen I turned on the light to Bob's tank, and the fish seemed to eye me, annoyed, until I removed the lid to the small tub of food and pinched a few flakes.

'Easily pleased, aren't you, Bob?'

I switched on the kettle, then grabbed my phone that I'd left in the kitchen junk drawer in an attempt to have a restful night. I checked to see if Howard had messaged, but nothing new had come in. I thought Howard might have updated me or at least asked if I'd got home safely. On the news, however, The Host and his Game was everywhere. Twitter, Facebook and the national press were dominated by what was happening. There was a new alert on the BBC News app, posted four hours ago, about the police being at Peterborough rowing lake in connection with an ongoing investigation. So far, the details of the latest Game hadn't been revealed but I knew it was only a matter of time. As the kettle clicked off, I heard Sam walking around upstairs, then a minute later she came into the kitchen wearing her dressing gown.

'Made you a coffee,' I said, handing over her mug.

'Thanks. So what are your plans for the day?' she asked.

'I've been asked to go in for a meeting this morning at nine. The gaffer wants to see me.'

'About the IOPC report?'

'Maybe, or probably just to assign me a list of places in the community to visit.'

'Well, that's something,' she said. She didn't ask about the latest video posted; she didn't ask if I knew anything. Sam was far too good for me.

'How do you think school will be today?' I asked, redirecting the conversation.

'Bloody hard,' Sam replied, taking a sip of her coffee.

'I bet there are lots of scared kids at the moment.'

'Most of them, yes.'

'But not all?' I queried.

'Some were riled up yesterday after the new video, ready for a fight. We had four separate scraps, three of them in the middle of a lesson.'

'Jesus. They should just close the school.'

'But a lot of parents work, so if we close the kids have nowhere to go. We have a duty of care.'

'Yeah, you're right.'

'A few of my most vulnerable students really concern me. These kids are on the edge as it is, without this. Yesterday,

I tried to find them all, to talk to them, tell them that we teachers are there to help, but really, what can we do after 3.15 p.m. when they go home? I gave a few of them my mobile number so if—'

'Is that a good idea? Students having your personal number?'

'No, it's not, but what else is there? Some of those kids are pretty much fending for themselves. They don't have anyone to comfort them. I figured I rarely use my mobile, anyway, so it wouldn't matter if it became a designated phone for work.'

'Kids might ring you in the middle of the night.'

'They might, but I want to help, especially those who don't have anyone to help them through all this. I just hope none of them need to pick up the phone.'

'I guess them knowing someone is there might be enough.'

Sam smiled. 'That's what I'm hoping.'

Sam regularly told me about a few of the kids she was most worried about. If I was their teacher, I probably would have given my number too. Even though our jobs were so different, they were both about helping people.

'Maybe today will be a little better,' I said.

'We both know it will be worse.'

'Do you want me to drop by in an official capacity?' I asked, hoping when I received my bollocking from Bradshaw I could appease him by suggesting I could help. I couldn't tell Sam I'd intended to the other day, but a panic attack stopped me.

'Really?'

'Sure. I think I'm going to be asked to be out and about anyway.'

'It's worth a try. Thank you, love.'

I kissed Sam and took my coffee upstairs to shower and get ready for my meeting.

'It's weird seeing you in that uniform again,' Sam said when she came up to join me.

'It feels weird wearing it.'

'Want a lift to work? I can drop you on my way in.'

'No thanks, love, I'll walk.' As a farewell gesture before I left the house, I kissed her and said, 'If I'm coming in to the school, I'll message before.'

As I stepped onto the pavement, I saw a woman leaning on Sam's car. I hesitated for a moment, but then, my police head firmly switched on, I approached.

'Can I help you?' I asked, my voice steady. I recognised her face, but for a moment couldn't place it – by the time I did, it was too late to react. The woman spat at me, hitting me on the chest.

'You're a disgrace. You shouldn't be in a uniform, you should be in jail. Murderer.'

I tried to respond as a police officer should, trying to defuse the situation, assert the power the uniform gave, but I faltered.

'It's been two weeks since you killed my son. And you get to carry on like nothing happened. I hope you burn in hell, you bitch!' She spat again, this time hitting my chin. I knew I should have responded, arrested her even, but the woman shoved me hard, and I stumbled back into the bush outside my house. I corrected myself, tried to speak, say something, but the words wouldn't come. She shoved me again, called me a bitch again, and once more, I was powerless.

'What the hell are you doing?' Sam shouted from the doorstep, alerted to what was going on. She stormed protectively outside in her dressing gown. 'Fuck off, before she arrests you.'

The woman, unprepared for conflict with another, stared at me one last time. 'You'll pay for what you did to my boy. You'll rot in jail one day, you mark my words.' Again, I knew I should say something, but still the words wouldn't come. Maybe she was right, maybe I should be punished?

'Piss off,' Sam said, drawing level with me, and Grayson's mum laughed a bitter laugh before stuffing her hands into her pockets and walking away. Only then did I breathe. Neither Sam or I spoke until the woman turned off our road and disappeared.

'Was that Grayson James's mother?' Sam asked.

'Yeah,' I said, pulling a tissue out of my pocket to wipe the spit from my face.

'Are you OK?'

I shrugged. 'Yeah, I'm going to have to be. I better go.'

'Karen, wait. Maybe you shouldn't go in today. Can't you ask to rearrange the meeting?'

I shrugged again, catching myself and stopping mid raise. 'I'll be fine.'

CHAPTER FORTY-FOUR

8.27 a.m.

I stepped into the office amid a sea of tired eyes glued to warm computer screens and sleepy voices talking to persons unknown on telephones. An array of takeaway containers, pizza boxes and coffee cups littered the desks. Paperwork was scattered around, piles of notes and photos and statements from the public. There was the smell of stale air and the hint of body odour from a room full of people who hadn't been able to have their morning shower. It looked like they had been here all night and hadn't slept. I should have been here, too, following up any potential leads. I'd failed, and that was compounded by the shame of not having dealt with Grayson's mother as I should have done. Her words looped in my head – I wasn't sure I would ever be able to pause her voice.

'*You're a disgrace. You shouldn't be in a uniform, you should be in jail. Murderer.*'

Bradshaw wasn't in his office, but I didn't doubt he was in the building somewhere, so I waited outside his door. From across the incident room, Howard caught my eye. I nodded, which he acknowledged before walking away towards the bathrooms.

Checking my watch, I still had ten minutes, so I followed. As I walked past Rawlinson's desk he looked up from his phone.

'What are you doing here?' he barked.

'Superintendent Bradshaw invited me in,' I replied confidently, pleased that after the incident on my doorstep I could still act as if I had a cool head.

'Well, his office is the other way. You shouldn't be walking around here, you're technically suspended, you know.'

'I'm on restricted duty.'

He offered a thin smile. 'After your little stunt last night, I wouldn't be so sure.'

'Stunt? I was trying to help, you…'

'You what? Go on, finish what you were saying.'

I bit my tongue, there was a time and place for the words I wanted to say to him, but now wasn't it.

'This is a murder investigation,' he hissed, as if I didn't know. 'I suggest you turn around.'

'I'm actually going to the ladies; do you feel the need to escort me?' I asked, unblinking.

'Just be quick. I don't want you lurking around where you're not welcome.'

'Can't promise I'll be speedy,' I said, and he looked away. 'You know how slow us women are. And I can't find anyone to come with me either. I'm not sure how I'll cope.'

I couldn't call him an egotistical prick, like I wanted to, so calling him out on his sexism was the next best thing.

'Just, um, I've got my eye on you, DI Holt.'

'In the bathroom? Bit weird, Rawlinson…'

Just before turning the corner on my way to the toilets I looked back, and he turned away quickly. I was sure there was a sign of a blush on his cheek. Smiling, I disappeared into the ladies.

'Howard?'

A cubicle door opened, and Howard stepped out.

'Hey.'

'So now we're forced into secret meetings in the ladies loo?' I said.

'Karen, I'm sorry, I had a gagging order out on me.'

'I guessed as much.'

'I don't want you to think...'

'Howard, it's OK, I assume it came from the top?'

'Yes, but through Rawlinson who was only too pleased to tell me if you and I talked, I'd likely be removed from the case. Possibly suspended.'

'Suspended? Bit extreme. He's probably bluffing.'

'I think he added that bit, I can't see Bradshaw throwing around threats like that.'

'Agreed. So what happened after I left last night?'

'The man, John Stroud, didn't make it,' Howard said, shaking his head.

'And the woman?'

'His wife, Maggie.'

'His wife?' I echoed, surprised. The Host's choice of a couple was an unsettling development. 'He's forcing us to consider how we would treat someone we love,' I murmured.

'Yeah.'

'Was she able to tell us anything new?'

'Nothing more than we already know. Robotic voice, motorbike helmet. Rules and time.'

'And the camera, I'm guessing?'

'Yep, he filmed it again.'

'Which means there's another video coming soon.'

Howard nodded.

'Have we got anything to work with, or are we waiting for him to lead?'

'There's one camera which caught some of last night's incident, a decades' old one on the roof of the rowing club building.'

'Do you have it?'

'Yes. But I don't know how to get it to you.'

I thought for a second. Rawlinson was no doubt watching like a hawk. I didn't want Howard to end up in trouble.

'Well, it's probably time to start thinking like a rule breaker if we're forced to be one. I'll get a pay-as-you-go phone. And I'll message.'

'A burner?'

'Uh-huh.'

Howard chuckled. 'Could you imagine us having to do this a month ago? Secret meetings in the ladies loo. You talking of getting a burner phone just so we can speak.'

'Yeah.' I smiled but it didn't quite reach my eyes. All this subterfuge because of what I'd done. I pressed on. 'Did you find the train symbol?'

'Yes. It was on a rock close to the water's edge.'

I nodded. 'Anything about the rock that seemed unusual?'

'It was lighter in colours than others around it. That's what drew my eye. It's man-made. Concrete or something. It's being looked at now.'

'So it was placed there.'

'Yeah. It must have been.'

'So that's our clue. Any ideas?'

'None so far, but we'll keep digging.'

'OK. I'd better go, before Rawlinson gets suspicious. When the coast is clear I'll message so you can sneak out.'

I left the loo and walked past Rawlinson, who pretended to work, and towards Bradshaw's office. His door was open and he was back from wherever he'd been. I messaged Howard, and moments later he too walked past Rawlinson. He noticed Howard and eyed me suspiciously once more. I tapped three times on the doorframe, Bradshaw looked up from his computer screen and smiled.

'Come in, Karen, shut the door, take a seat.'

'Thank you, sir.'

'Karen, look…' he began, his face pained, regretful.

'Sir, I can explain last night. I met Howard for a pint at the Woodman and then we walked along the river. It was pure coincidence we were close to the scene.'

'Was it?' he said, removing his glasses to fix his gaze on me. 'Honestly? You know I don't believe in coincidences, DI Holt; neither do you, I suspect.'

'No, sir,' I admitted.

'You were there because you knew the next murder had something to do with the river.'

'Yes, sir. I was following the adage, "take life where life began".'

'Yes, I was filled in on your reasoning.'

'It was DS Carlson that worked…'

'Karen, we both know that's not true.' His expression softened. 'Good thinking.'

'Thank you, sir.'

'I just wish I had more officers to follow it up.'

'Me too, sir.'

'Now, officially, I have to reprimand you. You know full well you shouldn't have been there last night, coincidence or not.'

'I know, sir.'

'Unofficially,' he said quietly, 'this investigation is a mess and I need my best people working on it. I know there is very little I can say to stop your mind working overtime, Karen. However, from now on in, if you have a thought, a notion, an idea, you come directly to me, is that understood?'

'Sir, if I could come back into the investigation properly, I know—'

'Well, you can't. You know my hands are tied. I had to beg the IOPC to allow you to come back on restricted duty to visit schools. How many did you manage before somehow worming your way back into this investigation?'

'Just the one, sir.' If I told him the truth – that I hadn't even made one – I'd not be allowed even on restricted duty.

'Karen, I want you back. But you have to play ball for the time being.'

'Understood, sir.'

'No more putting yourself in the thick of it, and I daren't ask what happened to your face.'

I opened my mouth to say something, but Bradshaw stopped me.

'I don't want to know. From now on in, Howard Carlson is off limits, he's under orders not to talk to you. I know you're close, but best to stay away, especially because it might look like you're trying to influence him on the Grayson James incident.'

'Sir, I wouldn't—'

'I know, Karen, believe me, I do, but the IOPC are keeping

tabs now. They got wind you might be breaking the limitations of restricted duty and have warned me, if they find out, you are in deep, deep shit.'

He didn't need to say how the IOPC got wind, it was obvious: Rawlinson. The snivelling prick.

'So to be clear, you'll be in uniform, only visiting schools. Nothing more. Understood?'

'Understood, sir.'

'And only speak to me from now on if you have any leads. That way, I will hear them properly.'

'Yes, sir.'

'Good, now get out of here, and as you leave, look pissed off.'

'Pissed off, sir?'

'Certain people requested I had a show of force today.'

'I understand, sir, thank you, sir.'

I got up to leave, but as I opened the door Bradshaw stopped me.

'Karen, I mean it, don't do anything stupid that forces my hand.'

'Yes, sir. Mind if I slam the door?'

'Not at all.' He smiled.

I stepped out of the office and slammed the door. Several heads looked up, Howard looked concerned, Rawlinson pleased. I didn't say anything but lowered my head and stormed out of the office. I booked out a police car, and once the keys were in my hand and I was heading to the lot to collect it, I messaged Sam, asking if she still wanted me to come in. She messaged back a thumbs-up emoji. Another message straight after saying to ring when five minutes away.

First, though, I needed to go and buy myself a burner phone.

CHAPTER FORTY-FIVE

The Host

9.16 a.m.

He sat with two scarlet-coloured pipe cleaners in his hands, bending and shaping them into a person. This one wouldn't go on the shelf with the small but ever-growing group of individuals, survivors, victims. Just like him. No, this one was going to sit on his desk, act as a reminder that he needed to be more vigilant than ever. He finished shaping it and could almost feel it watching him, wanting to speak to him. He placed it down next to his computer monitor and smiled.

'Hello, Karen, it's a delight to meet you properly at last. I'm looking forward to you playing The Game. You might be the best Player yet.'

CHAPTER FORTY-SIX

1.25 p.m.

As Sam and I got our lunch from the school canteen, I could feel many eyes on me, or rather my uniform. I tried to ignore it, as most pupils were just being curious, but there was one young person who particularly stood out – when she saw me she looked edgy and then quickly left. As she exited, she was already on her phone, texting away. I didn't get a good look at her, but her behaviour suggested she may have had a run-in with the police at some point, probably for drinking or loitering or something similar. Despite it being the twenty-first century, there was still a stigma around coppers. It had lessened in the eleven years I'd been on the force, but it probably would always be there.

A group of boys started to mess around; at first it was just boys being boys, but it quickly escalated to them throwing food at each other and rough-housing. Sam jumped up and as she approached they stopped. They were scared of being told off by their head of year. While Sam had a polite word with them, I checked my phone for a news update, then seeing Sam still distracted, I pulled out the cheap Nokia pay-as-you-go phone I'd bought to see if Howard had messaged back. Nothing as yet.

Around the canteen there was a sudden crescendo of noise, a hundred voices all calling at one another, then, shortly after, silence. I jumped up, knocking my orange juice over the table top, and headed to the closest group of teens who had fallen silent. Sam and I joined their small circle watching the screen of a Samsung phone. We knew what it was immediately. The familiar helmet of The Host filled the screen as he relayed his message. Then, the image switched to a point-of-view shot of two older, frightened people, and we watched as the latest Game began.

I should have confiscated the phone, told every single student to put theirs away, or risk being arrested. I knew they shouldn't see what was about to happen, they were all too young. I knew but did nothing. Despite anticipating the posting of this new video, I felt my diaphragm snap, like an elastic band that had been stretched too far. I was aware Sam was saying something to me, but her words sounded like they were coming from underwater as panic began to flood into my ears. There were too many people here, too many eyes on me, and I was powerless to move. Eventually, I managed to push out a feeble plea for the kids to put their phones away, and although I had no impact, my voice too meek, too small, it snapped Sam and the other teachers into action and they swept through the canteen, quickly confiscating phones from students. The kid with the Samsung handed it to me without being asked.

The video was hardest to watch yet, not because of its violence but its tenderness. After the man disappeared beneath the surface, the woman's wail of grief was so harrowing I could barely watch. Then The Host returned to the screen, closing with the same words as before. I expected the video to end there, but the image of the rowing lake came back onto the screen, and the scene kept rolling, albeit from a distance.

In the shot, the woman was sitting on the bank, her feet in the water. Behind her, the dog whimpered ceaselessly. I looked up, Sam was at the other end of the canteen, looking at her phone as young people around panicked. Before I could divert Sam, the video showed Howard and me running to help, the camera switching off once I was kneeling beside the woman, looking around for the victim, my gaze landing directly on the camera. In the final frozen frame, my despair clear to see. His voice returned over the image.

'To those in the video, if you think you're so smart, come find me. You were close, but not close enough. Perhaps this time, you'll have better luck. I will play tonight at 8.00 p.m. Maybe I will see you there, Karen Holt.'

Then the screen faded to black.

I couldn't move, nor could I hear anything around me, and I had to grab a nearby chair to stop myself falling. He knew my name. Somehow, he knew my name.

As my eyes met Sam's I could see her disappointment that I had placed myself in harm's way and maybe even put her in danger too. The Host's message was a warning, a threat directed at me. Around the room, phones that teachers had not managed to confiscate began to drop to tables and into laps. No one spoke. The video was too harrowing, too heartbreaking. But I sensed that fear wasn't the biggest emotion in the room, it was anger. Sam's anger.

'I wanted to tell you,' I mouthed.

Sam just looked at me, then shook her head before walking off, telling the students to begin to make their way to the hall. I didn't move. As the young people filed out a small girl, likely a year seven, tapped my arm, drawing my attention.

'You have to stop him,' she said, her voice delicate, tears in her eyes. Then she lowered her head and followed the crowd.

CHAPTER FORTY-SEVEN

Carlson

2.41 p.m.
Five hours and nineteen minutes until the next Game

Howard's phone alarm sounded, stirring him from a fitful sleep. Rolling onto his side he saw the time – if he snoozed he'd sleep for another hour, so he sat up, groaning deeply. The last few days had been hard; the lack of sleep, stress, physical exhaustion had all begun to show. Bradshaw insisted after Karen had left that he go home and get some shut-eye, even just a few hours. Stopping his alarm, he saw a message from Becca, and when it opened a video of Jess sprung to life.

'Hi, Daddy, I cannot wait to see you!'

'I can't either,' he replied, despite knowing it was a recording and she wouldn't hear. Jess waved and moved to play with her toys. The video spun and Becca filled the screen. Carlson felt his heart skip.

'Hey, Howard, so we are gonna aim for early evening, around teatime? That OK with you? I hope you're all right. I saw the video from last night. Call me if you need me, I mean it.'

The camera spun again, and Jess was back on screen.

'Say bye to Daddy.'

'Bye, Daddy!' Jess waved.

'Bye,' Becca echoed. 'We love you.'

The video finished and Carlson stared at the screen a little longer, the last image of his smiling girl melting away the aches he felt. He rolled out of bed, turned on the TV and flicked to Sky News. They were discussing what was happening, which wasn't a surprise. The shock came when he heard the news presenter say Karen's name.

'What the...'

Picking up his mobile, he searched on social media, his stomach dropping when he saw The Host had posted the next video. He watched it, blinking hard to stop a tear falling. At the end he saw himself and Karen run in.

'Fuck.'

Howard dressed quickly and headed out to go back to Thorpe Wood, knowing he would be needed. As he opened the front door, a person walking past jumped.

'Sorry!' Howard said, an automatic response.

'No, it's OK. You just startled me,' the person replied, smiling at Howard before lowering his head and walking away.

Howard jumped into his car and backed out of his drive, not knowing that the man he had apologised to – who'd just smiled politely – was, in fact, the same man he'd walked past on the day of the Second Game. The man he'd locked eyes with on the night of the third.

Three times in one week, Carlson had been within grabbing distance of The Host, and he hadn't even known it.

Emily Curtis > Peterborough Free Discussion

Hi, everyone, with what is going on, I have been elected to be an administrator for this Facebook page. It's probably a good time to recap the group's code of conduct we all agreed when joining. This group is to discuss anything happening in our city. If anyone is found to be abusive or sharing videos of the horrific crimes happening you will be removed from the group.

771 Comments

Johnny Ormo
Nicely put, **Emily**! I'm sure all members agree. I didn't know you were admin?

Emily Curtis
I approached the page owner last night, asked if I could help.

Johnny Ormo
That's really good of you.

Emily Curtis
I noticed that with The Host's attacks the page is a lot busier. I just don't want anyone to feel like they can use this page to stir up fear.

Johnny Ormo
I agree. Good for you.

Amanda Belkin

I just saw the latest video and it's truly horrific – for me it's the worst one. Imagine having to do that to someone you loved. And who were those two people in the video?

Johnny Ormo

I think they were police.

Amanda Belkin

God, they were so close to him and didn't even know.

Jack Anderson

I just want this bastard to be caught.

Johnny Ormo

Me too. I was afraid, but not now, I'm so pissed off. We need to stop this guy.

Emily Curtis

I hate that he can control us.

Claire Turner

Control us?

Emily Curtis

He's stating the times, so we all panic. We need to show him we are better than that.

Johnny Ormo

I hear you, **Emily**. But how?

Emily Curtis

I don't know. But I want something to happen, you know? We are all crippled by this thing, and he is thriving on it. He made a married couple play his evil Game. Enough is enough.

Claire Turner

Yes! I agree, I've been feeling this way since Roberta – who is he to play God? I'm tired of being afraid. I'm tired of trying to explain to my kids what is happening in the world. They are eleven and nine. They know something awful is going on. I shouldn't have to tell them what. The Host doesn't control us. We are in charge of our own lives.

Michaela Balfour

I'm with you all the way. If Jim can be a hero, I can too.

Jack Anderson

Guys, there's been a news update, shall I post it?

Amanda Belkin

👍

Jack Anderson

'The Host's' Reign of Terror Continues

A pensioner who was found dead at Peterborough's rowing club is the latest victim of The Host.

The wife of victim John Stroud, 68, who has been named

by neighbours as Maggie Stroud, 66, was arrested at the scene and is being questioned.

The latest video from the person calling himself The Host has been posted online, showing the scene where a fatality was reported. It appears Mr Stroud was killed on The Host's instructions.

A police spokesperson said: 'We are appealing for witnesses in and around the area of the rowing lake or Ferry Meadows between the times of 8 p.m–10 p.m. to contact us.'

The identity of the woman in the video The Host spoke to directly in his final message has been locally named as Detective Inspector Karen Holt.

Sources have told us DI Holt is believed to be currently suspended from active duty following the incident involving Grayson James. A spokesman for the Police Federation has refused to comment on her involvement in the case.

As of yet, there has been no news of the survivors, Michelle Reed, Richard Mullis, Milly Hallam or the minor, who cannot be named for legal reasons.

Jim Weston, the hero who jumped from the bridge, in order not to be a Player, still remains in hospital, under police protection.

If you have been affected by recent events, have your say **here**.

Emily Curtis
I think I remember reading about the Grayson James thing.

Amanda Belkin

I do too, God, could you imagine being her? What an awful few weeks at work.

Johnny Ormo

She's not even at work, she's suspended.

Amanda Belkin

So she's doing this off her own back? Trying to stop him.

Johnny Ormo

That's how I've read it.

Jack Anderson

Jesus. She's either brave, or stupid.

Emily Curtis

Guys, I've had an idea. Instead of hiding away tonight, what if we were out? What if we were more like this Karen Holt?

Johnny Ormo

Emily, I said I was angry, not suicidal.

Emily Curtis.

I mean, what if we created an event. Using #thePlayers. What if we got loads of us, hundreds of us out in the city centre? At all of the sights maybe. A show of force, a vigil for those who have had to play.

Jack Anderson

It's also a big 'fuck you' to The Host. That's actually not a bad idea.

Claire Turner

It's great. Enough of us, we will be safe.

Emily Curtis

And we can show him we are not going to take what he is doing anymore. Last night he targeted a retired couple, the night before, a kid. I say enough is enough.

Johnny Ormo

Fuck it, I'm in!

Claire Turner

Me too.

Jack Anderson

And me!

Amanda Belkin

Create the event, tag it in here. Let's see if we can fill the streets tonight as a big fat 'up yours' to The Host.

Emily Curtis

Even though we're all really scared right now let's show him we're not going to live in fear. It's time to take a stand.

CHAPTER FORTY-EIGHT

7.02 p.m.

Fifty-eight minutes until the next Game

Knowing I'd been only a matter of metres away from The Host at the rowing lake made my head spin. I didn't want to be caught up in this, I didn't want to be the centre of anything, I wasn't ready. But somehow, I was at the heart of it all now, and when The Host called me out in the video, I knew there would be massive consequences. I'd had a phone call earlier in the afternoon and stern words from Bradshaw with the instructions to go home immediately, lock the doors, stay inside. The IOPC would definitely know, and I was likely going to lose my job. The personal damage I was still working through. Sam was currently upstairs and I was sure I could hear her crying. I needed her, I felt myself drowning, but my actions had pushed her to the limits. I had lied countless times. It was right I was being held accountable. I needed her, but she needed to have some space from me, and I had to honour that. All I could do was watch the news helplessly, while waiting for a message or call from Howard that I knew wouldn't come. Not now. We hadn't – I hadn't – worked out

The Host's latest clue. I had failed to understand what that rock was telling me.

The city was in chaos. Thousands of people were in the streets, protesting, their actions in defiance of the terror that they all felt. The Host's latest attempt to strike fear into the hearts of the public – his compulsion to make the world see there was no good – had backfired on him. The hope Jim Weston sparked when he decided to throw himself off a bridge rather than hurt another human had become an inferno when the heartbreaking video of the Stroud couple went viral.

Peterborough was angry. Everyone covered it: ITV and Channel 4 featured it on the 6 p.m. slots. Sky News and the BBC were live throughout. I sat glued, watching it all. I could see officers I didn't recognise who must have been drafted in from Cambridge or Nottingham. I knew I should be trying to speak to Sam, beg for forgiveness, but I couldn't pull my eyes from what I was seeing.

People weren't just in the city centre, they were also at the scenes where the crimes had taken place: the Chinese, the nightclub, the library, the footbridge and the rowing lake were thronged by hundreds of people, placing candles, and paying their respects.

None of it changed the fact it was going to happen again, and with people out, needing policing, there would be fewer officers available to find The Host.

On Sky News they showed overhead footage of Bridge Street, rammed and defiant, a street that was getting progressively busier and busier, then they cut to a shot of a woman holding a small child somewhere amongst the crowd.

'I think it's important for people to be out together – we

can't let this man terrorise us anymore. He is trying to teach us all we are bad, so we need to prove that we aren't, that people are basically good.'

A person off-camera asked if that was why she had brought along her child.

'Yes, I want her to grow up knowing that this city is a safe place to be, where people look out for one another. We are a close-knit community.'

Another person came onto the screen, from another part of the burgeoning vigil. The young man looked like he'd had a few drinks, and as he spoke, he didn't look at the camera or the interviewer.

'This is what we should have done after the first Game – we will not let terrorists win. If we stick together, we have safety in numbers. We can fight terror with love.'

I wanted to believe him, but it didn't stick.

The camera switched to show footage of the vigil outside the Chinese takeaway. The studio reporter described the scene.

'... the site of the first crime, of course, was the Chinese restaurant in Fletton. As you can see from the images, dozens of people are in the area, laying flowers and lighting candles...'

The camera zoomed in on the ground outside the front door where a card to Timothy and Michelle sat open, the message showing the hashtag #protectednotarrested.

The next half hour's viewing consisted of the same scenes: footage from the city centre, the occasional interview, and images of the other areas where crowds were forming. Each time a new location came into shot that was busier than the last. And the clock ticked down.

Twenty-six minutes.

I was unable to blink as I watched the screen, looking for anything that might be a clue. Trying to work out what that bloody rock meant that was found by the rowing lake. Really, all I could do, all anyone could do, was hope that because the city had taken a stand, The Host's plans had been disrupted, and I hated it.

Because deep down I knew, even if tonight he didn't play, he would tomorrow, or the next day, or the next, and there was no way to stop him.

CHAPTER FORTY-NINE

The Host

7.43 p.m.
Seventeen minutes until the next Game

Moving effortlessly through the crowds, his song playing in his headphones, The Host enjoyed what he was seeing – confirmation that it truly was a wonderful life. People smiled and talked and drank. And he smiled with them. Their reaction was exactly what he had dreamed of, it was part of the reason the Stroud couple had been chosen. The world would either become fully docile and accepting, as he first thought, or agitated like this. People were incensed yet optimistic, they believed they could make a difference. Along with the anger, he heard conversations of hope. Hope was a dangerous thing. It can lift a person one moment and crush them the next.

In the throng of people, someone played music through a portable speaker, making those around toe-tap; The Host joined in too. Dancing to his own song, arms high above his head, reaching for the heavens. He didn't care what he looked like; he didn't care that some were laughing at him. He was high on his Game, he was high on the fact they were all there, because of him, and they would never know.

Up ahead, close to the archway that led to the cathedral – the very spot he knew The Game would work because of a homeless man and his dog – he saw a familiar face. A part of him knew he should give him a wide berth, and yet he just couldn't help himself. His invincibility, his invisibility insisted he approached. As he drew close to DS Carlson, he smiled apologetically and removed his headphones.

'Excuse me?'

'Is everything all right?' Carlson asked. For a moment The Host thought he might recall his face from only a few hours earlier, but the spectacle of the city masked him.

'Yes, sorry, I thought I wanted to be here this evening, but really, it's all a bit much,' he said, loving each word that slid off his tongue. 'Do you know whether the buses are running? I heard they weren't.'

'Yeah, it's a bit much for me too,' Carlson agreed. 'Let me radio, see if anyone is close to the bus station and knows what's going on.'

The Host smiled as DS Carlson turned his back and spoke into the closed-circuit radio on his shoulder. After a moment, Carlson turned back.

'Yes, all buses still seem to be running.'

'Brilliant, thank you.'

'You're welcome. Make sure you get home safely.'

'I will, thank you.'

The Host turned and walked away, back into the heart of the ever-growing crowd. Once he was confident DS Carlson could no longer see him, he turned back and headed down

Bridge Street towards his next location. Around him people held crudely drawn cardboard signs. WE WILL NOT BE AFRAID OF YOU, one shouted. Another said that The Host was a monster. They were right, he was a monster hiding in plain sight, a monster that looked just like them, that sounded just like them. He was the most wanted person in England, he was all anyone could talk about. They could grab him right now, stop him, stop The Game they so fervently protested against. But they wouldn't, because he was one of them, a mirror reflection of their innermost thoughts. Instead they smiled when he agreed with their signs, patted him on the back when he danced with them, hugged him when he spoke of defiance and courage and love instead of hate. He was just like them, or rather, they were just like him. As he made his way towards the site of his next Game, he saw another sign: WE WILL NEVER PLAY YOUR GAME. WE WOULD RATHER DIE.

They were like him; the only difference was he knew the truth. But they would get there, just like him; just like Michelle Reed and Milly Hallam and Richard Mullis and Maggie Stroud. Just like another would very, very soon.

Putting his headphones back on, he played his song, drowning out their noise. The ballad in his ears contrasted with the energetic and chaotic movement of the people around him. It was beautiful, like they were moving in slow motion. Swaying to his own rhythm, he moved towards his destination.

The Sixth Game was going to be perfect. He couldn't wait to see what would happen when they learned who the next Players were.

CHAPTER FIFTY

8.22 p.m.

Twenty-two minutes had passed since the time The Host had given, and the police were still diligently holding their posts. There was no sense of panic, no officers rushing to a crime scene. The news broadcaster who spoke over the images of smiling, dancing people, raising their glasses and toasting a victory over terrorism, couldn't hide their personal elation. Too much time had passed, and there had been no indication the 'Game' had been played. I didn't want to believe it until my phone began to vibrate in my pocket. Pulling it out, I looked at the screen; it was dark which confused me – then I realised it was the other one, the burner. And only Howard had the number. I took a deep breath and retrieved it, not knowing which way this conversation would go. I could hope, but hope seldom counted for much.

'Hey.'

'Hey,' Howard replied quietly, then after a beat, 'There was no call.'

'What?'

'There was no call, it seems people's reactions have spooked him.'

'Oh,' I said, unsure how to react.

'Yeah, I don't know if I trust it either.'

'Is that why you've rung?'

'Partly. Jim Weston was discharged an hour ago. He's back home.'

'I see.'

'Jim's wife has got a solicitor. The police cannot talk to him unless it's formalised.'

'Why the bloody hell would she do that?' I asked.

'I don't blame her. She's freaking out.'

'But he didn't do anything.'

'I guess, neither did the other survivors. She's got a point though, right?'

'Yeah, she has,' I conceded. 'But why are you telling me this?'

'We're going to try to get Jim into the station to talk. Rawlinson is leading.'

'Fuck.'

'Yeah, not good. I'm stuck here, in town, until the crowds disperse.'

'You want me to go speak to him?'

'Karen, I hate this, all of it, but if Rawlinson speaks to him first, he'll back poor Jim into a corner, make him feel like he did something wrong. He's too heavy-handed for something so delicate.'

'Howard, it didn't help when I spoke to Michelle.'

'No, you're right. However, Jim saw the conflicted side of The Host. Maybe he saw something that no one else has?'

'Yeah, maybe.'

'I just want this to end, I want to catch this fucker.'

'Me too.' Howard had got me thinking. There was no doubt The Host was conflicted on the bridge; it was likely to be the reason it didn't go to his 'plan'. He was off his Game; he might have slipped. Jim might have a detail that we didn't know. A way to find him. 'What's the address?'

'117A, Fulbridge Drive.'

'I can't promise I'll go, but I'll try.'

'That's all I can ask for. This all feels personal now.'

'Yeah, it does.'

I didn't say goodbye before hanging up the phone because behind me, Sam had entered the room and cleared her throat.

'Hi Sam,' I said quietly.

'Hi,' she replied, taking a seat beside me. Her eyes were puffy and red. 'Howard?'

'Yeah?'

Sam shook her head, her lips clamped shut as if she was trying not to say something. She took a deep breath. 'So what's happening?' she asked, looking at the TV.

'It seems that he didn't do it tonight.'

'Thank God.'

'Yeah,' I replied. Sam sensed I was unsure.

'Karen?'

'I don't know, I'm over-thinking it.'

'What was that about Fulbridge Drive?'

'The man who jumped, he's home again.'

'And Howard just told you that?'

I didn't reply but looked at Sam imploringly.

'No,' she said, matter-of-fact.

'Sam…'

'No, Karen.'

'I need you to see this from my perspective. This guy, this Host he is—'

'I don't care what he is, you are not at work, you aren't on this case. This maniac filmed you and spoke out to you directly in the last video. Karen, he singled you out by name. When will you realise this is dangerous?'

'I know it's dangerous, but Sam, my job has always been dangerous.'

'Not like this. This is different: a risk you don't have to take, and you bloody well know it.'

'What am I supposed to do, sit back and watch it on the TV?'

'Yes, that's exactly what you're supposed to do, just like me, just like everyone else is.'

'But it's my job,' I pleaded.

'Right now, it isn't, is it?'

'I can't just switch off, Sam.'

'Your job right now,' Sam continued, ignoring me, 'is to work on keeping this family safe, given that he knows who you are.'

Sam's words stunned me into silence. I had been so desperate to help that I hadn't even thought of the danger I might be putting Sam in. I felt ashamed at how reckless I'd been. Sam was right, I hadn't been keeping her safe and that realisation hurt, especially when we'd vowed to love and protect each other. The day I married my wife, I swore I would always put her first. And I was failing.

The TV behind us fell silent; I assumed Sam had turned it off, but Sam's eyes lifted to the screen, confusion painted on her face. The live footage of the city centre still played but now the crowd had fallen silent, their heads cast down, the night illuminated by a thousand phone screens.

'No, God, no,' Sam whispered, her hands going to her mouth. She looked at me as I grabbed my phone and went online.

It didn't take long to find what the crowds were staring at. The screen on my phone was filled with the image of the motorbike helmet. Behind him wasn't the same white wall as in his previous posts, this one was dark, he was somewhere new. I thought I could hear something in the background. Turning up the volume on my phone I put the speaker to my ear.

'What?' Sam asked.

'Shhh.' I replied, straining to hear. There was something there – a distant noise – but I couldn't pick out what it was. When he spoke, in the same robotic tone, I jumped and moved the phone away, I noted there was a slight echo that carried his words around the room. Wherever he was, it was big and spacious.

'I've enjoyed the false hope this evening. I've enjoyed the words of strength and solidarity. I've enjoyed how this city has decided to rise against me, to show me that you were no longer playing. Except you have.

'What you are about to see is unedited footage of a game I played tonight when you flooded the streets and were speaking of community and identity. A game I will play again...'

The screen cut to the image of a terrified young man, tears streaming down his cheeks. As The Host lay down a pair of hedge trimmers and a brick I looked to Sam who had turned grey.

'Lock your phone,' Sam asked, unable to look away.

'I have to see this,' I said quietly.

Sam didn't respond but left the room quickly. Once she was gone, I turned back to the screen and watched.

THE SIXTH GAME

'The camera is rolling; you need to say what we have discussed,' The Host said.

'Please…'

'You know what will happen if you don't.'

The young man, no older than twenty-five, looked directly at the camera.

'My name is Nistor Hofer. I am here, in Peterborough city centre, with my brother, Rusu. We have been instructed to play…' His voice trailed off as he began to cry. I watched as Nistor dropped to his knees sobbing, his right hand covering his face, his left rigidly tied to something; he was a prisoner.

'You don't want to kill your brother, do you, Nistor?'

'No, I would rather die.'

'You *think* you would rather die.'

The camera turned, and I could see a younger man with a cut on his head, also tied to something. If I had to call it, The Host had attacked the smaller brother, told the older to tie himself, and then instructed the younger brother to do the same.

'Rusu. You don't want to die, do you?'

'No.'

'Good, that's good.'

The Host turned back to Nistor, who had stopped sobbing. 'Tell our audience the rules.'

Nistor looked up at the camera. I don't think I had ever seen anyone so afraid. As he spoke, his whole body shook.

'Me and my brother have to fight, if I refuse, he will kill Rusu, if Rusu refuses, he will kill me.'

'And...'

'And if he believes we are not trying, he will kill us both.'

'Well done, Nistor. That's right; if either of you doesn't play properly, I will kill the other. Do you both understand?'

Nistor nodded, fresh tears rolling down his cheeks. Rusu slowly dragged himself to his feet and nodded also.

The Host stepped back, allowing the camera a view of brothers. The younger picked up the saw, the senior the brick. Neither of them spoke. The Host wound up his clock and placed it on the floor so they could both see it. Rusu was the first to strike, slicing through the air with the saw, slowing down just before it hit his brother on the arm, making him bleed, but not as much as it should have. Nistor pushed him back using the brick but there was no force behind it.

The camera moved as The Host stepped forward, and using a baton, the same he had in the nightclub, I watched as he hit Rusu across the back of his legs, sending him crashing down.

'Next time I'll aim for his face.'

Nistor charged at The Host, the brick high in his hand, screaming he would kill him, but as he approached, the binding on his wrist pulled taut and stopped him in his tracks.

'Tick tock,' The Host said.

Then it happened, the violence exploded.

As Rusu attacked Nistor it looked like he wanted to hurt, but not kill him. They had to make it look real, or the other would die. I couldn't imagine being in that situation. Having to hurt someone you loved, hoping it would save them if they then killed you in return. It was difficult to watch, difficult to listen to, and once it was over, both men were on the floor, one face down, blood pooling from a wound on the back of his head where he had been hit with the brick, the second, beside him, a torrent of blood coming from a cut on the inside of his elbow. I couldn't help but feel that some of their blood was now on my hands, because I hadn't stopped him when he called me out.

Once it was over, the video faded back to The Host.

'I want to pose three questions to you all.

'Question 1: You see a runaway train moving toward five incapacitated people lying on the tracks. You are standing next to a lever that controls the line. If you pull the lever, the train will be redirected onto another line, and the five people on the main track will be saved. However, there is a single person lying on that new track. These are the options. You do nothing and allow the train to kill the five people on the main track. Or you pull the switch, diverting the train onto the side-track where it will kill one person. What do you do?

'Question 2: What if you were on the track? You do nothing you die, to live you have to push someone else in front of the train. What then?

'The ultimate question: What makes you so special?'

I thought the screen was going to fade to black, but it didn't. The Host continued to speak:

'My final message is for DI Karen Holt. I know who you

are. I know you are looking for me, but your search will be in vain. Fear not, however, our paths will cross in time.'

I lowered my phone, my heart beating fiercely out of my chest. Looking behind me, I could see Sam's back as she stood watching the kettle boil. I hoped she hadn't heard the final message to me. The Host had forced me to act. Because doing nothing would make me just a culpable as him. Getting up, I put on my shoes and coat and walked into the kitchen.

'Sam—'

'I don't want to know.'

'I have to go.'

'No, Karen, you don't have to do anything.'

'I do, Sam, I do. I need to talk to Jim.'

'Who?'

'Jim Weston, the man who jumped.'

'You're talking like you know him, you don't, Karen. You don't know anyone involved. And you are not on this case.'

'He thinks he's smarter than me, I can use that agai—'

'Because he *is* smarter than you, he's smarter than everyone.'

'Sam, I have to.'

'You need to make a choice,' Sam said, silencing me. 'You can either stay here and support your wife, who's scared shitless by the way, or you can go out there searching for him.'

'Sam, that's not fair.'

'What's not fair is I'm scared for you, Karen, and you aren't.'

'Sam, please.'

'Choose, Karen. Choose to stay at home. Choose to see if you carry on with this, you'll get hurt, or worse.'

'It's not that simple.'

'Choose to accept that throwing yourself into this isn't dealing with what happened with Grayson James.'

'Sam—'

'Choose to show me I matter more.'

'You do matter more.'

'Do I?'

'Sam, people are getting hurt, people are dying. I need to stop him.'

I zipped up my coat and repeated, 'I need to stop him.'

'If you go, I might not be here when you get home,' she whispered, tears in her eyes.

I looked at Sam, my eyes brimming also, I hated seeing my wife so upset. But this was more than us disagreeing, this was life and death and he was speaking directly to me, meaning it was now fully my responsibility to stop him. It was time to get off the back foot and be proactive.

'I'm sorry,' I said as I kissed Sam, turned, and disappeared out of the front door. If The Host wanted me to play in his little Game, I would, and I would beat the bastard at it.

CHAPTER FIFTY-ONE

9.23 p.m.

I took my place on the back seat of the bus and rested my head on the cold glass, watching the houses go by. I should have taken the car for two reasons: first, it wasn't safe for me to be out, at any time of day, and second, if I had the car then Sam would likely not leave. But what kind of person would I be to stop my spouse doing what she felt was right? So the bus would have to do.

I knew Sam wasn't bluffing; I knew when I went home, she would be gone. Not because she was unreasonable, but because it was right. I knew that, and still I had to leave. The Game I was now being forced to play was one of small margins. A word here, an action there, could be all I needed to latch on to a new thread that I could pull and unravel The Host's tapestry. And time was ticking. The Host would play again, but more pressingly, Rawlinson would have his clearance to interview Jim Weston. And I needed to speak to him first. This was personal now.

By the time I arrived at Fulbridge Drive the streets were entirely deserted. As I alighted the bus, the driver smiled with a faint line of concern, then he closed the doors and pulled away. Finding number 117A, I hesitated before ringing the doorbell. It was late, perhaps too late, but Rawlinson would be there first thing, so it was now or never.

After a short wait, there was movement behind the frosted glass of the door, and I heard a safety chain being slotted into place, the snap of a lock, then the door opened just wide enough for half a tired face to show through. I knew from the TV press conference that it was Jim Weston's wife, Susan.

'What do you want?'

'I'm so sorry to disturb you so late…'

'What do you want?' she asked again, clearly in no mood for small talk or pleasantries.

'I was wondering if I could talk with Jim.'

'Are you press?'

'No.'

'Police?'

'Not strictly.'

'So that's a yes. If you want to talk to him, you'll have to go through our solicitor.'

Susan Weston began to close the door, and I saw my chance to find out something, anything that might help, fade away.

'I'm Karen Holt.'

The door paused.

'I'm the person The Host has mentioned, I'm the woman from the video by the rowing lake.'

The door opened again, the safety chain still attached. 'You nearly saved that man.'

'Yes, nearly, but I didn't.'

Susan paused, nodded, waited for me to continue.

'Have you seen the news? What happened earlier this evening?'

Susan nodded again. 'I thought we might have beaten him at his own game.'

'I did too. All I want, Mrs Weston, is to stop it happening again.'

'And you think Jim can help?'

'I don't know, maybe. But I hope you can understand why I'm here. I have to try at least,' I replied honestly.

'You said you weren't strictly with the police. What did you mean by that?' Susan asked, and I knew it was a test of some kind.

'I'm not on the case.'

'I think you're lying,' she said and began to close the door.

'No, wait. I'm not. I'm on restricted duty following an incident.'

'What incident?'

I didn't want to say it, but I had no choice. Susan clearly wasn't in the mood for any bullshit. 'A man died while being arrested.'

'I see – that Grayson James thing?' she asked. I simply nodded. 'You were involved in that?'

I nodded again.

'I'm sorry to hear that,' she said, catching me by surprise.

'I'm sorry about Jim. I just want to help everyone who has been forced to be a Player. They are all victims. All of them, Jim included.'

Susan closed the door, and after releasing the safety chain, she opened it fully.

'You better come inside. I'll go get him.'

'Thank you,' I said, stepping over the threshold to the Westons' home.

'Make yourself comfortable,' Susan said, gesturing to the living room as she took to the stairs. I nodded and entered, perching myself on the edge of their sofa. From above, I could hear voices, Susan's and a deep one belonging to Jim. It sounded like she was waking him.

As I waited, my eye was drawn to the mantelpiece above the fireplace. Pictures of Susan in her wedding dress, from maybe two or three years ago. Besides that, one of Susan, Jim and a young girl. The daughter posed between the two adults, but the girl leant ever so slightly towards her mother. Again, the picture looked recent. It told me they were a new family, and the daughter wasn't sure of Jim.

Footsteps came down the stairs. 'He'll be down in a minute. He's still a little sore.' She said when she joined me in the living room.

'From what I heard he was very lucky. You look like a really nice family.' I gestured towards the mantelpiece.

Susan smiled. 'Our wedding was eighteen months ago.'

'I see.'

'I married young, my daughter's father was a bad boy – you know the type all teenage girls are attracted to.' I smiled but didn't pass comment. 'Anyway, it all fell apart when my daughter, April, was three. He lives in France now, tries to come back a couple of times a year.'

'Are April and Jim close?'

'At first, no. Jim is sweet, he likes to listen, offer support. He's a really kind man. I'm not saying April's dad isn't kind, but Jim is attentive and sensitive. She found it a little – um, I can't think of the word.'

'Intense?' I offered.

She relaxed. 'Yes, intense.'

'But not now?'

'No. When Jim was forced to…' She didn't finish her sentence. She didn't need to.

From behind, a male voice spoke. 'Susan, love,' he said, his voice tired and sore as he limped towards her and gave her a hug before sitting down.

'Jim, take it easy. You should have shouted; I would have helped you down the stairs,' she said, helping him raise his left leg and place it on a pouffe.

'Mr Weston…' I began, trying not to stare at the bandage on his head, the bruises creeping under the bottom, extending towards his jaw. 'I'm so sorry to disturb you this late.'

'It's OK,' he smiled, several teeth were missing; it looked painful.

'Thank you for taking the time to talk.'

'Susan tells me you're the copper who was in that video, the one he spoke about?'

'I am.'

'But you're not working the case?'

'I'm not.'

'It might be the medication – it's made me a bit hazy – but I don't understand.'

'I want to stop this man. And I've been close,' I said. I told him what happened that night on the footbridge after he had been taken to hospital.

'Is that how you got that bruise?'

'Yes.'

'And then you nearly saved that man in the water?'

'Nearly, yes.'

'How did you know?'

'He's leaving clues, so far, I've been mostly able to work them out,' I said, not mentioning that I'd failed to work out the last one.

'I see. So it's a game you two are playing?'

'I guess you could say that. But I don't want to play at all. I want this to stop.'

'So how can I help? The police have already taken my initial statement from the hospital.'

'I want to know what happened *before* Lucas arrived.'

'Who?'

'The other Player. The kid.'

'Lucas. You know, they wouldn't tell me his name at the hospital. Well,' he paused to shift his weight and get comfortable, 'I don't know what else I can say. I found him on the ground, at first I thought he was hurt, until he rolled over and I saw the helmet.'

Jim related how The Host revealed himself. How Lucas walked past with a girl, and Jim had had to hide The Host from sight. When Lucas returned on his own, The Game began.

'He hid on the footbridge?' I asked. 'How?'

'He cowered beside me; I used my body to block him from view. I don't know why I didn't do something. I should have,' he said, as he began to choke on his own words. Susan rubbed her husband's shoulder, telling him he hadn't done anything wrong, and I waited, permitting the man his need to cry. Afterwards, he blew his nose and apologised.

'Don't be sorry, Mr Weston. And don't second-guess yourself. You handled the situation better than anyone else could have.'

'But—'

'In a game where someone had to die, no one did.'

'But the boy, I could have stopped him seeing it.'

'The boy is alive because of you, and he will get the help he needs after what's happened. None of it was your fault, love,' Susan said.

'Mr Weston,' I continued, 'I'm struggling to picture the scene. You said The Host hid on the bridge. How was he not spotted?'

'I blocked him from view. It wasn't hard because of his stature.'

'His stature?'

'Yes, he was smaller than me.'

'How tall are you, Mr Weston?'

'Five ten-ish.'

'And you say he was shorter?'

'Yes, a good five inches, I'd say.'

'Are you sure about the height?'

'Yes, a hundred per cent.'

Something didn't seem right about what Jim was saying. A knot formed in my stomach. 'Is there anything else you can tell me?'

'No, not really. He stopped the kid when he was on his own, the rest is in the video. I'm sorry I'm not much help.'

'No, Mr Weston, you are, you've made a huge difference in the case.'

'But you're no closer.'

'Maybe not, but the public perception has changed because of you,' I replied, praying that was still true after the latest hope-destroying video. 'You're a hero, Mr Weston. You saved a boy's life a few nights ago. Never forget that.'

He smiled. 'Thank you.'

I stood to leave, thanking both Jim and Susan profusely for their time, given the late hour and circumstances. As I stepped outside into the frigid air, I turned back to Susan, who had walked me to the door.

'Susan, thank you for allowing me into your home.'

She fixed me with a hard stare. 'Just stop this guy.'

'I intend to.'

As I walked away, the knot in my stomach wouldn't shift. In my mind, The Host was taller, taller than me. I was sure of it when I chased him. In light of Jim's story, I had to ask myself: had I projected Grayson James onto my depiction of The Host? I quickly dismissed it. No, my first instinct was right. I thought back to when I nearly caught him by the footbridge – he was definitely bigger than me, not the diminutive figure Jim had described.

It didn't make sense, but before I could understand why, the burner phone buzzed. A text from Howard.

Call me when you can. New developments to discuss.

CHAPTER FIFTY-TWO

10.08 p.m.

As I approached my house, I saw Sam's car had gone. Or rather, I had driven her away. Walking into an empty house felt strange. I threw my coat on the end of the banister; it slid off and fell to the floor but I didn't pick it up, I didn't have the energy. Although I knew Sam wasn't going to be there, I hoped she would be at the breakfast bar when I walked into the kitchen. But of course she wasn't. Sam was gone, as she had warned. I was destroying my marriage as I destroyed my career. I was hurtling further and further on a downward spiral which would soon spit me out at rock bottom.

Taking a seat, I rested my heavy head in my hand and watched Bob swim. I didn't blame Sam for leaving. I loved that about my wife, she was true to her word. She had a clear sense of what was right and wrong, which was everything I had been lacking these past few weeks. I could have sat there all night, my head in my hands, wallowing. But what would it achieve? Sam wouldn't come home, and I wouldn't be any closer to stopping The Host. There was time for self-pity but it wasn't now. I forced myself onto my feet, and walked over to the sink to splash my face with cold water. I felt more alert once I had, and that was when I saw a note waiting for me on the side.

I've gone to stay at Mum's for a bit. Please think about why you are doing this.

If you change your mind, you know where I'll be – your side of the bed will be waiting. I love you,

S X

The idea of being in a warm bed, the duvet pulled high, the arm of the person I loved wrapped around me, and a full night's sleep was tempting, more than that. I knew if I called, said I was on my way, Sam would wait up. Despite being upset and angry with me, I knew she loved me as much as I did her. One quick call and I would feel safe. But I knew I wasn't going to call, not her anyway. Instead, I rang Howard back. After three rings, he answered. No pleasantries, no greeting.

'We've found the sixth crime scene. Both dead.'

'Shit.' I knew from seeing the film, they were likely both badly injured, but both dead? That was new. In all the games, someone survived – they had to be alive to keep the story living forever. With both Players dying, it explained why there was no phone call, and why the video was posted online a lot earlier than the others had been. But I had to wonder, what would that mean for the Host?

'Where did you find them?'

'In the basement of a closed-down coffee shop, on Bridge Street.'

'Bridge Street – that's where the news footage was coming from.'

'Yep, one hundred or so feet from the crowds.'

That was what I could hear in the video, the faint noise in the background. It was the crowds on the streets nearby. The Host said he was going to crush hope – when the world knew they were celebrating so close to where The Game was being played, hope would indeed be dead. He was right under dozens of police officers, literally. And no one knew.

'Karen, the basement was under refurbishment. Debris everywhere.'

'I could see in the video.'

'It's not confirmed, but that rock – the one at the rowing lake – looks like it was from here.'

'Fuck.'

'Yeah, fuck. Did you speak to Jim Weston?'

'Yeah.'

'Anything?'

'Maybe. If you can, could you check the other CCTV footage from the library? I can't see how tall The Host is in either the Chinese or the footbridge incidents. It's not clear.'

'Sure. Why?'

'I got a sense of him being taller than me. Five ten-ish, but Jim Weston said he was small in stature and thought he was about five five.'

'OK, I'll have a look.'

'It might be nothing.'

'I gotta go, Bradshaw is here. I'll message later.'

'Don't tell him we've spoken. If the height discrepancy comes up, say you had a hunch, the idea can't come from me. I was supposed to go to him with any ideas, but...'

'Yeah, how would you explain to him you'd been to see Jim Weston? Don't worry, I've got your back.'

Howard hung up, and I started digging through my messages from him, bringing up the CCTV footage he had sent me from the Chinese takeaway again. I was missing something. I watched him: the swaying, the preparing, he reached up and turned on his GoPro with his right hand. I pulled up the CCTV footage from beside the footbridge. Did his build look different from before? It was hard to tell in the low light and poor-quality picture.

Trying again, I looked at the GoPro image The Host had posted after both crimes, trying to see if one was from a higher vantage point than the other. In both videos the image sprang to life when he reached up to his helmet to turn on the camera. Taking a screenshot of the first moments in both videos I compared the pictures. I hoped to confirm my thoughts, but again, it was impossible to tell.

I was just about to give up, when I noticed something different in the two pictures. In the Chinese, The Host's right hand was in the first shot, captured as he lifted it down after turning on the camera. In the second his left featured. Going back to the CCTV videos I watched them both again. At the Chinese, he turned on the GoPro with his right hand, pulled the weapons out of the bag with his right hand, laid them down using his right hand. On the bridge, the order was the same, but even in the low light, I could see the hand was different. Left every time.

The difference in behaviour, the height discrepancy, the difference in the hand used. We weren't looking at someone with two personalities. We weren't looking at someone who was feeling the pressure of public perception.

We were looking at two different people.

Closing the videos, I went to call Bradshaw but stopped myself. I shouldn't have seen the CCTV footage and would likely get in deeper shit. Instead, I messaged Howard. This had to go through him.

> Get Jenny from profiling to draw up a character of The Host from the footbridge – forget the other videos, just the footbridge. I'll explain when we talk.

After I hit send, I went back to looking at the videos. Trying to find something else that was staring at me and I'd missed. Now I had worked it out, it was obvious they weren't the same person – to me, anyway.

Despite the latest crime being the most horrific and only a few hours old, I kept coming back to the Fourth on the bridge. I watched The Host pace, wipe his hands. I could almost hear him talking to himself inside the motorbike helmet. If I had to choose one word to describe him, that word would be conflicted.

If it was another person entirely, like my gut was telling me, and if they were still conflicted, I could use that. I had to find them first or get them to come to me. It was a big if, and with that came a big risk. If I could pull on their doubt, make them feel safe and understood – if I could give them a way out – I could use that to find the other. The real Host.

I knew what I had to do. I knew it would no doubt cost me my job but I had no choice. I could be wrong about all of it, but if there was even a one per cent chance I was right and there *was* a second person involved, I had to try.

Logging into my Facebook, I tapped the upload button, changed the format from a picture to a video, and began to record.

DAY 7

9 February 2019

'BLOOD BROTHERS' TRAGIC END. THE HOST STRIKES AGAIN, CRUSHING HOPE FOR THE CITY OF PETERBOROUGH

The City of Peterborough is in a state of shock after a moment of hope quickly turned to terror as The Host committed the sixth terrifying and brutal attack on the city and its people. Following the death and subsequent video of **John Stroud**, the people of Peterborough participated in a vigil in the city centre as a sign of defiance at the time The Host stated the next 'Game' would be played.

At 8.24 p.m. – twenty-four minutes after The Host's stipulated time – there had been no indication his crime had taken place. As the city began to celebrate, The Host posted his latest video showing the attack on two young men, brothers Nistor and Rusu Hofer.

The Host also took the opportunity to directly address **DI Karen Holt** who took to social media to respond in an attempt to stop The Host continuing his rampage on the city. In her **video message**, she said:

'I know there is a part of you that doesn't want to do this, a part of The Host that believes this is wrong. A part that has doubts. I am speaking to you. Reach out, let us help you, let's work together to stop this. You know where I am, so find me.'

Her message has been seen over 100,000 times on social media. DI Holt and Cambridge Constabulary have yet to comment.

Amanda Belkin > Peterborough Free Discussion

Has anyone else seen that video? What the hell is that police officer thinking?!?

Johnny Ormo

She is going to end up dead.

Jack Anderson

I think she is being clever, trying to appease him in a way he understands.

Amanda Belkin

What do you mean, **Jack**?

Jack Anderson

Well, he likes a big audience, doesn't he? I think she knew if she posted anything, especially after she was named, it would go viral. It's had like, what, 100,000 views or something. I bet he has watched if for sure, and who knows? It might make him stop.

Johnny Ormo

Of course it won't. This guy is a psycho. I agree with **Amanda**. All Karen Holt has done is make herself vulnerable. She's gonna end up dead if she's not careful.

Claire Turner

At least she is trying.

Amanda Belkin

But it was desperate, don't you think? There is no way he is gonna hand himself in.

Claire Turner

I agree, but what else could she do?

Johnny Ormo

Keep quiet, let the police do their job.

Jack Anderson

She is the police.

Claire Turner

Guys, has anyone seen **Emily**? Is she OK?

Jack Anderson

Emily left the group last night.

Claire Turner

What?

Jack Anderson

I messaged her after, you know, it happened, and she sounded broken. She said she was responsible, because it was her idea to defy him.

Michaela Balfour

No, he was going to do it regardless of what we did. Her idea gave us hope.

Johnny Ormo

But now what? Last night we had hope, we arranged a congregation of people, in the middle of town, and he still killed right under our noses. Where I stood last night was within fifty metres of where he played. Fifty. How can you stop someone who can do something like that so close to so many people?

Jack Anderson

I was close too. I saw the body bags coming out.

Amanda Belkin

Jesus!

Jack Anderson

Yeah, Jesus. This guy could literally pick off anyone if he wanted.

Claire Turner

I agree. None of us are safe.

Johnny Ormo

Me too. That's why I think that police officer, Karen Holt, is going to get herself killed.

CHAPTER FIFTY-THREE

10.14 a.m.

Bradshaw had seen my video and I had been summoned. Walking into work felt a lot like it had the day after Grayson James died: the sideways looks from colleagues who knew, quiet whispering when they thought I was out of earshot. I knew I was putting my neck on the chopping block when I posted that video on Facebook last night. But it was for the right reasons – I just hoped Bradshaw would see it that way. I know I should have spoken with him first, but I hadn't wanted him trying to stop me.

Just before I reached Bradshaw's office door, a hand grabbed my arm and pulled me towards a quiet corridor outside the buzzing incident room.

'Karen, what the fuck?'

'Howard, let me explain.'

'You have any idea how much shit you are in?'

'Yeah, I suspect a bit.'

'A bit? The whole fucking world has seen it. You're gonna get yourself sacked. Or worse, Karen.'

'I can explain.'

'You bloody need to, because it looks like you've got a death wish.'

'Howard, you know the height discrepancy I ask you to have a look at – it's not one person with conflicting personalities, it's two people.'

'*What?*'

'In the CCTV videos, one is right dominant, one is left. I didn't notice until Jim Weston raised the height difference. There are *two* of them.'

'Are you sure?'

'Yes, I am, and I think Jenny will agree. Have you spoken with her yet?'

'No, not yet.'

From behind I heard someone clear their voice, and when I turned, Bradshaw was leaning in the doorway. He didn't say anything but raised his eyebrows and walked back towards his office.

'Shit, I'd better go.'

'Yeah.'

'Before I do… did you find the train image?'

'Yeah. I'll fill you in later.'

Head down, I walked back toward Bradshaw's office and tapped lightly on the door.

'Come in. Close the door, take a seat,' he said, not looking away from his computer screen. I did as instructed, readying myself for the bollocking I was about to receive. After a moment, Bradshaw looked up, sighed, dropping his shoulders. I assumed he'd not been home since it all began.

'Sir, are you all right?'

'Just…' he hesitated.

334

'I'll be quiet.'

'Yes, please, thank you,' he said with an air of defeat. 'I have watched you, Karen, right from when you started as a bobby to the day you passed your exams and became a detective – a thumping good one, I might add. I know it's not been easy for you, with the demotion and now the IOPC investigation, but I need you to know, I am always in your corner.'

'Thank you, sir.'

'You have a good gut for policing, you see the things others don't. So I didn't want to assume the worst when I saw this.' He turned his computer screen, to show my Facebook video. 'DI Holt, do you want to explain what the bloody hell you were thinking?'

'Sir, I know what it looks like.'

'Do you really?' he asked earnestly.

'I can explain.'

'It better be bloody good.'

I told Bradshaw exactly what I told Howard.

'Are you sure? Two people?'

'Yes, sir, I think so.'

'And how did you come by all this information?' he asked, unblinking.

Shit.

'You've seen the CCTV footage, I'm assuming?'

'Yes, sir. I have seen some of them.'

'How exactly have *you* identified the height discrepancy when I've got an office full of people combing through it all, dozens of times, without reaching that conclusion?'

'Sir, I…'

'This morning Rawlinson has spoken with Mr and Mrs

Weston, and although Mrs Weston didn't say so outright, Rawlinson believed they have already been spoken with. I wonder how that could be possible, DI Holt?'

I opened my mouth to say something, protest my innocence, justify my actions, but the words wouldn't come.

'And now I'm going to ask about your face. Besides visiting Jim Weston, just how closely involved have you got yourself?'

'Too close, sir.'

'Jesus wept,' Bradshaw said, getting up and moving towards his window.

'It wasn't something I planned.'

'Wasn't it?' he asked, snapping his attention back to me.

'No, sir, that's the truth. I promise.'

'I just don't know what to believe anymore.' He held my gaze until I looked away, ashamed of how bad it had all got, and all behind his back. 'But I did specifically state that if you had any ideas you should come directly to me.'

'I know, sir. I forced DS Carlson to share with me and, once he had, I was worried if I came to you with my ideas, he would get into trouble. It's all my doing, sir, and I take full responsibility for it. I messed up.'

Bradshaw sat back in his chair, rubbing his hands through his hair. 'I'm assuming you've asked for corroboration on your theory of it being two people?'

'Sir, I—'

'Yes or no?'

'Howard asked Jenny in profiling.'

'You are making this very difficult for me, DI Holt.'

'Sir, I miss my job, I miss the work I do. The Host is making people kill; I can't help but want to stop him.'

Bradshaw nodded towards me; I hated seeing the disappointment in his eyes.

'Because of your little stunt with the video, I'm getting pushed from the very top, and I mean, the very top. The IOPC are considering your dismissal.'

'I'm sorry, sir. I just want to stop this guy.'

'We *all* want to stop him, but no one else is popping up all over the internet, calling him out, are they?'

'No, sir.'

'It was reckless. You've put yourself in danger. From today, there will be a police protection officer with you at all times.'

'Even at my house?'

'Even *in* your house.'

'Inside my house, no, sir—'

'What choice have you left me? You have a target on your back now, Karen. Do you not understand? You'll be escorted home, and then two PPOs will be stationed with you. It's either that, or we send you away entirely.'

'Sir, please, don't ground me, we are so close—'

'DI Holt, it's decided. Is Sam at home?'

'No, sir, she's with her mother.'

'We'll send someone to collect her too.'

'Sir, leave Sam out of this.'

'DI Holt, I don't need to remind you how dangerous this man is. Sam is in this because you are. She needs protecting too.'

'Please, sir—'

'Karen,' he warned, leaning back in his chair and removing his glasses. He rubbed his eyes, the exhaustion clear on his face. When he spoke again, his voice sounded fragile, like it might crack at any moment. 'This has come from way above me.'

I slumped back in my chair, mirroring Bradshaw, and covered my face with my hands. Bradshaw assumed I was trying not to show I was crying and shifted awkwardly. I didn't want to cry, I wanted to scream, I wanted to tell him they could do whatever they felt necessary, I wasn't walking away. But I would lose my job, and possibly Sam. I'd already done enough damage driving Sam away and now the police were going to turn up at her mum's house.

'Karen, I really wish it didn't have to be like this, I really do, but you've brought it on yourself,' Bradshaw offered sympathetically.

There was a tap at the door, and after being ushered in by Bradshaw, a young uniformed officer took one small step inside. 'Ah, your lift has arrived. Will you give us a moment, please? DI Holt will be right out.'

The young officer nodded and backed out of the door, too nervous to speak.

'They get younger and younger,' Bradshaw said, trying to smile and lighten the mood.

'Yes, they do.'

'Karen, promise me you'll not do anything stupid?'

I didn't reply but nodded. 'Sir, Howard was only talking with me at my insistence.'

'DS Carlson is his own person. He could have said no, despite how insistent you can be.'

'He was only looking out for me, sir.'

Bradshaw sighed. 'He is on thin ice, I hope you realise that.'

'I understand, sir.'

'Now, get out of here. No more recklessness. I can't stop you thinking, so if you have any ideas, you get one of the officers who will be posted at yours to contact me. Say your thoughts, but that's it. No groundwork, no investigating and for God's sake, no more videos. Understood?'

'Yes, sir, can I just apologise to Howard before I go?'

'Make it quick.'

I left the office, beelining for Howard, who was startled at me approaching.

'Bradshaw knows we've been speaking. Tell him everything we've talked about.'

'What about you?'

'Bradshaw thinks I'm in danger, so I've now got PPOs and am under the strictest orders not to leave the house. It's shit.'

'But he's right. You need to be careful.'

'Before I go, tell me about the train symbol.'

'It's dark green.'

'Aren't they usually black?'

'Yep, but this one is green, and in the smoke there was an image, a lion. It's the logo for the army cadets.'

'Are you sure?'

'It's pretty similar.'

'It seems too obvious.'

'Maybe he's taking larger risks. He really thinks no one can stop him.'

'Or he's getting lazy?' I said, aware of the young officer behind me wanting to move me on. 'There are only so many places connected to the cadets. Find him, stop him, Howard.'

From behind I heard Bradshaw clear his voice. He stood in his doorway, arms crossed. He gestured with a nod for

Howard to join him before walking back inside, the door left open.

'Be careful, OK?'

'I will. Take it easy, Karen. See you on the other side.'

I wanted to hug him, but eyes were watching – Rawlinson's beady little pair amongst them – so I gave him a nod.

'DI Holt?' the young officer interrupted.

'I'm ready. Let's go,' I said as I began making my way to the parking bay. As I got into the passenger seat of the car, and we pulled away, I looked back at the station that had been my second home for over a decade, not knowing if I would ever be allowed back.

CHAPTER FIFTY-FOUR

The Host

10.53 a.m.

Playing with his little pipe-cleaner figurine, bending her limbs unnaturally, he imagined it was in fact a voodoo doll, and with each manipulation parts of Karen Holt were breaking. Sadly, it wasn't true, but a nice thought regardless. Drawing it close to his face, he spoke to it.

'Very soon, you and I shall meet, properly. I'm excited, Karen, can you feel it? A deep, internal buzz of our inevitable coming together. You caught me off guard before. Next time, I'll be ready. Next time, I'll be waiting for you.'

Pulling the figurine closer, he tweaked its head, making it perfect.

'I hope you're thinking of me as much as I'm thinking of you.'

He set it down carefully, sat back in his chair and sighed. He had to be patient – timing was everything, more so now than ever because of Karen Holt. She would play, when it was time, and to help, he had to use the girl again. She wasn't to be trusted to facilitate The Game, not after Jim Weston. But her observational skills were useful to him. His instruction to her had been clear – which house to watch, to not be seen or engage with anyone, and to pose as a homeless person again to keep the low profile she had perfected over recent weeks. He had entrusted her to leave the train stencil in a place he'd specified. She had a lot to prove, so he didn't doubt she would meticulously stencil it in the exact spot.

The next Game had begun, and he would show Karen Holt that she would never be as smart as him.

He reached to pick up fresh pipe cleaners, but remembered that both Players had died in the surprising and challenging Sixth Game. He knew they would fight. Besides Jim Weston, who would have if he'd been there and not the girl, they all fight. But both of them dying wasn't what he expected. He expected the younger to live and the older brother to sacrifice himself. And as much as the outcome was good for crushing hope in the audience, it annoyed him that there would be no one to join the others on the shelf. No one to understand him, to be like him. The death of both his Sixth Players was yet another deviation from his plan, his vision. But he pushed the annoyance down. Because the Seventh Game was in motion and would be his best work yet.

CHAPTER FIFTY-FIVE

11.49 a.m.

As we arrived home, I had tried to ask the young officer, Kane, to wait outside as I needed a moment to clean, but he insisted he was under the strictest orders from Bradshaw not to let me out of his sight. I reluctantly showed Kane to my living room before walking into the kitchen to tidy up.

As I washed up the single mug and breakfast bowl, I thought about calling Sam to forewarn her she would be visited by the police, but I suspected they had already made contact. I also wanted to beg for forgiveness for placing her in such a shit situation. I didn't want to talk to Kane, so I busied myself in the kitchen by filling a jug and watering two plants on the windowsill. Once the jug was empty, I washed it and placed it on the draining board before reaching for the fish food. Pinching a few flakes, I opened the top of the tank to sprinkle it in.

'Hey, Bo—'

I stopped short. The flakes fell from my fingers onto my shoes and the kitchen floor. Inside the tank, belly up, floated the fish from the night Sam proposed.

343

The air seemed to stop, the world had become mute, all that existed was me, and the dead fish. And from somewhere deep in my stomach, a rising tide of grief that wanted to burst. I thought about that magical night when Sam and I had been so happy. Straw under our feet, the air above our heads lit with a thousand lightbulbs from rides and stalls. The smell of candyfloss.

It was just a fish, just a stupid little fish that had way outlived its life expectancy, and yet, despite knowing that, I began to cry. I was crying because Grayson James resisted arrest. I was crying because I was the one who took James to the ground. I was crying because a man was terrorising the city and I couldn't help myself. I couldn't cope with a room full of people. I couldn't ring my own mother through fear she would see straight through the front I'd been putting up. Worst of all, I had pushed away the one woman who'd stood by me throughout. As the tears fell, the front door opened, and I heard Sam's voice.

'Please do not follow me – I understand why you're here but we still need our own space and privacy,' she said as she kicked off her shoes and stormed into the kitchen.

'Karen, I hope you realise they just—'

She froze mid-sentence.

'Karen?' she said quietly, tentatively taking a step closer. I didn't move. 'Karen?' she repeated. Her tender, urgent tone was too much, and I lowered my head to my chest and began to sob. 'What's happened?' Sam glanced in the direction I was facing and saw Bob. 'Oh, love.'

'We got him on the night you proposed.'

'I remember.' She stepped towards me, wrapped her arms around me and I sobbed even more.

'Sam, I'm so sorry. I'm a mess, and I don't know how to make it better. Are we in trouble? Because of what I've done, how I've been?'

'That night, at the fair, when we won Bob, when I got down on one knee and asked you to be my wife, I wanted to be with you to share all the best moments together.'

'I get it.'

'But –' Sam continued, cutting me off – 'I also wanted to be there for the harder times too. I wanted to marry you because I want to share it all, good and bad, with you.'

'I'm scared that we are—'

'Karen, nothing will stop me loving you. Not even all of this.'

'He is dead, because of me.'

'Karen, I know we're not talking about the fish. Grayson is dead because he made a choice. He forced you to respond.'

'I could have not stepped in to arrest him.'

'And do nothing when Howard was in danger? If you hadn't, you wouldn't have been doing your job.'

'I could have stayed on my feet, not gone to the ground.'

'Your training states you need to go to the ground, doesn't it? Karen, look at me.'

I met Sam's gaze and she reached out to catch the tears that fell onto my cheek, wiping them away with her thumbs. 'You did nothing wrong. Nothing. You can crush yourself with guilt, or you can accept that it was a tragic accident, deal with it and move on. You are in charge of that.'

'But a man died because of something I did.'

'He did, yes, he did die. But you can't let this define you and the career you love. You have to find a way to get past it.'

'I just want to make it better, that's all I want to do.'

'I know, love. I know.' She kissed me on the forehead and pulled me closer. 'We'll get through this together.'

Kane cleared his throat in the doorway, and Sam turned to face him. I looked down at the floor. The other officer who had accompanied Sam home stood awkwardly behind.

'Sorry to interrupt. We think it would be best if we based ourselves in the kitchen.'

'Yes, of course, can you give us a moment?' Sam said. Kane gave a nod, stepping back.

'Sam, I'm really sorry for doing this to you. I know I've messed things up by trying to stop The Host. I just thought if I did, it would make me feel OK again.'

'I understand, and can I tell you a secret? If it was the other way around, if it was me, I might be trying to stop The Host too.'

'Really?' I said, fresh tears beginning to well.

'Really. Soon The Host will be caught and the IOPC investigation will be over and you'll be free to return to work. This will all just be a bad memory we can look back on when we are old.'

'I hope you're right.'

'It will be, I promise. Get out of your uniform; if we are under house arrest, we should at least be comfy. Go on, I'll sort out in here,' Sam said, walking to the cupboard under the sink, retrieving a small net. Despite me having been a police officer for so long, and having seen so much in that time, I couldn't watch her put Bob in the bin. I left the room, coming eye to eye with the police officer who'd brought Sam home. A face I knew, PC Jake Sommers.

'Hello, DI Holt,' he said politely.

I didn't reply, but gave him a nod and went upstairs. In our bedroom I looked outside on the street. A few people milled around, curious as to why there were two police cars outside our property. I closed the curtains, hoping that if I blocked out the world, I would also shut out the Host. Of course, deep down I knew that wasn't going to happen.

CHAPTER FIFTY-SIX

The Host

4.42 p.m.

'You can go now; I'll be there imminently.'

'Shall I wait until you get here?'

'No, that won't be necessary. You've done what I've asked, now the Seventh Player has arrived, I have no need for you to stay.'

'But—'

The Host hung up, he didn't have time to mollify her. She had done what he needed; it was now time for him to take over. Grabbing his rucksack and helmet, he made his way to the door. A message pinged through. It was the girl again, infuriatingly. Once he had shared everything with her, but now she had become all but obsolete. Removing his phone, he read her message.

Two other people have arrived, a woman and a little girl? Were you expecting this?

No.

Will it cause any trouble?

He smiled to himself, their arrival was unexpected, but he could use that to his advantage.

In fact, all being well, it will guarantee the outcome I want.

CHAPTER FIFTY-SEVEN

7.58 p.m.

After dinner, we found ourselves in the living room and the officers stayed in the kitchen. It didn't take them long to relax enough to make their own cup of tea, which helped us settle too. Still, not an ideal way to spend an evening together.

'This is a bit shit.'

'But it won't always be like this, will it?' Sam offered, taking my hand in hers. Sam was right, it wouldn't be forever. One way or another, they would catch The Host. I still hoped he had slipped up, or was blinded by his own arrogance with the last clue. I hoped I'd get a call from Howard, telling me he was in custody, it was over, they had beaten him at his own game. And the IOPC investigation would come to an end, the words definitive in black and white, declaring my innocence, or guilt. I smiled to Sam, squeezed her hand and looked back to the TV. Jake popped his head into the living room.

'DI Holt, Ms Clarence.'

'Please, it's Sam.'

'Sam, would either of you like a cuppa?'

'Thank you, Jake. I'm assuming you have been instructed to stay all night?'

'I'm afraid so, ma'am.'

Jake turned on his heels and made his way to the kitchen to join Kane.

'Well, I never thought we'd be bringing men home.'

'Oh Sam. I'm so—'

'Enough.' She cut me off. 'It was a joke, it's done, besides, it could almost be like a mini-break, right? I mean, we can't do anything but watch TV, read, talk. It will be kinda nice. Look at us, curled up on a sofa, in our pyjamas with two police officers who look like kids in the kitchen. We *are* getting old. I swear, if we end up watching *MacGyver*…'

I smiled. 'I love that even when things are at their worst, you still manage to see some light. Thank you.'

With a fresh cup of tea in our hands, courtesy of Jake, and the living-room door closed for a bit of privacy and normality, it was nice to have some much-needed downtime together. We were only half paying attention to the TV playing in the background, some drama about homelessness. As I sipped my tea, my eye glanced upon a young woman whose character had escaped a violent home and had taken to the streets. It reminded me of the two homeless girls I had seen recently.

Then, that familiar, intuitive tug stirred from within. I jumped up, moving quickly to the kitchen. As I entered, both officers sat up straight.

'DI Holt, is everything all right?'

'I need to get hold of Superintendent Bradshaw. It's urgent.'

'Yes, ma'am, use this,' he said, handing over his mobile.

I took the phone and rang Bradshaw's office direct. He had barely said his name when I told him my thoughts.

'Sir, I saw a homeless girl close to the Chinese, and then another along the river on the night John Stroud died. Sir, it's the same girl, *she* is the second Host. The girl was out there, she's vulnerable, she can be reached.'

'Are you sure it was the same girl?'

'Yes, sir, I am. She isn't sleeping rough, she's posing as someone who is – to watch.'

'Why pose as someone homeless?'

'Because people don't see the homeless, do they?'

'OK, what does she look like? We can get officers out there to try and find her.'

'Sir, I know this is going to sound strange, but I can't shake the feeling she is young, like a college kid.'

'A college kid?'

'Yes, sir. No older than eighteen.'

'How sure are you?'

'I can't be a hundred per cent. She looked young, really young. She's just a kid.'

'OK. We'll get onto it, put out a plea for anyone who knows anything. Reassure her she can come to us discreetly, and if she helps, she will be protected.'

'But don't make out that we know there is more than one of them doing this.'

'Agreed, we'll keep that close for now. When we have anything, I will make sure you know.'

'Thank you, sir. Good luck.'

The line went dead, and I handed the phone back to Jake.

CHAPTER FIFTY-EIGHT

The Host

9.04 p.m.

It was time to play the Seventh Game.

The woman and the child had stayed. Perfect. He had more than enough leverage to ensure his Players followed the rules of The Game. They would play against each other, for their daughter. The only problem he had was getting inside. He knew from a quick Google search that DS Howard Carlson was ex-army. He knew that he'd not stand a chance against him, not without leverage. So he had to lure him out for a while. Removing his mobile, he unlocked it, and dialled the freephone number the police had dedicated for information about him.

'I need to speak to DI Karen Holt,' he said when the line connected. There was hesitation on the other end. The mechanical voice-altering device made him instantly recognisable.

'I'll put you through,' the call handler eventually said. After a moment, the line connected to the police. Before they could finish their sentence, he cut in.

'This is The Host, get me DI Holt.'

On the other end of the phone, the officer panicked. He dropped the receiver, fumbled to pick it up, then he said he would put him on hold just for a moment, to connect with someone in the office. Thirty seconds later, another voice came onto the phone.

'Where is Holt?'

'She is indisposed.' He knew she had gone; he had seen with his own eyes she was under house arrest when he stood outside her home, with a few other onlookers, as she closed her bedroom curtains.

'Who is this?'

'This is Superintendent Bradshaw. You can speak with me in her absence.'

'No.'

'I assure you, it's fine.'

'If Karen Holt is indisposed, I will speak with DS Howard Carlson. I'll call back in thirty minutes; if he is not there, someone will die.'

Hanging up the phone, The Host sat back and waited. It didn't take long for the lights to come on upstairs in the house. He watched DS Howard Carlson put on a fresh shirt. Minutes later, Carlson stepped out of his front door, closing it quietly behind him, before dashing to the car, firing up the engine and driving away. He would be at the station within fifteen to twenty minutes.

Satisfied he wouldn't return, The Host approached the house. Crossing the deserted road, he confidently walked up the garden path, and rang the doorbell. A light flicked on in the hallway, and the woman opened the door. She started to ask if he had forgotten his keys, assuming it would be Carlson. Before she could react to seeing the motorbike helmet, he slammed into the door, knocking her back into the house. She hit the floor hard, tried to scramble to her feet, but he climbed on her, forcing her back to the ground. With one hand on her mouth, the other pinning down one of her arms, he whispered for her to be quiet.

'If you scream, the child will die.'

She nodded, tears streaming down her terrified face.

'Good, let's make a phone call, shall we?'

CHAPTER FIFTY-NINE

Carlson

9.15 p.m.

Carlson was driving at close to eighty miles an hour along the dual carriageway that cut through the heart of the city. The roads were quiet, and he swerved round those who were out and abiding the speed limit. His phone rang, and Becca's caller ID came up on his dashboard display.

'Howard, you need to come back,' Becca said, sounding distraught.

'Becca, I need to be in, that maniac—'

'Jess has hurt herself.'

'What? What's happened?'

'She fell out of bed,' Becca said between sobs. 'She is really hurt. Come home, I'm freaking out.'

'OK, I'm coming, is she conscious?'

'No. I can't get her to wake up.'

'OK, try not to panic. Is she breathing?'

'Yes.'

'Ring an ambulance, I'm coming.'

Carlson knew that The Host calling in was important, but Jess was more so, and without hesitating he spun the car around, and began to head for home.

THE SEVENTH GAME

DS Howard Carlson pulled up on the drive and, barely raising the handbrake, he jumped out and let himself into the house. Inside, it was dark, and quiet. He sensed straight away that something was wrong. Becca should have been shouting for him. Lights should be on. Something had happened, but it wasn't that Jess had hurt herself. The instinct was confirmed when he saw a small patch of blood on the floor by the front door. Jess couldn't have hurt herself there, could she? As a parent he was worried. He wanted to call out, find his daughter. But something was clearly wrong and he knew he needed to stay calm and use his training. The discipline, emotional detachment, and if needed, the ruthlessness he knew he had in him came to the surface. Taking three tentative steps towards the stairs, a voice rang out from the living room. Not a word, nothing intelligible, but a sob. Becca.

Three steps in the other direction, and he was in the doorway to the living room. With his hands raised, he took the fourth and fifth step to enter. The room was empty. Another sob came from beyond the double doors that led to the extension out back. In the shadows of the room, he could just about make out the shape of something – it was too tall to be Becca. Again, he wanted to call out, but refrained. As the rest of the room came into focus, he could see what the shape was. Becca was standing on a chair, blood on her face. Her mouth had something stuffed inside and had been stuck shut with tape. He could see the rope around her neck that was attached to the exposed wooden beam that ran across the ceiling. The rope was thick, and even in the low light, he could tell it was tied correctly and wouldn't fail.

Carlson raised his fingers to his lips, telling Becca to keep quiet. She nodded back, understanding, and he took his eye from her to scan the room, looking to find Jess. From the furthest corner, the darkest space of the room the shape of The Host stepped out. Carlson assessed his height; close to six feet tall, this wasn't the second, unsure version – the one he could reason with, talk down. It was him, the real Host, in his home. And in his arms, his hand clamped around her small head, was Jess. His other hand wielded a hammer. Jess was sobbing, and Carlson could see she had wet herself. Carlson's stomach dropped, and he wanted to be sick, only the soldier in him stopped that happening.

His training took over. Assess. Understand. Act.

'You don't have to hurt her,' Carlson said calmly, trying to hold The Host's eye through the darkened motorbike helmet visor.

'And I won't, if you and your lovely partner play a game with me.'

'Let her go, and I'll play whatever you want.'

The Host laughed, the voice-altering device making him sound much more sinister.

'No, DS Carlson, I think I'll hang onto her.'

'Just don't hurt her.'

'You have my word. I know what you think will come next, but this time it's different. You see a runaway train moving toward people lying on the tracks, DS Carlson. You are standing next to a lever that controls the line. If you pull the lever you save five people. However, there is a single person lying on the side-track. A single life, what would you do?'

'Pull the lever.'

'And be responsible for killing a person.'

'Better to act than do nothing at all. Better to save the many, not just one.'

'I see. Most would do nothing, just abnegate their responsibility. But then, you know about killing, don't you, DS Carlson? Now, answer me, with my Game, how would *you* play? What if you had to kill, or be killed?'

Carlson didn't say anything in reply and in the silence that hung over the unanswered question, Jess cried out.

'Daddy?'

'It's OK, darling, everything is going to be OK.'

'Of course, you have played before, haven't you?' The Host continued. 'We all know the answer to that one. Here are your choices tonight. You can either kick the chair, and watch the mother of your daughter die. Or you can take her place. Do nothing, and I kill your child.'

Becca sobbed behind her gag, Carlson wanted to comfort her, but daren't take his eyes off The Host.

'If you hurt my girl, I'll kill you.'

'So be it, we all die eventually. But I think you wouldn't want your girl to be hurt, would you, Howard? Ready to be a Player?'

Carlson didn't reply, and taking his cue, The Host reached above his helmet and pressed record on the mounted GoPro. The rules were set. The Game was in motion.

'So DS Carlson, what is it going to be?'

'I don't want my daughter seeing.'

'Fair enough,' The Host replied as she cried for her daddy.

'It's OK, darling. Hey, Jess, look at me, sweetie.'

Jess looked at him, desperate and afraid; it broke his heart.

'Everything is going to be OK, I promise.' Carlson looked at The Host, repeated his only demand. 'I don't want her to see this.'

The Host took off Jess's pyjama top, tied it around her head, covering her eyes.

'Turn her around.'

The Host did as he was asked. 'There. Now, DS Carlson, it's time to play.'

'And what happens after I do?'

'The same as always. I leave.'

'Jess will be unharmed?'

'Yes, just like either you or the woman.'

Assess. Understand. Act.

Carlson looked again at the hammer. He knew even though he was fast, if he sprang for The Host, he wasn't 100 per cent confident he would land on him before the hammer could come down on his daughter's small, precious head. The risk was too much, the stakes too high. He had assessed. He understood. Now he had to act.

Turning to face Becca, he told her the same words he told Jess. It would all be OK. Stepping up onto the chair, he removed the noose from around her neck, and helped her down. She ripped the tape from her mouth and gagged as she pulled the sock from within. She made to dash to Jess, but The Host stopped her. She turned back to Carlson as the noose slipped over his head. His eyes locked on hers.

'Becca, listen to me, because this is really important.'

Becca didn't speak, but nodded, tears streaming down her cheeks.

'This is not your fault. You couldn't have done anything different. This was my choice. I need you to know that. Say it, Becca, say it.'

'This wasn't my fault.'

'I mean it. You're a great mother, the best, you and Jess, you're going to be OK.'

Becca nodded again and closed her eyes. Carlson looked back to The Host.

'You'll leave them alone,' he said.

'You have my word.'

Carlson nodded, his jaw muscles flexing, as he mentally prepared. He took a deep breath, exhaled loudly, and looked at Becca once more.

'Becca, darling, turn around. I don't want you to watch.'

'Howard—'

'Please, for me. For you. After, don't look at me. Just leave and get help,' he said, turning his attention to The Host. 'Let them be together.' The Host paused for a moment, then nodded and Becca ran to Jess's side, hugging her daughter, kissing her head and telling her it would be over soon. Becca looked once more to Carlson, and he smiled at her.

'Babe, turn around.'

Becca did so, and held their daughter close. For Carlson,

everything else faded into nothing. There was no rope, no Host, no fear, no hammer held in a white-knuckled grip above his daughter. Just the two most important people he was blessed to know, that he was honoured to have in his life. Seeing them, back turned, holding each other, was more than he knew he deserved. Becca stroked their daughter's hair, quietly whispered reassurance, and it was the most beautiful and heart-wrenching image he would ever see – something he would carry to wherever he went next.

'I love you girls, now, and always. It's going to be OK; everything is going to be OK.'

Carlson rocked the chair, and as it went over the tipping point and fell, he didn't take his eyes from the girls he loved until the world faded into nothing.

DAY 8

10 February 2019

CHAPTER SIXTY

12.42 a.m.

I bolted upright, a noise snapping me awake – I didn't know what – and then I heard it again, a knock. Sam stirred beside me.

'Babe? You all right?'

'Yeah, I thought I heard…'

It happened again, a few light taps on the bedroom door. I rolled out of bed, threw on my pyjama top and trousers.

'Coming.'

As I opened the door, Sam hid under the covers. The light outside in the hallway blinded me temporarily and when my eyes adjusted, I knew something was wrong. Jake looked like he had been crying.

'What's happened?'

Jake looked up at me. 'Ma'am, I've been instructed to take you to the station.'

'To the station? Whose orders?'

'Bradshaw.'

'Why? What's happened?'

'Ma'am, I…' he hesitated, unable to finish his sentence, or likely, not allowed too.

'OK, give me a minute.'

He nodded before turning and heading back downstairs.

I closed the door, turned on a bedside lamp and began to dress.

'Karen, what's happening?'

'Bradshaw wants me to go in.'

'Really?' Sam sat upright. 'Why?'

'I don't know. They won't tell me anything.'

'And you don't know why you're needed back?'

'No, maybe they found something and need me to work out what it is. Maybe Howard has twisted Bradshaw's arm to let me come in and look at it with him?' I said, but I didn't think that was the case at all.

We drove most of the way to the station in complete silence. I had tried asking Jake what had happened again, hoping my persistence would pay off. But he wouldn't tell me anything and instructed me to turn my phone off which only added to my sense of unease. When we arrived at Thorpe Wood, dozens of people were outside, holding a candlelit vigil.

'Jake? What the fuck has happened?'

'Don't talk to anyone, Superintendent Bradshaw is waiting,' Jake said, opening the car door and walking beside me into the station. Once inside, I made my way to Bradshaw's office and knocked on the door.

'Sir, what's happened?'

'Sit down.'

I did as he asked whilst he closed his office door. Bradshaw sat down beside me, his body turned in, feet parallel, facing my way. He leaned in as he spoke. I read his body language, it was textbook 'I'm about to deliver some bad news'. He was preparing to offer support.

'There was another attack this evening,' he said.

'We were wrong about the link to the cadets?'

'No, not strictly speaking. It was linked to that, but not in the way we thought.'

'So where was it? What happened? What do we know about those involved? Who is on the scene?'

'Karen, there is no easy way to tell you this, but thirty minutes ago, a new video was posted, from inside a house.'

He stopped, swallowed. Took a breath, and in that short moment I tried to work out where he was going.

'It was DS Carlson.'

'What was DS Carlson?'

'In the video.'

'Sir, I don't understand?' I said, hoping the dots I was connecting were sequenced wrong. I wanted it to be that Howard was in the video, like before, because he nearly stopped it.

'The video was from inside DS Carlson's home. Howard…'
He stopped and lowered his head.

'Is he OK? Sir, is Howard OK?'

'No, Karen, I'm really sorry, he's gone. He was the latest victim. Howard is dead.'

I knew what Bradshaw was saying, but the words wouldn't process, they became disjointed, broken, struggling to find their natural order. Bradshaw said something else, I could see his mouth moving, but I couldn't hear. He reached out and touched my arm, and I had no feeling. Not until his words settled. Howard was dead. Howard was gone.

'Karen, I know how close the two of you were. We are all here for you, if there is anything I can do…'

I nodded, bit my bottom lip, held my breath. Tears filmed

over my eyes, making Bradshaw's features soften and blur. I blinked and a thick tear dropped onto my cheek. I caught it quickly, wiped it away. Now wasn't the time to cry.

'Karen, if I can do anything…' he reiterated, as if unsure of what else to say, but there was nothing, no words would make this right, no gesture would bring Howard back.

I grabbed the chair I had been sitting on and threw it as hard as I could. It hit the wall opposite, bounced, landed on its side. Three officers ran in from the incident room, and Bradshaw stopped them with an extended hand. They backed out, the door closing behind them. I wanted to kick the shit out of something, and contemplated attacking the upturned chair again, but the disruption caused by the advancing officers stopped me. And then the fight in me died. Standing with my back to Bradshaw, I crossed my arms, chin resting on my chest. I tried to breathe but didn't dare.

'Karen, I'm truly sorry.'

I nodded, unable to speak as my chest tightened, and pins and needles shot into my hands. I focused on my breathing, slowing it down to steady myself. I needed to help, I needed to catch the fucker who killed my friend.

'We will get this son of a bitch, I promise.'

'Have you found the stencil?'

'No, but we will.'

I nodded again, bit my lip. Held in my rage, my grief. 'I need to see the video,' I said quietly.

'No, absolutely not.'

I turned, the fire in my gaze startling Bradshaw. 'I'm not asking, sir; I need to see the video.'

CHAPTER SIXTY-ONE

1.37 a.m.

The video lasted for only five minutes fourteen seconds. It began with The Host's usual message, then it faded to Howard. He was on the screen for only three of the five minutes fourteen seconds. The final image of Howard before The Host reappeared was one that would stay with me forever.

'Where are Becca and Jess?' I asked quietly.

'They are safe.'

'Public reaction?'

'They're already back in the streets. More vigils, more candles, quite right too.'

'And the organiser of the vigil?'

'No one specific, as far as we can tell. People have found their own voice with this.'

I nodded; my eyes glued to the screen.

'It seems, DI Holt, you didn't catch up. Pity, you can always try again. The next Game is in motion, and I will play at 10 p.m. tonight.'

The screen went dark, and I could see my reflection. My shoulders were slumped, my head heavy. The clue was clear as day. The cadets' symbol wasn't pointing towards a building, but a person. Howard had even told me many times he was a cadet and I still didn't see it. He had targeted Howard, and he dangled it in front of my face. He was smarter than me, and it had cost Howard his life.

I couldn't help but shoulder the responsibility for what I had just seen. If I kept out of it, like I had been ordered on several occasions, The Host would have no reason to target Howard. I had dragged him into this, made him be my eyes, made him come with me to the rowing club building where The Host filmed him and – thanks to the media – identify him. I didn't doubt I would have played if The Host could have got to me. Howard was my substitute. I had been rash with my video, and after, I only focused on Sam, not thinking for a second I was also putting Howard's life in danger. No one would say it, no one would need to, but Howard's death was on me.

'Karen?' Bradshaw said, placing a hand gently on my shoulder. 'I don't know the first thing to say here. But...'

I took a deep breath, squared my shoulders, pushed out my jaw defiantly.

'Play it again.'

'Karen, I don't think—'

'Play it again. I need to hear the message again. This guy hides his clues in plain sight. He will have given us something to go on.'

'No, you need to step away from this.'

'We don't have any more time to lose.' I looked at my watch. 'We've got less than twenty hours until The Host plays his eighth game.'

When Bradshaw didn't argue, I leant forward and replayed the video. I heard nothing new in The Host's words, nor did Howard say or do anything that could generate a lead. I took solace from that. His final moments were filled with nothing but love for his family. He wasn't thinking of work, of regret, just love. As it should be. Once the video stopped, I sat back, my head lowered.

'Can you even begin to imagine what Becca and Jess are feeling right now?'

'No,' Bradshaw said.

'Can I contact them?'

'It's best you didn't, not right now.'

'When you speak to them, tell them I'm truly sorry.'

'Of course. Karen, can I be frank?'

'Yes, sir.'

'This is fucking shit, all of it. And I don't know how we are going to stop him.'

'Yeah,' I replied. What else could I say? The Host was one step ahead, one thought quicker. We knew from the beginning that he was clever, but so far he'd outsmarted everyone.

'Sir, we need to find that train mark.'

'We have a team in Howard's house right now, if it's there, they'll find it.'

'It won't be inside. The Host stencils before he…' I couldn't say before he played, before he made my friend kill himself. 'It will be outside, somewhere close to Howard's house. He hasn't left a clue in the video, not that I can see anyway, so the clue will be with the train.'

Bradshaw nodded, grabbed his phone and stepped away to make the call no doubt to one of those drafted in from other forces, as it would be impossible for anyone in our team to be objective and process the room properly. As Bradshaw spoke in clipped, commanding tones to the officer on the other end, I knew I needed to get up. Showing defeat wouldn't stop him, it wouldn't bring The Host to justice, nor would it avenge Howard. I would have time later to process all the sadness, regret, shame and grief I was feeling. But now was not that time. Now I need my rage to be in the driving seat. Standing took much more effort than it should, and as Bradshaw gave instructions, his back turned, I slipped out of his office. I needed to act and find The Host. I needed to end his Game, with or without help.

As I stepped into the incident room, the atmosphere was subdued, people were working, trying to follow leads, speaking with neighbours, accessing all available CCTV in the area. Dealing with the press, too. As I walked to my desk and sat down, each colleague fought a battle to scrutinise and yet not look at me. I sensed everyone felt as leaden as I did.

My desk was still covered in notes I had scribbled weeks before, notes about the Grayson James investigation. I saw a question on a scrap of paper I'd scribbled to myself the night before we went to his house. *Flight risk?*

I knew the answer now, I probably did then too. The night before we attempted to bring Grayson James in for questioning, Howard and I had gone for a meal together. We knew, with the evidence building against drug-dealing Grayson James, his arrest was imminent. We shared a curry, drank a few beers, speculated on how soon it would be until we would raid his house. We were just waiting for the CPS to green-light it. I thought we were still a few days away, Howard bet it would be the following morning. He was right.

I stopped myself remembering that evening; it was the last time I felt OK, the last time we'd managed a conversation that wasn't about a suspect's death or the national interest. The last time he and I were just friends.

Standing up, I had to move to shake myself from thinking too much about Howard's last moments. Collecting the notes stuck to the side of my monitor, I threw them in the bin. I wondered about Howard's own notes on this case. Did he have any thoughts on The Host that we hadn't had the chance to discuss? I wandered over to his desk, and sat in his chair. His desk was clean, there were pictures of Jess as a newborn, a toddler covered in food, her first day of school. And one of him, Becca and Jess together, recent, smiling for the camera. It felt strange to be in a space that was his. He'd only been gone a few hours, and yet it felt like the chair had been long abandoned. But he wouldn't ever be forgotten, not by me, not by the team, nor the world. My eye was drawn to a single Post-It note on the top of his monitor, a question in large, capital letters.

IS HE RETURNING TO THE SCENE OF THE CRIME?

I got up and went back to my desk. Bradshaw had finished his phone conversation and hastily joined me as I sat down and tried to log in.

'Karen?'

Although my password worked, and allowed me to access the home page, as soon as I tried to log on to the internet, I was blocked. My restricted duty only allowed me to see emails.

'Shit.'

'Karen, what's happened?'

'Sir, I need to go online – can you lift my block.'

'I can't, it's an IT thing. Use my office.'

I didn't wait for him to lead, and before he entered the room, I was already sitting at his desk, logging on to YouTube.

'Karen, what is it?'

'Sir, Howard had a note on his desk, it's made me think. It's been well documented that serial killers sometimes return to the scene of the crime, to relive what they have done.'

'Sure, think of Manson, think of Son of Sam.'

'Right, to name a couple. What if ours is doing the same?'

'But how would we know? We have no profile of him, only that he is male, wears a motorbike helmet, and is around five feet nine. It's not a lot to go on.'

'I'm not thinking about him. I'm thinking about her. If it's who I think it is, I've seen her face.'

'Could you pick her out of a crowd?'

'Maybe.'

YouTube loaded and I typed in PETERBOROUGH CITY CENTRE VIGIL. After a few seconds, videos loaded. The first one on the list was what was happening right now in the city in response to Howard's death. Grief panged in my stomach, but I fought it back. Scrolling down to the third video, I clicked the link. It was the footage from the Bridge Street vigil, a reporter talking with a swarm of people behind. I watched them, hoping to see the young girl amongst the faces. But I couldn't. I loaded another video, one from outside the Chinese takeaway, close to the underpass I first saw her. She wasn't there either.

'Fuck,' I said, feeling the thread begin to slip from my grasp.

'What if she was back at the place where she felt the most guilt?' Bradshaw asked. He was right, she would go back to where she committed the crime. To *her* location. No more than ten seconds into a video of a reporter on the footbridge over the A15, I saw her in the background.

'There,' I said, standing up so Bradshaw could get a look at her.

'How sure are you?' he asked.

'A hundred per cent, sir. That's the girl.'

Bradshaw nodded, and played some more of the footage. She wasn't aware she was in shot, and I could see her twitching, her anxiety close to spilling over.

'She looks terrified,' Bradshaw said.

'She is, sir. I think she was sold on the ideology of our guy – a girlfriend, perhaps, who is desperate to be close to him. But in practice, she isn't in the same place as he is.'

'But she's trying.'

'Yes, sir, she's trying.'

'So how do we draw her out?' he asked quietly. 'She's been back to her scene; I doubt she'd go again and there is no way she was the one in Howard's house.'

'Agreed,' I said.

'So we have to make her feel responsible for what happened tonight.'

'But how?'

'Karen,' Bradshaw began, his face suddenly not looking so drawn and beaten, 'what if we did something we shouldn't?'

'What do you mean, sir?'

'What if you posted another video?'

'Sorry?'

'The whole world knows you and Howard were partners, friends. What if you spoke out, in an unofficial capacity again? What if you said someone knows who he is, and by hiding him, they are just as responsible? Then you could ask the public to hold a vigil at Howard's home. State that you've gone into hiding, for your own safety. Say you want people to pay respects, light candles at his house like they did for the others, because you cannot be there to mourn your friend. Let's give it a set time, say noon.'

'Wouldn't it be better to hold the vigil in the evening like the others?'

'No, we want to get to her and have time to squeeze until she tells us where he is.'

'And you want me to use Howard's death to draw her out?'

'It's horrific, I know, but it might just work.'

I thought about it, wondering what Howard would say. I could hear him telling me to nail him, do whatever it took.

'Karen, I know it's really shit to even think about doing this, but if there is a glimmer of hope—'

'I'll do it. I'll do anything to stop him.'

CHAPTER SIXTY-TWO

9.17 a.m.
Twelve hours, forty-three minutes until the next Game

I thought I could hear Howard's voice. Jolted awake, I opened my eyes and looked around for him. But then it hit me, Howard was gone, and I'd never hear his voice again. Sam, who was sitting next to me on the sofa, took my hand.

'How long did I sleep?' I asked her.

'Ninety minutes, tops.'

'And you? Have you slept?'

'No. Not since you got back earlier this morning,' she said, shaking her head.

From the kitchen, I heard Jake talking and a moment later there was a knock on the living-room door.

'Sorry to disturb you two, it's Superintendent Bradshaw,' he said, holding out a phone to me.

'Sir.'

'We found the train stencil, across the road from Howard's house.'

'Any obvious clues?'

'One thing about this train is different to the others.'

'What is it?'

'One of the train's wheels is a small compass.'

'A compass?'

'I'm sending it across to this phone now.'

'I'll put you on loudspeaker.'

The mobile pinged and the image of the train symbol filled the screen. The first wheel of the old steam train was definitely a compass. The needle was pointing a few degrees south of east. The train symbol and compass were in the usual black they had been in all but one. Only the needle wasn't. That was in the same green as yesterday's train symbol, Howard's symbol. The Host was goading me. He knew I would hate myself for not seeing his clue yesterday, and he was rubbing it in my face.

'What do you think it means?' Bradshaw asked.

'The east of the city, perhaps?'

'I thought that too. We have people out already, trying to find the next train mark. If we find it, we can be in place before him. But as you know, the city is big; it could mean the East of England Showground, or somewhere like Eye, Parnwell. Christ, even as far out as Whittlesea, or anywhere else east side of the city. It's a needle in a haystack. We need the girl to help us narrow our search. It's time to draw her out. Are you ready? Remember everything we discussed you'd say?'

'Yes, sir, I'm ready.' My nerves began to twitch. The first time I posted a video, it was reactive, in the moment. I wasn't so sure about it this time. Using Howard's death to bring out the girl felt cheap. And waiting to do it made it staged. I wasn't an actress and prayed it wouldn't show. I hoped I didn't forget any of the points Bradshaw insisted I say. I thought of

Howard, I thought of Becca and Jess who would have to live the rest of their lives without him. I had to do this for them.

'Good luck, Karen,' Bradshaw said, hanging up the phone.

Turning to Sam, I smiled. 'Can I have a minute?'

'Sure, I'll be right outside.'

Opening up my camera, I turned it to video mode and looked at myself in the screen. My eyes were puffy and blood-shot. My skin drawn and as pale as I could ever remember. Stress showed itself on my neck in the form of a rash that was creeping up and under my jaw. In any other context, I wouldn't want anyone to see me, but now, as I hit the record button, I knew that very soon many would. The recording had begun, and taking a deep breath, I spoke.

'I am DI Karen Holt. I am the officer who tried to help Maggie Stroud by the rowing lake. I am the one The Host has been speaking to. I am the woman who pleaded to the side of The Host that I know doesn't want to do this. I begged for you to stop.

'Last night, at just after 1 a.m., a video was posted of my –' I paused, swallowed, fought with myself to not cry – 'friend and partner DS Howard Carlson. We know what happened, we all saw the sacrifice he was forced to make.'

I blinked, a single tear escaped and ran wildly down my cheek.

'Due to the threat on my life, I cannot be actively involved in this investigation. But what hurts most is I cannot see my best friend's surviving family to comfort them and pay my respects.'

I paused again, collecting my thoughts. What I said next was important to get right.

'The police know that The Host is acting alone. But surely

someone must know something. By not coming forward, by not talking to the police and aiding us in stopping him, you are just as culpable for DS Carlson's death. His daughter will now grow up without a father, his partner will forever remember that awful night. Someone knows more than they're telling us, and I blame you as much as I do The Host. As far as I'm concerned, you have my friend's blood on your hands.'

I wiped tears from my eyes.

'I've been informed the police will allow people close to his house soon. I want nothing more than to go myself, light a candle for my friend, for his courage, for his sacrifice. But I cannot. So I ask the public, will you go light a candle, offer your prayers? Please, will you do it for me? It won't bring back a good person, but it will help those who have survived him, including me, deal with what The Host has done to him and his family. Today at noon. I will watch on the news to see the tribute you're making on my behalf.'

I took a breath, ready to launch something towards The Host, a defiant comment about how we would stop him but as I opened my mouth, the words wouldn't come. Stammering, I stopped the video. I didn't review it, didn't hesitate, I just uploaded it, and locked my phone.

Cradling my head in my hands, massaging my temples, I took deep breaths and tried to stop the headache that was beginning to push behind my eyes. The door opened, and Sam came and sat beside me.

'Is it done?' she asked quietly.

'Yeah, it's done.'

'OK,' she nodded. 'All we can do now is wait.'

CHAPTER SIXTY-THREE

The Host

9.54 a.m.
Twelve hours and six minutes until the next Game

As he watched Karen Holt's desperate video, he bent and shaped two more pipe-cleaner figures, one smaller than all the others, and placed them both with the group on his shelf. Jess and Becca. Turning back to his computer, he picked up his Karen Holt figurine, straightened her legs, held her arms up into the air, like she was reaching up towards God. He pitied her for the depths to which she would sink to try and win. And following her second Facebook stunt, he would humiliate her, embarrass her. All her video did was tell him the police were completely powerless to stop him. He had won.

Once the video had finished, he rang the girl; he needed her again for the next Game. The phone rang and rang, and there was no answer. Hanging up, he tried again, this time the phone went straight to voicemail.

Johnny Ormo > Peterborough Free Discussion

Guys, have you seen the newest Karen Holt video? I can't believe the Seventh Player was her friend. How fucked up is that?!? Is anyone going to the vigil?

1,482 Comments

Jack Anderson

I can't watch any more of The Host videos but I have seen Karen Holt's. I cannot believe The Host killed a police officer, and her friend.

Amanda Belkin

It's good you've not seen the actual video. It's horrific, he died saving his partner and child.

Jack Anderson

THERE WAS A KID IN THE HOUSE WHEN IT HAPPENED??? 😨

Amanda Belkin

His daughter.

Jack Anderson

Oh fuck. I hope she didn't see her daddy die 😨

Amanda Belkin

From what I can tell, she was in the room.

384

Jack Anderson

The Host is pure evil. **Johnny,** I'm wasn't going to go to the vigil, but I am now.

Johnny Ormo

Good, I'll see you there. I hope the rest of you come too.

CHAPTER SIXTY-FOUR

11.58 a.m.

Ten hours and two minutes until the next Game

Knowing I wouldn't be allowed to go for myself, all I could do was sit on my sofa, with Sam beside me and Jake in the doorway, and watch the news coverage of Howard's house. To the rest of the world, this was good television, a melodrama. But actually it was real life.

With the cameras rolling live, I watched as well-wishers drifted in, slowly at first, then, with each passing minute, the swell of people intensified. I was nervous because we had pinned so much hope on this working. I hadn't thought about the consequences if it didn't. We were using Howard's death to try to lure out the girl. If she came, we could perhaps claim it as a victory. If she didn't, I knew I'd likely crumble. I could only carry so much guilt.

More and more people came, with flowers and cards. They came carrying teddy bears for Jess. They lit candles on the footpath outside his house, despite it being in the middle of the day. Some had their placards, #FIGHTTERRORWITHLOVE. A clear message to The Host, again, despite the fact that love was not winning this fight, love was killing, love meant a good man had to hang himself.

As I watched, more and more came, so many the police had to shut the road and redirect traffic. I tried to keep focused as I needed to concentrate on watching the crowds to see if the girl arrived as I hoped. I prayed she felt compelled to join the crowd, that her guilt was thick and sticky, something she couldn't shake free from no matter how hard she tried, a quicksand, dragging her down.

As the report spoke of Howard, a picture of him filled the screen. He was younger, dressed in his pressed uniform, smiling proudly at the camera. My dear, dear friend. I remember when we first met, how we both clicked straight away, how I knew we would be more than work colleagues; I remember the day he told me they were having Jess. How he giggled with joy, like a kid at Christmas.

He was too good a man to have died in such a horrible way.

So wrapped up in my memories, I didn't notice the disturbance in the crowds until Sam nudged me. In the live footage, several of our undercover officers were moving quickly through the crowd. One of them showed her badge, and the crowds gave some space, I saw the girl standing between two officers, their hands on her wrists so she couldn't run.

'Karen – is that her? Is that the girl?' Jake asked over my shoulder.

'Yep, that's the girl.'

CHAPTER SIXTY-FIVE

2.19 p.m.
Seven hours and forty-one minutes until the next Game

'Well done, Karen, your idea worked perfectly,' Bradshaw said as I entered his office and shut the door, leaving Jake outside. The other PPO, Kane, had stayed at home with Sam.

'Is she talking?'

'Not yet. I need to be clear, Karen. You shouldn't be here.'

'Why am I then, sir?'

'Because Howard shouldn't have done what he had to do. This is more than a job, this is personal. For now, the rules are forgotten. You have always been closer to this guy. I need you to help me stop him. The girl is in with her solicitor and social worker.'

'Social worker?'

'You were right, she's just fifteen.'

'Jesus.'

'Yeah, Jesus. Rawlinson is about to go in. I want you to watch the interview.' Bradshaw and I walked into a small room, adjacent to interview room two and watched through a monitor as Rawlinson entered, sat down and began to interview the girl.

'Hello, I'm Detective Inspector Paul Rawlinson. Can I ask your name?'

'Jessica Thomas.'

'Jessica, do you know why you have been brought in today?'

'No comment.'

'I want you to understand the reasons why, and know we are able to help you. I assume, as you were at the vigil, you know about what is happening in the city?'

'No comment.'

'Can you tell me anything about it?'

'No comment.'

Up close, I knew I had seen her somewhere other than by the Chinese and by the river. She was a student at the City Academy, Sam's school. She was the girl who I saw bustle away in the canteen. I should have placed her there and then, if I did, Howard might well still be alive.

As Rawlinson asked questions, the girl shifted every few seconds in her seat, not knowing what to do with herself. And with each question asked, she looked to her solicitor, begging with her eyes to be guided in the right direction. Rawlinson showed her the footage of herself on the night of the vigil at the overpass and when she signed the statement, he commented on how she was left-handed like The Host in that video.

Each time he stated a truth, the girl looked for support, but her solicitor didn't meet her gaze. Instead she was noting everything down, no doubt trying to work on a plea bargain. After an hour, it was agreed that they should have a break, because of her age, and Rawlinson left the room. Alone with her solicitor and social worker, and in Rawlinson's absence, the girl began to sob. The social worker whispered something I couldn't quite make out, but no doubt reassuring her that she was a victim. And she was right, the girl was a victim. Yes, she had done something that would be unforgivable to Jim Weston, Lucas Mathews and their families, but I sensed she had been swept up in this. The Host was always going to play his Games. There was hope for her, but if she didn't cooperate, and another person died, there would be no reprieve.

The door to my left opened, and in stepped Rawlinson.

'I'm not gonna get anywhere with her.'

'Well, we need to keep going,' Bradshaw said. 'This is a critical time.'

'I've been on a loop for over an hour. She isn't going to budge. I'm gonna really lean on her.'

'No. She might be caught up in this mess, but she is just fifteen.'

'So what now?' Rawlinson said, irritated.

I didn't comment but watched Jessica. She was tapping her foot; at first it was light, but the longer we left her, the more anxious it became. The solicitor stood to excuse herself, no doubt using the small window to collect her thoughts before beginning to negotiate a plea for her client's immediate release and witness protection. As she was buzzed out of the room, the social worker leant in, resting her hand on the girl's shoulder, and asked how she was. Jessica shook her head. Fresh tears fell.

'Remember, when the police come back in, you don't need to say anything. But you need to think about what will happen if you don't tell them something that could help their investigation.'

'Am I going to get into a lot of trouble?'

'I don't know. I hope not. But if you can help, you need to. This is serious, you know that, right?'

The girl nodded. 'I don't want to talk to that man.'

'And you don't have to.'

The solicitor came back in, smiled curtly towards Jessica and the social worker.

'Any ideas?' Rawlinson asked of Bradshaw and me.

'Just keep going, reiterate that we know of her involvement, tell her she needs to help us stop this,' Bradshaw said.

'And tell her we want to help The Host,' I added.

'Help him? I wanna hurt him,' Rawlinson replied.

'Me too, but she is drawn to him, she wants to protect him. Tell her we only want to help. Let's soften her.'

Rawlinson nodded and left for the interview room once more. He started by reconfirming that he knew she was involved.

'Tell him,' the girl interrupted, speaking with the social worker.

'Jessica says she doesn't want to talk to you.'

'Jessica, we want to—' Rawlinson pushed on.

'My client reserves the right to not speak to anyone.'

Jessica spoke up. 'I want to talk. I just don't want to talk to him.'

Rawlinson flashed a look to the camera, before returning it to Jess. 'OK, Jess, who do you want to speak to?'

'Karen Holt. I'll only speak to Karen Holt.'

CHAPTER SIXTY-SIX

3.27 p.m.

Six hours and fifty-nine minutes until the next Game

As I opened the door, I smiled, suggesting to Jessica I was calm, in control, happy to be there to talk with her. But in truth my heart was pounding and my chest felt tight. I didn't want to be the one to have this conversation. I didn't feel strong enough. The clock was ticking, we had less than seven hours to go, and still no idea what The Host's latest clue meant. Unless I found out from the girl where the Eighth Game would be played, someone else would die, and The Host would start again. Perhaps it was my anxiety, but I couldn't help feel if we didn't stop him now, we never would.

Taking my seat, I introduced myself to the solicitor, social worker, and Jessica, before resuming the interview. I knew the tape would likely be useless, because I wasn't technically allowed in the room. But all agreed our priority was to stop The Host.

'Hello, Jessica, I understand you wanted to talk with me. What did you want to tell me?' I started, hoping my voice remained level and calm.

The solicitor chipped in. 'Remember, Jessica, you don't have to say anything, and you shouldn't. I highly suspect DI Holt shouldn't be in this room. If I'm right, you will be out of here very soon.'

'That's OK. You don't have to talk to me, Jessica,' I said, ignoring the threat. 'Just listen. We've met a few times, haven't we? If I recall, we nearly walked into each other in your school. Am I right?'

'What do you want to ask DI Holt?' the solicitor said.

I ignored her. 'Jessica, it's a nice name. Howard's little girl is called Jessica too, did you know that?'

Jessica shook her head.

'No? She's six. She's my goddaughter actually. Now she has to grow up without a daddy. That's going to be really tough for her.'

'I didn't know that he had a daughter.'

'But you knew he was a target?'

'No, honestly, I was just told to watch the house.'

'By who?'

'Him.'

'Who is he?'

Jessica paused for a moment, and I could see she was about to throw out a 'no comment'. I needed to keep her talking.

'Tell me about the Chinese takeaway. Why were you there?'

'He wanted me to see what happened after. Report back.'

'How long did you watch for?'

'All night. After you and I spoke, I got spooked and left.'

'Why did he pick the Chinese? Why Michelle Reed and Timothy Smart?'

Jessica hesitated again, unsure if she should continue. I flexed my hands under the table, till my joints burned.

'Jess, can I call you Jess?' I asked, feeling like I was betraying my fatherless goddaughter by saying her name.

'Uh huh,' she replied, staring at her hands, now meshed together on the table, her right leg ceaselessly tapping underneath.

'Jess,' I swallowed, 'I want to help people. Surely you understand that, right? I just want to help people, like I couldn't help my friend, Howard.' I felt my diaphragm tighten further.

Shit, not now. Please not now.

Jessica looked up, caught my eye, and I blinked several times.

'He wasn't just my partner, Jess; Howard and I were friends.' My voice was shaking now.

Push it down.

'Oh.'

'How did he choose Michelle and Timothy?'

'He didn't choose Michelle. Timothy was the one he watched.'

'Why?'

'Timothy went to the takeaway every week, at the same time. He spoke nicely, held the door open for others. He was kind.'

'And that's it? Timothy was chosen because he was kind?'

'Yes. The Host wants everyone to see that kindness doesn't really exist. Even in those who were truly good.'

'And the second, in the nightclub?'

'I don't know. But the library, it was for the same reason. Both involved were good people, truly good people,' she said quietly as tears began to fall, landing on the table.

'And then you had a turn.'

Quietly, Jess began to sob, and as she spoke, she did so quickly, I could sense, the lid had boiled over, and it would all spill out.

'He was worried if I didn't actually do it, I could bail.'

'He made you be The Host, to keep you from talking.'

'He said if I did, I'd go to jail too.'

'And you love him.'

'Yes, yes I do.'

'And you wanted to keep him happy.'

'I wanted him to see me again, like he did before this all began.'

'But it didn't go to plan.'

'The man—'

'Jim Weston?'

'Yes, him. I was told there was no such thing as a good person, but when he moved to jump, to save the boy, I saw that there was. He saved that kid. He…' She trailed off; her words stuck in her throat as the night on the bridge came back to her. I could see it shook her to the core. Changed her. 'He didn't ask me to try again, because I'd get it wrong.'

'Would you have wanted to?'

Jess shook her head. 'No. I couldn't. So I said I'd watch, to see if you or anyone else was close. I knew he was beginning to obsess, even if he still didn't know who you were.'

'Was that hard for you? The fact he was obsessing?'

'With each Game he became more distant and the more distant he became, the more I didn't understand why anymore. Especially after the married couple.'

'Maggie and John Stroud,' I said.

'Yes, them. When people went into the streets…' She trailed off, tears streaming down her cheeks.

'And then he played The Game with the brothers.'

'Yes, the brothers.'

'Who had to kill each other.' I needed her to know who was involved, I needed her to know what had happened. She was skimming the important details to protect herself. I understood, I had done the same in the past. But this was real, this needed to be faced.

'Yes, killed,' she said, barely at a whisper. 'And for what? I don't know anymore.'

'But you did once.'

'Yes. I did. And then, when your police officer…'

'DS Howard Carlson,' I said, despite how hard it was to say his name. My eyes filmed over. I tried to wipe them discreetly, but the girl saw.

'DI Holt, I didn't know whose house I was watching, not at first. Then the woman and the girl.'

'Becca and Jess—' I said quietly.

'When they came, I told him to stop.'

'Did you?'

'I wanted to.'

'But you didn't, did you?'

'I was scared, I *am* scared. I'm scared of how much trouble I am in; I'm scared that when he finds out I am here, he'll…' She began to sob into her hands. I exchanged a look with the solicitor, and the social worker. We all understood she was a young person who had been manipulated into this. I knew she would still have to face the law for what she did. But I hoped, even where Howard's death was concerned, they would bear in mind she had been coerced. She was still just a child and she had been groomed.

'Jess,' I said, lowering my head to try to draw up the teenager's eye. 'Jess…'

She wiped her eyes with the ball of her hands, before smearing her nose onto her jumper sleeve, the action making her look younger.

'*Jess*,' I said for the third time, and when Jess looked up to me, I didn't dare blink.

'We need to stop this. We need to help him, he is unwell.'

She nodded, shifted in her seat, pulled down her jumper sleeves to cover her hands.

'Jess, do you know where the next Game is taking place?'

'Uh-huh.' She nodded.

'I need you to tell me where it is. I need you to help me help him. This needs to end, you know that, right?'

Jess nodded, wiped her nose again, hid more of herself inside her jumper.

'Jess, where is The Game?'

'I…' she paused.

'He will never know you told us. I have been close before, as far as he will ever know, I worked out the clue. Where is he going?'

'It's a pub,' she said quietly.

'Good, that's good, Jess – do you know the name of the pub?'

'No.'

'What can you tell us?'

'It's a boat.'

'The pub? The pub is a boat?'

She nodded. 'On the river.'

'Jess, that's great. Thank you,' I said, standing up and

leaving the interview room, the teenager's sobs muted only once the door was closed behind me. I took some measured breaths. I wanted to be sick, but I needed to move. Time was not on our side. Going back into the observation room, I looked to Bradshaw. He nodded a 'well done' in my direction. And I felt fresh tears press.

'Does it fit? Could it be that her lover has told her to send us down a false trail?' Rawlinson asked.

'No, it fits. The clue is a compass, right? The needle pointing east.'

'Right, what's that got to do with a boat pub? As far as I know, there are none east of the city.'

'There isn't. The Game is going to be played on the Hawser.'

'The Hawser?'

'Yep. The pub is the bottom of the barge. The top...'

'A restaurant called East Point,' Bradshaw said, catching up.

'It fits, in the clue left behind, the compass needle is pointing to just below east. He didn't mean east of the city, he literally meant just below East. The Hawser is just below East Point. The girl is telling the truth. Sir, that's where he'll be.'

CHAPTER SIXTY-SEVEN

8.41 p.m.

One hour and nineteen minutes until the next Game

Over the few hours since Jessica told us the location, we'd listened intently as Bradshaw himself led the team and got them into place to ambush The Host. Bradshaw asked over the radio every now and then for an update. Each voice came back, sounding off that all was quiet, and that, despite searching, there was no sign of the train stencil, the one thing that would confirm categorically we were right, and the teenager hadn't lied. Time was ticking, and I started to worry I had been mistaken.

I felt completely at a loss, sitting in the empty police office whilst the entire force was out, stalking a barge on the river, waiting for The Host to arrive. I could see Jake was at a loss too, having to stay with me, despite me telling him and Bradshaw it wasn't necessary. He paced, clock-watched, checked the radio was still working when all was silent for too long. I wanted nothing more than to be there, with them, but Bradshaw pointed out two problems with that. The first was despite him calling me in, despite me speaking with a key witness, I was still, in the eyes of the IOPC, on restricted duty. I began to argue against it, but I couldn't contest the second, more obvious reason. My second video had gone viral. I wouldn't be able to move without someone seeing me. Going home wasn't an option either, because then I wouldn't be able to listen to the closed-circuit radio Bradshaw had left with Jake.

A voice came over the radio. 'I've found it.'

'Confirm, over?'

'The train is here, under a bench in the pub's beer garden,' the voice said, quietly. His confirmation that the train had been found cemented the fact that we were right.

'Good. Sit tight, everyone. He will come,' Bradshaw said, then, silence.

I stood up, began to pace the room, looked at the clock, its ticking relentless and deafening. I grabbed my cold coffee and took a sip, looked at the clock again. I put down the cup and ran my fingers through my hair. Paced some more. Time seemed to slow to a complete stop. It felt like I was waiting for hours, and only minutes had passed. Sitting down once more, I rubbed the bridge of my nose, trying to move the tension somewhere else. It would soon be over. We had him; we had the bastard.

CHAPTER SIXTY-EIGHT

The Host

8.44 p.m.
One hour sixteen minutes until the next Game

Walking over the bridge that crossed the River Nene, he dared to look down towards the Hawser on its bank. It should have been a quiet, wet Sunday night, and yet, several people were sitting at a bench, pints of beer in their hands, barely speaking to one another, none were smoking, it was too cold for non-smokers to be outside. Something wasn't right. Stopping midway over the bridge, he leant on the wall and pretended to text on his phone, so he could watch. For a while, they did nothing but chat occasionally and sip their drinks; one checked his watch often, kept exchanging a look with the man opposite, like they were waiting for something. Then, he flashed a glance under the table, to the exact place The Host put the train mark.

They knew he was coming.

He had viewed Karen Holt's second video as desperate but it was in fact something else entirely. He assumed Holt was trying to draw him out, but now it appeared she wasn't after him, she was after the girl. And the girl had been caught. How else would they know exactly where he was going to play?

The barman and his regular drinker who were supposed to be The Players in his Eighth Game had been given a stay of execution. He would return to them, but only when Karen Holt was out of the picture. Instead, it was time to bring to life his back-up plan. He wanted to commission this plan a few days from now, but Holt had forced his hand. She had manipulated his Game, and it was time to make her understand once and for all she wasn't special. She was just the same as everyone else and she would be the next Player.

They say every single person in the world is connected to everyone else within six degrees of separation. In a small city like Peterborough, it was likely to be only three. But his research had showed him that for him and Karen Holt, it was just one person. One that linked them both. And it was that one person that would now make Karen Holt play.

CHAPTER SIXTY-NINE

9.21 p.m.
Thirty-nine minutes until the next Game

My phone buzzed in my pocket and I was surprised to see it was Sam. Until then, I hadn't realised how much I needed to hear her voice. I excused myself from Jake, and stepped into another room.

'Hi, Sam, I'm so glad you've—'

'Karen Holt.' A voice came back, metallic, robotic. The shock of hearing him made my legs give and I fell into a nearby desk.

'No, please. Don't...'

'Hurt her? That's up to you now, isn't it? You are just a piece in my Game.'

'OK, all right, just, please. Don't do anything to her,' I begged.

'That all depends on you, now doesn't it? You see a runaway train, DI Holt. What do you do?'

'I don't know.'

'Interesting, I would have thought you'd be someone who would act. Soon we'll know, won't we?'

'What do you mean?'

'Come to your lovely wife's school. We'll be waiting. And DI Holt, I don't need to tell you to come alone, and tell no one, do I?'

'Wait, I need to know she is…' Before I could ask if Sam was unhurt, the line went dead. I lost the ability to move. My mind tried to catch up with what just happened. I was preparing myself for The Host being arrested, and now, I was the next Player in his Game. And the woman to whom I owed my happiness and stability was caught up in it. My chest began to feel tight, and my hands started to burn once more. I fought like hell to push the torture down, but I was failing, I couldn't catch my breath. I stumbled into a wall, and before I fell, Jake caught me under the arm.

'DI Holt, are you OK?'

Push it down, Karen, you cannot let slip, he'll kill her.

'DI Holt?'

'I'm fine, it's just a lack of sleep.'

'Sit down, let me get you some water.'

You don't have time to sit.

'Jake, I just need to splash my face and drink more coffee. Could you…?'

'Of course. You sure you're all right?'

'Yes. Fine,' I said. I had no time for my anxiety or grief. Sam was being held, and I needed to act. As Jake walked towards the kitchen to make a coffee, I waited until he was out of sight, and once he was, I moved.

Going into Bradshaw's office, I searched for his car keys. He'd climbed into a patrol car when he left earlier, and so his was still in the basement car park. I searched his desk and thankfully, there they were.

I walked as quietly and a quickly as I could towards the basement. As I pulled out of the station's underground car park – no sign of Jake behind me – every fibre in my body told me to drive as fast as I could to Sam's school, but I forced myself not to. I couldn't attract attention. I had to do as he said, knowing, if I deviated, he would kill Sam and post her all over the internet.

As I joined the A15, heading north, the roads were as quiet as they might be at three in the morning. Most people were scared to be out, and rightly so. No one knew where he would strike. Not even Bradshaw and the team who were waiting at the river to catch someone who would never arrive. Ahead, there were around a dozen people standing on the bridge that Jim Weston had jumped from. Another vigil, another peaceful demonstration. Most were fearful, a few were still defiant. I tried to drive as quietly and steadily as I could, but it didn't matter if I was silent or not, The Host knew I would come.

After all, it was his Game. His rules.

CHAPTER SEVENTY

The Host

9.27 p.m.
Thirty-three minutes until the next Game

At first, when he was digging into the life of Karen Holt, he struggled to believe it. And yet, here she was. In her classroom. Bound and gagged. She had been a teacher in his school for years. The woman who had tried to help him at his lowest was connected to Karen Holt.

It was beautiful.

He liked Miss Clarence, but he was being forced to play the hand he didn't want to play. It was a game he had started, Karen Holt had changed the rules, interrupted the flow. She left him no choice. He knew Miss Clarence would want to help a desperate student. So when he called her on the number she gave him and begged her to come see him outside of the school, he knew she couldn't say no – even though it meant she'd have to give the young officer in her house the slip. He didn't know how she managed that but she had, because she cared.

She was just like Jim and Richard and Alexandru and Maggie and the rest of them, too kind for her own good.

Miss Clarence tried to say something behind her gag. But now was not the time to listen. Now was the time to reflect. To plan. Unzipping his rucksack, he pulled out the figurine and put Karen on the desk beside her wife. Then, turning up the music in his headphones, he allowed himself to be wrapped up in the moment. He let the music take over as he left the room and began to lay the trail for his next Player.

Soon she would come, soon Karen Holt would die. She had become the beacon of hope. The world had started to look to her to be its saviour. For this Game, there would be yet another twist in the rules – and it would be just for her. It would start in a similar way to the brothers' game: if she didn't hurt her wife, she would die. She could only kill herself once Miss Clarence was badly injured. So in his video, he would make the world see Karen Holt attacking her wife. And then they'd see Karen Holt's dead body, and they would all think she had lost The Game. That final thread of hope would turn to ashes. Karen Holt had become a thorn in his side, but now, she would be the one to ensure his message would be delivered. After her, he might not ever need to play again.

CHAPTER SEVENTY-ONE

9.39 p.m.
Twenty-one minutes until the next Game

Outside the school entrance I turned off the engine and stepped out into the cold night. As I reached the main reception, there was a crudely drawn arrow on lined paper Sellotaped to the door. I followed the directions and turned down the side of the huge building. There was another arrow telling me to turn left, so I did, and noticed that the gate that led to the playground was ajar. The hinges squeaked angrily when I opened it wider, and I froze, listening to hear if anyone approached. All was quiet.

Walking into the playground, the place felt haunted for the lack of children. I saw another piece of paper stuck to one of the basketball posts. Following the instruction led me to an open door. I expected to see a light source from within but the endless corridor before me was dark, lifeless. A handful of steps took me inside, then another arrow told me to keep going. As I descended into the darkness of the school corridor, a spark flickered in the back of my mind. The Game was his, and his rules were precise. For the city, for me, it was all so horrific, but to him it was only a game.

But what if I stopped playing by his rules?

He was scared; he had tried to push me away by calling me out, knowing I'd be removed from the case. But realising I wouldn't ever back down, he had grown desperate. Sam was a lure to get me to come to him, and he was smart enough to know I would die before hurting my wife. I knew in that moment he wouldn't hurt Sam. He wanted me to hurt her or, more likely, he wanted me to die in her place.

Taking my phone from my pocket, I dialled Sam's number. The phone connected, rang twice and The Host answered.

'Are you lost, DI Holt? I thought I'd made my directions clear.'

'No, I'm not lost. I'm in the school.'

'So why the phone call?' he asked, and even through the voice manipulator, I could tell he was smirking. 'Begging me to reconsider?'

'No.'

'No?'

'If you want me, if you want Sam and me to play your Game, you're going to need to find me first.'

CHAPTER SEVENTY-TWO

The Host

9.42 p.m.
Eighteen minutes until the next Game

The Host stood stunned for a few seconds. This was not part of his plan. This was not the way it was supposed to go. He threw the mobile, screaming in frustration. The voice-altering software struggled to adapt to the sudden outburst and decibel level. As the phone exploded on impact with the wall above Sam's head, she jolted. The Host grabbed the nearest school table and flipped it, sending it clattering into chairs and knocking them over like skittles. Sam screamed behind her gag, and in doing so, she distracted him so that his focus splintered.

This was going to be a fuck up, just like the bridge, if he didn't control himself. He had planned this all for so long; he'd withdrawn from his friends and sacrificed everything just to make sure the world understood what he had lost. Karen Fucking Holt was not going to screw it up.

Turning to face Miss Clarence, his chest rising and falling like a caged animal primed to kill, he stepped towards her and grabbed her face in his hand. Her tears ran over his dirty fingernails. He began to squeeze, his fingers digging into her cheek so hard he could feel her teeth through her thin flesh. One of his fingers was close to her eye; it took every ounce of energy not to squeeze until it popped out. Shouting in her face, he released her and stepped back, taking a moment to collect himself. She looked so small, so fragile, bound with cable ties to the cast iron radiator that was from when the school was built in the 1960s. The commanding head of year that she had been to him was all but lost. He felt sorry for her, she wasn't supposed to play, and yet, here she was, sobbing incoherently. Fear had crippled her ability to think or act.

Removing the motorbike helmet, he considered her for a moment, then tore off the tape that held her mouth shut.

'There has been a slight change to the plan,' he said.

'Theo? No, no,' Sam sobbed, shock desiccated her features, making her look old and haggard. 'Theo, what are you doing? Please, you have to stop this.'

'We are way beyond that, Miss Clarence.'

'I don't understand,' she cried.

'You of all people surely must understand,' he said, genuinely hurt. 'I've told you everything, you know everything about that day. About what happened. You must understand why I need to do this.'

'Theo, please.'

'Tell me you understand.'

'I can't.'

'They let her die, they let her die and then they were called heroes, like she didn't matter.'

'She *did* matter, as do you.'

'No one matters if she doesn't, and no one is good if she can die and people can be praised for it.'

'Theo, you don't have to do this.'

'Why can't anyone see? Michelle Reed, Milly Hallam, Richard Mullis, Maggie Stroud, the brothers Nistor and Rusu, all "good people" – all could and did kill.'

'Theo, this has to stop. You cannot kill good, it exists in everyone. Including you.'

'The good in me drowned with my mum.'

'Theo, that's not true.'

'I'm so disappointed, Miss Clarence.'

'Theo…'

'Sit tight. We will play soon enough; I just need to go and collect your wife.'

CHAPTER SEVENTY-THREE

9.44 p.m.
Sixteen minutes until the next Game

I heard footsteps on the floor bounding in my direction. He wasn't trying to mask his approach. Arrogance, or perhaps panic obviated the need to tread carefully. I sidestepped into a recess under a flight of stairs that led to the upper floor and hid in the dark corner. I watched him barrel past me and was shocked to see he wasn't wearing the motorbike helmet. As he pushed open a set of double doors and disappeared away, shouting my name, I felt the hope that my wife wasn't dead collapse. The Host had managed to hide his identity from all of the victims and survivors. But Sam could ID him, and I would be able to as well. He wanted us to play, and he wanted us both to die.

Crawling out from under the stairs, my shoulder sticky with cobwebs, I kept low and ran in the direction The Host had come from. I looked into every classroom window, hoping I would see Sam behind the glass, and with each empty window I peered into my fear grew.

As I opened a fire door and continued down the corridor,

I saw light coming from one of the rooms ahead. Breaking into a run, I drew level and looked through the glass. The light was faint, but I could see enough to make out the shape of Sam on the floor by the window. I covered my mouth with my hands to stifle my sobs. She was tied up, like the Hofer brothers had been, but she was alive. I stepped inside, and Sam panicked – began to scream, so I moved quickly, placing my hand on her mouth to trap in her terror.

'Sam, it's me. Take a breath, I need you to be silent.'

Sam nodded, her fear melting into relief, and I removed my hand.

'Karen—'

'Are you hurt?'

'No.'

'We need to get you out of here,' I said.

'It's Theo, The Host, it's Theo, my student.'

'Sam, you have to be quiet. We need to get you out of here,' I said in hushed tones as I worked on the cable ties. She nodded.

'You're coming with me, right?'

I didn't say anything as I fought to remove her from the radiator. The cords were tight, so I grabbed a pair of scissors from the desk and began to cut through the thick plastic that was biting into Sam's wrists. I noticed a small, red pipe-cleaner figurine on the table but ignored it. After several attempts, I managed to hack through, and Sam's arms dropped to her side. I didn't wait for Sam to nurse her wounds or shake blood back into her lifeless limbs before digging her under her armpits and dragging her to her feet.

'Sam, we have to get you out of here. Please, you have to do

414

exactly as I say then we'll both be safe,' I urged, and opened the classroom window. The drop was only a few feet onto a gravel border of the asphalt playground. Nothing obstructed the drop, which wasn't high enough to cause any harm.

'Come on,' I demanded, and in shock, Sam drew by my side. 'Climb on the windowsill, I'll help you out.'

Sam climbed up awkwardly. Then, throwing one of her legs out of the window, she straddled it for a moment before the other joined on the outside of the ledge. I held her until she was ready, and then Sam jumped. She landed heavily, let out a little yelp as she hit the floor.

'Sam, have you got your phone?'

'No, it's by the whiteboard, he broke it.'

I looked behind me, sure enough, there it was, the screen smashed. I passed her my mobile phone through the window. 'Find somewhere to hide. Ring Bradshaw. Tell him what's happened.'

'Wait – you're not coming with me?'

'No. When he sees you're gone, he'll either try to find you, or slip away.'

'Karen, what are you doing?' Sam begged as I began to close the window once more.

'Ring Bradshaw, hide somewhere, stay low until he arrives. I can't let him get away again,' I said, retreating to go and find The Host.

CHAPTER SEVENTY-FOUR

The Host

9.48 p.m.
Twelve minutes until the next Game

He felt panic; it was something new. He often felt grief, shame, anger, hatred, frustration, but for a long time, not panic. The last time was that moment just before he and his mother had held hands, listened to that song and accepted they would drown. That day that made him who he was. The day he watched two strangers make a choice and save him over his mother.

He needed to regain control of his emotions, his status. He couldn't find Karen Holt, couldn't hear her moving around the school, playing her childish game of hide and seek. She thought she would outsmart him, and for a moment, she had by luring him out. But if she thought she was going to win a game that was of his design, she was sadly mistaken. She would either comply, or he would kill Miss Clarence without The Game being played. It might muddy his message, but things had gone beyond that – they had, if he was honest, after the incident with Jim Weston.

As he entered the classroom again, his stomach dropped: his teacher was gone.

'No!' he yelled, running over to the radiator. The cable ties were on the floor, and on the windowsill a pair of scissors that had been on the desk when he'd tied the teacher up. Karen Holt had been in; Karen Holt had snuck past him and freed her wife. He had foolishly slipped up, and both were gone, and he didn't doubt that they had already contacted the police who would be on their way to arrest him. He needed to leave, quickly.

The battle was lost, but his message would live on. It was time to regroup, go into hiding, start again somewhere else long after the dust had settled. His message was global. He could play anywhere he wanted. He would have to disappear and be patient until he knew they would never find him. His work wasn't done. Not until they all understood. Grabbing the motorbike helmet, he made his way towards the door, but something caught his eye and stopped him. On the whiteboard, a rudimentary drawing of a steam train, above, an arrow, and beside it, in large capital letters, a question.

IT'S NOT YET 10 P.M.

DO YOU STILL WANT TO PLAY?

THE EIGHTH GAME

I hoped he was enticed by my challenge and would follow my arrows to the sports hall, where I waited for him. When I heard footsteps approaching, I felt relief and terror in equal measure. He had taken the bait, which meant Sam was safe and hopefully Bradshaw had got the message and was on his way. But until then, he and I would be alone, and he would want me dead. I just had to buy a little time until help arrived.

As the gym doors opened, The Host stepped in. His motorbike helmet was back on. He walked confidently towards me, and as he drew close, he spoke. The voice, altered, as always, rang out.

'Hello, DI Holt.'

'I'm glad you could make it,' I replied, hoping my fear didn't show in my voice.

'I know what you're doing. You're keeping me busy until back-up arrives.'

'How have you drawn that conclusion?'

'It wasn't difficult. You freed your wife, gave her your phone, told her to call it in, and now you're enticing me, knowing I would be curious to see you eye to eye, even though we have already met albeit briefly.'

'Yes, thank you for that, it hurt like hell,' I said, tapping the side of my head where he'd hit me with the motorbike helmet.

'You startled me,' he said by way of apology.

'You think you've got me all worked out, don't you?'

'Don't I?'

'Partly,' I said, as I started to move towards the light switches on the far right-hand side of the gym. 'I did free my wife; I did help her escape out of the window. But…' I pulled out the burner phone I'd bought to speak with Howard. 'My phone is still in my pocket.'

'Interesting. Were you not tempted to call the police?'

'Tempted, yes. But I wanted to speak to you.'

'I see, and avenge your partner?'

'We'll have to see, won't we?'

I flicked the switch and the ceiling lights hummed to life. The old fluorescent tubes lit up, weak at first, but growing with intensity as they warmed. The Host looked up, and as he did, I slipped the phone back into my pocket.

'So, DI Holt, are you suggesting that you and I become Players in my Game?'

'That depends.'

'On?'

'On whether there will be repercussions for anyone I love.'

'No repercussions.'

I moved again, circling back the other way, putting myself further away from the exit. I knew he would assume I was making a mistake, removing my only chance of escape. I hoped he wasn't right. He would be closer to the exit, and closer to the police who would hopefully see the gym lights on and come charging in. He took a look behind him, which gave me a second to look at my watch.

9.58 p.m.

'Two minutes,' I said, and I suspected he smiled inside that helmet.

I had to buy a little more time. Bradshaw would be close by now, I just had to wait until he found us.

'Theo.' Saying his name caught him off guard, and his body recoiled, just a step, but it was enough for me to know he wasn't feeling in control anymore. 'You see a runaway train moving toward people lying on the tracks. You are standing next to a lever that controls the line. If you pull the lever, you save five people. However, there is a single person lying on the side-track. A single life…'

'I'm flattered to be quoted, DI Holt,' The Host said, removing his backpack and placing it on the floor in front of him.

'I think what you have done will be quoted for a long time,' I replied, hoping I was playing to his ego.

'That's my plan.'

He drew open the rucksack and emptied it on the floor. Out fell zip ties, a hammer, a small hacksaw, a Stanley knife, a thick chain and a pair of garden shears. Standing up, he reached above his head and turned on the GoPro. I flashed a look at my watch.

9.59 p.m.

'I decided not to use conventional weapons with my games. Knives and the like would be too easy to identify, so everything here is from a garden centre or this school. If only someone had thought to check, you might have been able to stop me.'

'Maybe, or maybe you are just too smart.'

'DI Holt, are you trying to butter me up?'

'Just allowing everything to be said, while we have time.'

'I see. A catharsis of sorts.'

I saw something in the high windows directly behind The Host: lights. Car lights. Bradshaw was here, he was coming in. The lights went out, and I could swear there was the faintest sound of footsteps coming into the building. It would be easy for them to find us; The Host had laid a trail into the school, as I had done from the classroom to the gym. They just had to follow the arrows. For a second, I thought The Host heard the footsteps too. But the helmet would buffer out quieter sounds. I needed to keep talking, keep him distracted for a little longer.

'Ask me again, what I would do if I was by the track.'

'Do you have an answer now?'

'Yes, I do.'

'OK, I'm fascinated by you, Karen Holt. I'll bite. You see a runaway train. What do you do? Throw the switch or watch them die?'

'If it was the first time it happened, I'd throw the switch, saving five people.'

'But in the process killing one.'

'Yes. Killing one. It's something I know I can live with.'

'Of course, you know all about killing someone, don't you, DI Holt?'

'As do you.'

'No, no. I've never killed anyone. Hurt, yes, but never killed,' he said, crouching down to pick up the hammer. He felt the weight of it, flipped it in his hand, nodded. Satisfied he had chosen his weapon well, he stood and continued. 'I've just allowed people to find the part of themselves that could kill. Until tonight, that is.'

'So, yes, first time, I would throw the switch. But this isn't the first time it's happened, is it?' I said, continuing, ignoring his threatening stance and words. 'It's the eighth.'

'So?'

'I'd know the train was coming, wouldn't I? I'd stop the train before it could happen,' I said.

Understanding, he stumbled backwards and as he spun for the exit, we both saw torchlight coming towards us through the crack under the gym door. He panicked, trying to find a way out – being caught wasn't part of his campaign. When he realised he had been played, and cornered, he turned to face me once more.

'You bitch!'

The gym door burst open and three officers charged in. Raising the hammer high above his head, he ran towards me. I lifted my hands to try as best I could to save my skull from being crushed. Then, he stopped, his body going rigid, the hammer falling from his grasp just before he fell to the ground, the taser cables embedded in his back.

As the police officers dropped their weight onto his body so he couldn't move and placed him in handcuffs, I staggered back against the wall. I could barely catch my breath, my own internal hammer pounding so hard, I was sure I would die. The Host was dragged to his feet and they began to remove him from the gym. As they left the room, I slid down the wall, put my head in my hands, and slowed my breathing down, regaining control.

'Karen!' A voice came from the back of the gym, and as

I looked up, Sam was coming towards me. I tried to get to my feet, but my body wouldn't comply – it didn't matter, though, because Sam dropped to her knees and grabbed hold of me.

'Oh God, I thought you were going to die,' she sobbed.

'Shhh, it's all right, Sam, I'm fine. Everything is going to be OK. Everything is going to be OK.'

ONE WEEK LATER

THE HOST'S TRAGIC
IDENTITY REVEALED

Ross Cooper for the *Peterborough Post*

Further details have emerged about the identity of The Host, the fifteen-year-old boy behind the violent 'Games' that brought Peterborough to a standstill and made headlines across the country.

Although the boy cannot be named for legal reasons, it is widely believed that he was a student at the City Academy. And according to fellow students, he had faced personal tragedy of his own.

A family member unaware of his crimes revealed that his mother, a nurse, had died the previous year in a car accident in which the suspect himself was involved.

Exactly a year before the death of Timothy Smart, the suspect and his mother were involved in a car accident, skidding off the road into a water-filled dyke close to Ramsey.

A couple who do not wished to be named recalled that upon witnessing the accident, they had to make a 'horrific choice' as to who they would save and chose the teenager.

There has yet to be any published information as to charges or a court date.

A service of remembrance honouring the victims Timothy Smart, Alexandru Stoica, Roberta Richardson, John Stroud, Nistor and Rusu Hofer, and Detective

Sergeant Howard Carlson is due to take place next week at Peterborough Cathedral.

DI Karen Holt, the officer in the centre of this crime, has yet to return to work.

Jack Anderson > Peterborough Free Discussion

I know it's all over, but I read an article online about The Host, did anyone else see it? I hated the guy, but now, reading this, I don't know what I think anymore…

39 Comments

Claire Turner

I can't believe he lost everything and no one helped. He was just a fifteen-year-old kid.

Johnny Ormo

Doesn't change what he did though, does it? I still think he is evil. Regardless of what comes out now, all those people died because of him.

Claire Turner

Have you seen what's been said online about when they went into The Host's address?

Johnny Ormo

No?

Claire Turner

They found loads of pipe-cleaner models of people. So fucked up.

Johnny Ormo

Jesus.

Claire Turner

Gets worse, the feature I read also says that they found evidence of The Host having multiple social media accounts, they didn't say any names, but did say one of those accounts was used to set up the vigil on the night the brothers played.

Amanda Belkin

What, do they mean Emily?

Claire Turner

It seems so, I have since tried to make contact, her Facebook page is blocked.

Jack Anderson

Shit 😱 Can't believe we were talking to The Host this whole time!!!!

Claire Turner

I guess that's the power of social media, we can all hide behind it, pretend to be someone else.

Jack Anderson

I know, but he fooled us, I thought Emily was real, she looked real. It's so scary.

Amanda Belkin

Yeah. It is. We all chatted like we were the same. She was just like us.

Claire Turner

Online, we can be whoever we want.

Jack Anderson

It's crazy, if it's true, The Host was an admin on this page, The Host pretended to care when we spoke of fear and offered kind words to those of us who knew someone who had to be a Player. Emily, or rather, The Host organised the vigil in the city, and then played right under our noses.

Johnny Ormo

Goes to show, anyone could be a Host, hiding in plain sight, waiting for the next Player...

ACKNOWLEDGEMENTS

Well, we are here again. For me, this the hardest part of writing a book, as there are so many people to thank for the journey I have been on! I find it all a bit overwhelming at how many people are in my corner, and how lucky I truly am, I struggle to know where to start. But start I shall.

Firstly, I need to thank my editor, Katie Seaman. Writing *The Players* has been the toughest undertaking of my career so far – this book has challenged me, and I need to thank you for being there every step of the way. This book has changed from a rough idea into something I am incredibly proud of, because of your hard work. I'm so excited for what is next for us. Let's keep pushing the boundaries and I cannot wait to see where it takes us.

Also, a big thank you to the team at HQ: Melissa, Izzy, Fliss, Harriet, Sammy, Hannah and Darren. The work you do behind the scenes in helping me find readers is something I'm so grateful for, I just wish I could tell you more often.

Thank you to Jon Appleton for such wonderful work on the copyedit of this book and to Kate Oakley and Lisa at the Brewster Project for THAT COVER! Every time I look at it, I get giddy.

To my agent, Hayley Steed, you are my rock. There has been several meltdowns on this journey, and every time I felt myself unravel, you have sewn me back together again. Even during the difficult time of lockdown, you have always been there, and I honestly count my blessings. You do so much, without even knowing it. I am so proud to have you as my agent, and to be part of the Madeleine Milburn Agency.

To the man who came into a takeaway about two years ago, and told me I was going to die, I doubt you will read this, but despite scaring the s*** out of me, I need to thank you. Without your ridiculous prank or genuine homicidal thoughts (I still don't know which one it was) I wouldn't have had the idea for *The Players*. And to the man whose name I never learned, who was braver than me, and scared him away, thank you also, for you know, not letting something awful happen.

For help with the police research in this book, thank you Police Constable Kirsty Hulley and Police Constable Chris Smith. Chris – thank you for showing me around Thorpe Wood Station; without your insight and patience, I would have struggled to reflect the inner working of a station I needed to in *The Players*. Kirsty, thank you for always responding to my messages when a random question pops into my head. I take up a lot of your time, and I'm very grateful to you both.

Thank you to Louise Jensen, John Marrs, Phoebe Morgan, Lisa Hall, Cally Taylor, Lucy Knott, Louise Beech, Sarah Bennett. It's been a tricky time to be a writer, thank you for being around, offering advice, sharing stories and helping when things have gotten tough. How lucky am I to know you guys?

Richard Taylor, when I first told you about 'the game'

you led me to the trolley problem, which is so influential to the story and the ethical debate around *The Players*. Your idea opened up this book for me. Cheers buddy. Darren Madison, we talk about everything, thank you for being around for me to chew your ear off when I get excited about writing.

Writing a book is never easy, writing a book during a global pandemic has been especially tough, and without online book communities, I would have felt a little lost, so I want to thank everyone at The Book Club (TBC) and The Fiction Café Book Club for helping me realise that although we've been locked down, we haven't been alone.

To my family – thanks for understanding what it is I'm trying to do, and being in my corner as I do it. This road wouldn't be one I would travel without you.

And finally, to my son, Ben. Without you, there is no motivation, no determination, and no inspiration. And I will forever try to repay you for this.

READ MORE THRILLERS FROM DARREN O'SULLIVAN, THE MASTER OF THE KILLER TWIST

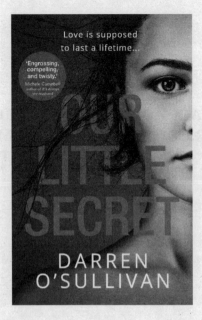

A deserted train station: A man waits. A woman watches.

Chris is ready to join his wife. He's planned this moment for nearly a year. The date. The time. But he hadn't factored in Sarah.

So when Sarah walks on to the platform and sees a man swaying at the edge she assumes he's just had too much to drink. What she doesn't expect is to stop a suicide.

As Sarah becomes obsessed with discovering the secrets that Chris is clearly hiding, he becomes obsessed with stopping her, protecting her.

But there are some secrets that are meant to stay buried . . .

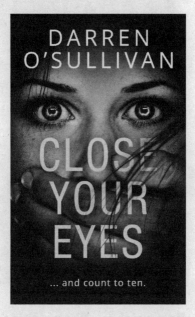

He doesn't know his name. He doesn't know his secret.

When Daniel woke up from a coma he had no recollection of the life he lived before. Now, fourteen years later, he's being forced to remember.

A phone call in the middle of the night demands he return what he stole – but Daniel has no idea what it could be, or who the person on the other end is. He has been given one warning, if he doesn't find out, his family will be murdered.

Rachael neds to protect her son. Trapped with no way out she will do anything to ensure they survive. But sometimes mothers can't save their children and her only hope is Daniel's memory.

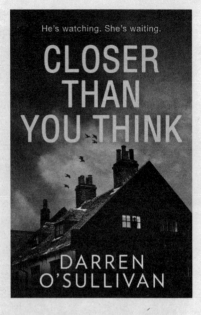

He's watching. She's waiting.

CLOSER
THAN
YOU THINK

DARREN
O'SULLIVAN

He's watching. She's waiting.

Having barely escaped the clutches of a serial killer, Claire
Moore has struggled to rebuild her life. After her terrifying
encounter with the man the media dubbed The Black-Out
Killer, she became an overnight celebrity: a symbol of hope and
survival in the face of pure evil. And then the killings stopped.

Now ten years have passed, and Claire remains traumatised
by her brush with death. Though she has a loving and sup-
portive family around her, what happened that night continues
to haunt her still.

Just when things are starting to improve, there is a power
cut; a house fire; another victim found killed in the same way
as before.

The Black-Out Killer is back. And he's coming for Claire . . .

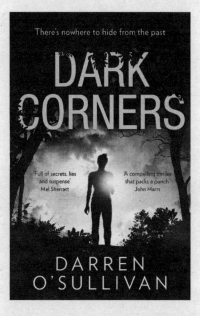

There's nowhere to hide from the past

DARK CORNERS

'Full of secrets, lies and suspense'
Mel Sherratt

'A compelling thriller that packs a punch'
John Marrs

DARREN
O'SULLIVAN

You thought you'd escaped your past.

It's been twenty years since Neve's best friend Chloe went missing. Neve has never recovered and promised herself she'd never go back to that place.

But secrets can come back to haunt you.

When Neve receives news that her first boyfriend Jamie has gone missing, she's forced to return. Jamie has vanished without a trace in a disappearance that echoes the events of all those years ago. Somebody is watching and will stop at nothing until the truth about what took place that night is revealed . . .

ONE PLACE. MANY STORIES

Bold, innovative and
empowering publishing.

FOLLOW US ON:

@HQStories